FOUNTAINS and SECRETS

A LIVIA AEMILIA MYSTERY

FOUNTAINS and SECRETS

LISA E. BETZ

BREAKTHROUGH
CHRISTIAN PUBLISHING

Fountains and Secrets © 2021 by Lisa E. Betz. All rights reserved.

Published by Breakthrough Christian Publishing - PO Box 1011, Ketchum, OK 74349

Breakthrough Christian Publishing is honored to present this title in partnership with the author. The views expressed or implied in this work are those of the author.

This book is a work of historical fiction. Names, characters, places and incidents are products of the author's imagination and are used fictitiously to depict a period of early Christian History within the Roman Empire, and with the exception of public figures, any resemblance to any persons is coincidental.

No part of this publication may be reproduced, stored in a retrieval system, or transmitted in any way by any means—electronic, mechanical, photocopy, recording, or otherwise—without the prior permission of the copyright holder, except as provided by USA copyright law.

ISBN 979-8-9907557-4-1 (Paperback)
ISBN 979-8-990-7557-5-8 (eBook)

Library of Congress Catalog Card Number: 2021920968

DEDICATION

To my father, Alan Ford Ellis.
You taught me to be an
independent, confident woman.
Thank you for always loving me,
believing in me, and supporting me
in my creative endeavors.

CONTENTS

DRAMATIS PERSONAE

THE **H**OUSEHOLD OF **A. M**EMMIUS **A**VITUS

Livia Aemilia—An unconventional young lady eager to whip her new household into shape. She can't resist a good mystery.

Avitus—An aristocrat with a new wife, an old enemy, and a dark secret.

Roxana—Livia's spunky handmaid. Always eager to snoop.

Momus—Avitus's doorkeeper. The cheerful one.

Sorex—Avitus's personal slave. Smarter than he looks.

Timon—Avitus's secretary. Talented with words, figures, and ferreting out information.

Grim—A dour bodyguard. He may not be as unpleasant as he seems.

Brisa—Avitus's housekeeper. A foe of dirt, disorder, and threats to the status quo.

Nissa—A young slave with a bad attitude.

Nemesis—A sneaky, sardine-snatching black cat.

Family and Friends

Senator Publius—Avitus's older brother. He has enemies in the senate.

Hortensia—His ambitious wife. A snob.

Curio—Livia's brother, who has useful friends.

Pansa and **Placida**—A baker and his wife. Livia's spiritual mentors.

Jonas—A freedman who's gone missing.

Damaris—Jonas's sister, who is apparently not married to a weaver from Pompeii.

Fabia—Livia's friend, with better taste in art than in men.

Aunt Livilla—Livia's widowed aunt. An inspiring role model.

Senator G. Octavius Laenus—The former water commissioner of Rome. A friend of Aunt Livilla.

Acquaintances and Strangers
(both helpful and suspicious)

Senator Gracchus—He gets what he wants by any means possible.

Gimpy and **Hairy**—A pair of troublemakers.

Hermas—A weaver who takes care of others.

Judith—A weaver who believes in dreams.

Dap—A clever boy who likes cats.

Parmashta—A spice merchant who doesn't sell chickens.

Sarai—A blind beggar who cares for doves.

Babak—A talkative silk merchant with a missing slave.

Nahla—His wife. She has exquisite taste in frescoes.

Zeno—A slave who knew too much.

Eleni—A sassy pastry seller who can keep a secret.

Brother Titus—a.k.a. Asyncritus. A physician.

Cyzicus—A landlord with questionable morals and useful contacts.

Fullo—A grouchy tavern keeper.

Ozias—He knows how the water system works.

Prochoros—A short-tempered foreman who lost something.

Nepos—A mysterious seller of marble. Unless he's really someone else?

L. Cornelius Scaevola—A wealthy merchant having a house renovated.

G. Ulpius Optatus—Another wealthy merchant having a house renovated.

Fornax—A water engineer with bad eyesight.

PROLOGUE

He'd sworn never to set foot on this block again.

It looked innocent enough, much like a hundred other back streets in Rome: Two women chatting beside a corner fountain while they filled water jars, a group of boys playing at gladiators, men in work-stained tunics and scuffed sandals entering a tavern for a cup of cheap wine after a long day's work. But this block held dark secrets.

He turned to his companion. "Is this where it happened?"

She nodded. "I recognize the tavern."

"I'm sorry to drag you back here, but I had to be sure." He pointed to the dark slit of an alley between the tavern and a neighboring building. "Is that the alley where you witnessed the crime?"

Another nervous nod. "Can we leave now?"

"One more question. When you first saw the attackers, which doorway did they come from? Was it that one?" He pointed past the tavern to a newly painted door in the next block.

His companion gasped. "How could you have known?"

"I only suspected."

And now, he was sure. The door belonged to a large residence undergoing renovations. He'd run afoul of the bullies guarding the house three days ago. They'd sent him home with a black eye, bruised ribs, and a warning never to come back to this block.

He hadn't intended to. And then his companion had brought him an alarming tale of a young man being beaten to death in an alley by men who fit the description of the ones who'd attacked him.

Same location. Same thugs. It couldn't be a coincidence. And he had a pretty good idea how the two incidents might be connected.

"Can we go now?"

"Yes, sorry." He scanned the street, suddenly conscious they'd been standing still for too long. Time to leave before someone recognized him.

"I've seen what I needed to. Turn around and head back the way we came."

He'd escort his companion to a safe place, then go directly to his former master and give an account of everything he'd discovered about this place and its secrets. They'd gone eight paces when a whistle pierced the air. Men emerged from the freshly painted doorway. Four of them.

Too many. It would be impossible to defend both himself and his companion from four assailants in the open street. "Into the alley, quickly."

When his companion hesitated, he grabbed her arm and propelled her into the foul-smelling alley ahead of him. It was barely wide enough for two men to pass. The close quarters would even the odds. Allow him to hold off their attackers long enough for her to get away.

Twenty paces in, he stopped. "Keep going."

"But—"

"Don't argue. Just go. Don't stop until you reach the Temple of Castor. I'll meet your there."

With a sob of fright, she ran on. He turned to face his enemies.

CHAPTER 1

Livia set the final rose bush in position and stood back to survey her handiwork. She was surrounded by mounds of dirt, baskets of wilting plants, and three sweaty, dirt-smudged slaves who were darting anxious glances at the mess she'd ordered them to make in her husband's tidy home. She ignored them and slowly spun around the *peristyle*, the colonnaded courtyard that served as the central hub of her new house. Livia mentally expanded the roses, oleander, viburnum and other plants, imagining how they'd look next year in full bloom.

Yes, that would do nicely. What had been a dull expanse of shrubs and paving stones would become a cheerful, flower-filled space.

"What a lovely garden this will be, my lady," said Roxana, Livia's maidservant. She was a small, feisty woman a few years older than Livia who'd been bubbling with excitement for days as she helped her mistress gather the plants for this project.

"Thank you." Livia matched Roxana's grin, then pointed to the flowers at the maid's feet. "But it won't be lovely unless we get these plants into the ground and watered. You dig those lilies in while Momus and Nissa fetch more water. We need to give all these plants a good drink."

The three slaves obeyed. Livia had become mistress of the house two weeks ago when she'd married Avitus. Her husband was the younger son of a senator, which meant he'd inherited an impressive pedigree but only a fraction of the family's fortune. His lack of funds explained why he lived in a modest house. His scholarly, phlegmatic temperament explained why he hadn't spent a single *sestertius* on home decor in the eleven years he'd lived here as a bachelor.

That was a fault Livia would begin to remedy today. Late summer wasn't the ideal time to transplant, but those who waited for ideal conditions rarely accomplished much. Better to act when the chance came, and hers had come today while her husband was busy attending a trial in the forum.

While the others were outside filling water jars at the public fountain, Roxana gave Livia a mischievous grin. "Won't the master be surprised when he sees what you've done?"

He certainly would. Avitus had given Livia permission to add flowerbeds to the peristyle, but how would he react when he saw the full extent of her alterations? She didn't know, because she barely knew the man. He spent most of his time reading law scrolls and composing speeches. He seemed to enjoy his dusty scrolls more than human company. Even his wife's.

It wasn't as if Livia had expected a doting husband. Marriages among Rome's upper classes were made for practical reasons, but she'd assumed her husband would share something of himself. Wrong. He'd not offered a single anecdote about his past, and when she asked, he changed the subject. So frustrating.

But now wasn't the time to ponder her enigmatic husband. She knelt and eased a rosebush into its hole, carefully tamping dirt around the roots. Another hour of work and all the plants were safely in the ground. Livia stood and brushed the dirt from the old ankle-length tunic she kept for dirty jobs like this. (And for trailing suspects, but that was another story.)

"Good work, everyone. Almost finished. Nissa, fetch more water. In this heat, everything needs another good drink."

Nissa wordlessly picked up a water jar and trudged off. The girl was a recent addition to the household. She was young and healthy, strong as an ox, and sullen as a mule. But she did what she was told, and that was all Livia cared about today.

"Roxana, you can sweep the pathways while Momus rakes the flowerbeds smooth. I want everything looking perfect before Avitus gets home."

Roxana grabbed a rake and handed it to Momus, Avitus's door-keeper. "Look lively, you old lump."

He crossed his brawny arms and glowered down at the petite maid. "Don't get snippy with me, girlie."

Roxana only grinned. Momus wasn't as fierce as he looked. He'd once served as bodyguard to a traveling merchant, but age and an injury had put an end to his fighting days. Now he tended Avitus's door, performed odd jobs, and put up with Roxana's sass.

"Admit it," Roxana said to him, "you're as amazed as I am over what the mistress has accomplished. Doesn't it look wonderful?"

"Looks different, that's for sure."

But was it *too* different? Would Avitus take one look and forbid her from touching anything else in the house? *Stop it*, she scolded herself. Avitus wasn't a tyrant like her father had been. He was a reasonable man who treated others with decency. Besides, if the sorry state of his house was any indication, he didn't have strong opinions on garden design.

Livia turned to find Brisa, Avitus's housekeeper, standing in the kitchen doorway. The prickly old woman had been watching from the shadows all day, muttering and shaking her head. She was the kind of woman who saw any type of mess as a personal affront. Now that the project was finished, perhaps Brisa could relax. Livia beckoned her over. "Do you like my improvements?"

Many thought Livia odd for asking a slave's opinion on anything, but she had embraced the teachings of a Jewish rabbi named Jesus, who taught that all men and women should be treated with respect and love. She felt strongly on this point, and she wouldn't have married Avitus if he didn't treat his household slaves with kindness.

Her husband didn't share her unusual religious beliefs, but he'd built a reputation as a lawyer who helped unimportant people fight legal battles against more privileged opponents. Livia didn't know what motivated Avitus to go against his fellow aristocrats in court, but she suspected his damaged skin was the primary cause. He'd been burned as a boy, leaving unsightly scars on his cheek, arm and chest. She sensed the accident had left scars on his soul as well. For a boy already prone to shyness, facing jeers over his damaged face must have eaten into his soul.

She was only guessing, of course, since Avitus had not bothered to share any details about the incident. Whatever his reasons, he treated those of lower status with more courtesy than most of his peers. Livia admired him for it. And she hoped he would admire her handiwork.

"What do you think?" she asked Brisa. "Will Avitus be pleased?"

The old woman sniffed. "The master prefers everything to be orderly. This is a jumble." She waved a hand at the flower beds. "No straight lines. No symmetry. It won't be what he's expecting, not at all."

No, it wouldn't. Livia preferred the wild beauty of nature to the stiff lines and trimmed bushes of a formal garden. Avitus wasn't a hidebound traditionalist, but would he be pleased with her artistry, or would he only notice that his orderly world had been upended? She truly didn't know.

Would it always be this way? Would they remain strangers living in the same house, sharing the same bed but little else? There were worse fates, but she wanted more.

Aulus Memmius Avitus stood at the edge of the small crowd and listened to his older brother, Publius, deliver his closing argument. Rome's legal disputes were heard in the broad public forums where any passerby could stop to watch, but this lawsuit wasn't sensational enough to have drawn much of a crowd. A simple dispute regarding a shipment of olive oil. Publius's client claimed that 20 percent of the shipment was damaged. The defendant claimed he'd delivered the full load intact.

Winning the case should have been as easy as calling reliable witnesses who had seen the damaged amphoras of oil. Except that two days before the hearing date, all the men Avitus and Publius had enlisted to testify had withdrawn. Avitus hadn't needed to ask why. The answer was obvious.

Senator Gracchus.

Gracchus had been an open sore in their lives for years, thwarting justice by any underhand means he could find. This wasn't the first time Gracchus had intimidated witnesses into withdrawing their testimony, so for this case Publius had been prepared with additional witnesses.

Publius finished speaking. Gracchus rose to deliver his final speech for the defense. All educated Roman men of the elite class were expected to provide legal aid to their *clientes*, men of lesser power or status. Thus, Avitus's childhood tutor had drilled them endlessly on the finer points of rhetoric and law, enabling both brothers to argue legal cases with confidence and finesse.

In contrast, men like Gracchus had never bothered to become well-versed in the legal codes. His closing remarks were vague and delivered in a tone as stirring as the recitation of a grammar textbook. Apparently, he knew he'd lost and wasn't even trying to sway the judge's opinion.

Avitus met his brother's eyes and gave a slow nod. He'd been watching the crowd and the senator who'd been assigned to judge the case. Publius's cogent arguments and adept use of oratory had erased any question of who was at fault. This time, despite Gracchus's thuggery, they had defeated him.

For once, justice would prevail.

This victory was important for Publius's career in the Roman senate. He hoped to run for the office of *aedile* next year. Defeating Gracchus, even in so minor a case, would gain him popularity among the many senators who despised Gracchus and his clique.

As an added benefit, Publius would be in a benevolent mood tonight when he hosted Avitus and Livia for dinner. Married life would go easier if his wife got along with his brother, and tonight would be Livia's first dinner at Publius's home.

Livia was a free spirit, independent and unpredictable. Nothing like the tediously conventional women Publius had suggested Avitus marry over the years. Those women had seen only his damaged face and awkward way with small talk. No one but Livia had bothered to notice his mind or appreciate his courage. She was a rare gem. But could his brother see past her unconventional opinions to accept her? And could Livia see past her mistrust of aristocracy to accept Publius?

The crowd hushed, drawing Avitus from his reverie. All eyes

turned to the judge sitting on his tribunal. The judge glanced at Gracchus, who gave a tiny nod.

Avitus's blood froze.

Had Gracchus bribed the judge? Despite all their efforts, had their enemy thwarted justice and smirched their honor yet again?

The crowd erupted in angry murmurs when the judge proclaimed the defendant not guilty. Outrage surged through Avitus's body, tightening his jaw and sending bile up his throat. Curse their enemy to the lowest level of Hades!

He turned to scan the length of the forum, plotting an escape route. He wanted to get out of there before word of the trial spread. Avitus turned to Sorex, the tall ex-gladiator who served as his bodyguard. "Let's get out of here. Help me avoid anyone I know."

The big slave nodded. That was one of his many fine qualities; he never spoke when a gesture would suffice. And he'd served his master long enough to understand that Avitus didn't want to talk to anyone.

Instead of heading home, Avitus strode out to the Field of Mars, a broad plain north of the forum. He didn't dare return home until he'd worked off the fury jangling every nerve. Livia would be alarmed to see him so upset, and she'd demand to know what was wrong. Her questions wouldn't stop until she'd heard the whole sordid tale.

Livia hated injustice as much as he did. If she learned the details of the case, she'd demand they take action. Last spring, when her father had been murdered, Livia had attempted to track down the killer single-handedly. The gods only knew what she'd attempt to do if she learned Gracchus had bribed the judge.

She didn't know the history of the feud between Gracchus and the Memmius brothers. Nor was she aware how dangerous Gracchus could be. If she meddled in his affairs, he would make her suffer.

Therefore, it was imperative Avitus bring his roiling emotions into control before facing her. Only when he could say his enemy's name aloud without a twinge did he turn his feet toward his house near the top of the Quirinal ridge, one of the so-called seven hills of Rome. (Technically there were nine hills within the city walls, but the populace never let facts interfere with tradition. So seven it was.)

Avitus entered the blessed quiet of his house. And stopped dead.

In the space of single day, his serene peristyle had been transformed into a riot of color. Publius had warned him a wife would wreak havoc on his cozy bachelor existence. He'd been prepared for her to bring a woman's touch into his house. But this…

His wife stood in the center of the space, watching him intently. Livia would not be considered a classic beauty, but she had a vibrancy Avitus found appealing. Her dark hair was wound artfully atop her head, a few stray strands clinging to her damp face.

"Greetings, Husband," Livia said. "I hope the trial went well?"

He shook off the shock and answered in a completely even tone. "We lost on a technicality. I see you've been busy."

She nodded. "What do you think?"

A perilous question. It was never wise to blurt out one's opinions without considering the consequences. Especially when speaking to one's wife.

"I had no idea so much could be planted so quickly. You must be exhausted."

"Not really. Making something beautiful energizes me. Do you like it?"

His tenacious wife wouldn't be put off, so he ran his gaze over her work, looking for something safe to comment on. Clumps of flowers ran helter-skelter around the edges of the space, creating a floral boundary between the colonnaded walkways and the sunny central patio. There was no discernible pattern to her design, and yet—the more he looked, the more he saw that the total effect was one of balance, not chaos.

Interesting. The design lacked straight lines or symmetry, yet the whole was pleasing. Avitus began to relax. "I was not prepared to arrive home and find my house so transformed. But now that I have gotten over the shock, I see you've created a combination of textures and colors that form a harmonious whole. The result is stunning yet soothing. I might call the effect wholesome."

No, that wasn't quite right. He slowly rotated, taking it all in. "I believe nurturing is a better word. A place that gives life."

Livia rewarded him with a smile that warmed his heart. Like everything about his wife, her smile was exuberant and genuine. "Thank you. I was hoping you'd like it. I chose my favorite plants."

"It's lovely. I can't imagine my sister-in-law designing a garden with this much artistry."

That won him an even bigger smile. Maybe he would figure out how to survive marriage after all. He smiled back. "I look forward to telling Publius about it tonight."

Anything to avoid talking about the case.

"Before we depart for your brother's house, can we discuss the dining room?"

Avitus blinked, momentarily confused by the change of subject. "Is there a problem?"

"Several," she replied gravely. "The dining couches are salvageable, but the lumpy cushions will have to be replaced. The frescoes are decades old. The paint has flaked off in several places, and two panels are so mildewed that even Brisa's most strenuous scrubbing can't remove the stains. We'll need a fresco painter to redo the walls. I want to start looking for one in the morning. Do you have any objections?"

Yes! Dust. Noise. Workmen invading his privacy. But all he said was, "No." The project would keep Livia's attention away from inquiring about Gracchus and the lawsuit. The more he distracted her from that topic the better.

"My sister-in-law has redone all the main rooms in my brother's house. You could ask her for her suggestions this evening. I'm sure she'd be happy to advise you."

Uh oh. He recognized that squint.

He should have known Livia wouldn't welcome the advice of a sister-in-law she barely knew. Especially one as pushy as Hortensia.

He cleared his throat and feigned a change of mind. "On second thought, it might be better if you didn't bring it up. Once Hortensia sinks her teeth into a subject she fancies, there's no stopping her. Publius and I will give you our undying gratitude if you promise not to mention it."

Success! Livia's furrowed brow relaxed.

"You make Hortensia sound like a gorgon," Livia said. "Is Publius really so badly under the thumb of his wife?"

"I'll let you decide that for yourself."

CHAPTER 2

Livia and Avitus rode to Publius's house in a hired litter. Avitus's elder brother lived on the Viminal Hill, a short walk from the house Livia had grown up in. Not that the two families had ever crossed paths. Livia's father had been an ambitious merchant-turned-landlord, while Avitus and Publius came from a distinguished line of senators. Avitus assured her the gap in status would not matter to his brother or sister-in-law. Tonight's dinner would prove him right.

Or not.

Livia was determined not to allow any snide remarks to anger her. Followers of Christ were to forgive rather than take offense. Unfortunately, Livia's heart was quick to react and her mind was quick to think up an acid retort. She prayed the Lord would help her control those tendencies tonight so she could remain gracious and above reproach.

"About tonight's dinner," Avitus said, a detectable note of concern in his voice.

Uh oh. Was he afraid she would embarrass him?

"Yes?"

"I should warn you that Publius hates to lose, so we mustn't mention today's lawsuit."

That wouldn't be a problem. She had no interest in legal cases. "Thank you for the warning."

She felt the tension go out of him. Odd he was so worried about that. She'd heard nothing about Publius having a temper. "Anything else?"

"There's someone who wants to meet you. A freedman named Jonas who used to serve as Father's bodyguard. He was fond of me, and he wants to see for himself that I've chosen a suitable wife." Avitus gave her a rueful look. "He may ask probing questions."

No wonder her husband was concerned. He avoided personal questions like the plague. Livia, on the other hand, wasn't afraid to talk about herself.

"Don't worry. I look forward to chatting with him." Especially if the conversation offered her a chance to learn more about Avitus.

Her in-laws' house was as large and grand as she'd imagined. The entryway led into an atrium large enough to house dozens of visitors waiting for a meeting with Publius. The frescoes covering the atrium walls were tasteful but predictable. Ditto for Publius's formal study, which they passed through on the way to the large peristyle that filled the center of the house. The garden's plantings and walkways had been laid out with geometric precision. Exactly what she'd expected from her rigidly formal sister-in-law.

Publius gave them a cheery wave and beckoned them to join him at a grouping of benches beyond the peristyle's central fountain. He was a more gregarious version of Avitus, plump and round-faced, with a ready smile. In contrast, Avitus was lean and wiry, with a narrow face and intense dark eyes.

A slave glided to them and offered a tray of delicate glass cups. Honeyed wine. A tad over spiced, but refreshing in the heat that lingered even though the sun was about to set. As she sipped her wine, Livia deftly guided the small talk toward her husband.

"I understand this is the house you and Avitus grew up in?"

"Yes," Publius said. "Although we've done extensive remodeling since then. Father would have apoplexy if he could see the place now. He hated change."

From the little Livia had heard, their father had hated pretty much everything. "And what would your mother have thought?"

"She and Hortensia shared similar taste in clothing and jewelry, so I imagine she would have approved."

The brothers' father (Senator Publius Memmius Pulvillus the elder) had died eleven years ago, and their mother had died a year or so later, shortly after Publius had married Hortensia. Livia wished she could have met Avitus's mother and asked her about Avitus's childhood. Instead, she'd have to wheedle what she could from Publius. "Despite the changes, I imagine the house is full of memories."

Publius nodded, smiling.

"Livia has begun to redecorate our house," Avitus announced abruptly.

Drat the man. She was sure he'd done it on purpose.

"I've given her free rein to do as she pleases," Avitus continued.

"Then you're a braver man than I am." Publius turned to Livia. "I suppose he's making you spend your own money on improvements rather than sending him into penury?"

She nodded.

"I understand you and your brother inherited the bulk of your father's estate?"

"We did," Livia said. "Father left legacies to his siblings and my mother, the rest went to Curio and me."

"Wasn't there a squabble over a property?"

"Only a farm in Ariminum where my father grew up." Her father had come from an unimportant town a good week's travel northeast of Rome. "The issue has been resolved, and we're not on speaking terms with those relatives anymore."

"Ariminum?" One eyebrow rose in censure.

Oh, fish pickle! Why had Livia reminded Publius of her lowly origins? She braced for condescending comments about provincial cousins with thick accents. Instead, Publius chuckled and shook his head. "Not much foresight on their part, alienating a wealthy relation. Good fortune for you and your brother, though, eh?"

"Yes." Livia smiled at him, grateful for his cheerful tact.

"Tsk, Publius." Hortensia arrived, her kohl-darkened eyebrows pinched in censure. "You promised not to discuss legal matters tonight."

She was almost as tall as her husband and perhaps five years younger. Her face was all sharp angles. Nobody would call her pretty, but she made up for it in poise and presence. One probing look from her intense eyes warned that she was a force to be reckoned with.

After greeting Avitus, Hortensia turned her formidable gaze on Livia. "A sister-in-law at last. Finally, someone who will converse on a subject other than law. Left to their devices, these two will spend the entire evening discussing commentaries of old cases written by long-dead jurists." She gave her husband a severe look.

He grinned sheepishly and asked Livia which chariot team she favored. That led to a lively discussion about the relative merits of the Reds (Livia's favorite) versus the Blues (Avitus) and the Whites (both Publius and Hortensia).

Slaves appeared with a basin and towels, and the group took their places on the dining couches. By the time the first course was finished, the conversation had shifted to politics. Hortensia was as informed as the men, but Livia wasn't interested in the minutiae of aristocratic circles and their constant maneuverings. Avitus had no pretensions of becoming a senator. A political career required huge sums of money to subsidize gladiatorial games, buy lavish gifts for supporters, and otherwise win public favor. The family had barely been able to finance Publius's bid for a senate seat.

Livia let them talk while she studied the room. Stylish, but boring. The paintings were predictable, the kind found in dozens of houses, using stock characters stenciled into the plaster and then painted to suit. The floor featured a mosaic of subtle geometric patterns with a border of ivy. Quality materials. Quality workmanship. No originality. But perhaps the artists who'd done the work were capable of more, given a chance? Dare Livia ask her sister-in-law for names, or would that invite Hortensia to proclaim herself Livia's design consultant?

She was jolted back to the conversation when she heard her name.

"Jonas told me he wanted to meet Livia," Avitus said. "Where is he?"

Publius beckoned the wine server hovering beside his dining couch. "Inform Jonas that my brother would like to see him."

Finally, another chance to coax information from her hosts. "Tell me about Jonas."

"He's the crusty old bodyguard who taught us our sword skills," Publius said. "Father freed him in his will, but Jonas still resides in the household. Avitus was his favorite. He spent hours practicing his footwork while I was in the forum with my friends."

That didn't surprise Livia. She'd witnessed her husband's fighting skill firsthand when he'd rescued her from the grip of a murderer. It was one of many fine qualities he kept hidden.

"I imagine you and Avitus held friendly competitions on many subjects?"

"Indeed, we did. We vied for praise from our various tutors. I was the better orator while Avitus bested me in the study of jurisprudence. He was also the better musician. Do you know he used to make up songs?"

"Only when I was five," Avitus said, a rumble of anger in his deep baritone voice. "What do you think about the progress of Claudius's aqueducts?"

Publius barely batted an eye at his brother's abrupt (and rude) change of subject. "The city can use the extra water, but I'm concerned the project has distracted the water commissioner from maintaining the existing pipes within the city. The Viminal Baths have been plagued with leaks lately."

Rome's water was supplied by seven aqueducts that brought fresh water from far-off springs directly to hundreds of public fountains, as well as private homes. Their previous emperor, the madman known as Caligula, had begun work on two additional aqueducts and Emperor Claudius had ordered them to be completed.

At least this time Avitus had changed the subject to something she could participate in. "I heard the new aqueducts are likely to be plagued with leaks. It that true?"

Hortensia raised one perfectly plucked eyebrow in surprise. At Livia's statement, or the fact she was capable of adding something intelligent to the conversation?

Avitus nodded. "They say Claudius is in a hurry to get them finished, and as a consequence the commissioner has allowed shoddy workmanship."

"It wouldn't surprise me," Publius said. "I'm sure every dishonest contractor has been bidding for a share of the imperial coffers."

The wine server returned, accompanied by an older man with the grave carriage of a servant who held authority. The steward, Livia guessed.

Publius gestured for him to speak.

The servant bowed gravely. "Forgive me, my lord. Jonas isn't here."

An angry knot formed in Avitus's stomach. Jonas had promised to be here tonight, and Jonas was a man of his word. Always. Avitus frowned at his brother's steward. "What do you mean, Jonas isn't here?"

"He can't be found, sir. He left the house and hasn't returned."

Avitus felt his temper rising. Had his brother been so furious after the trial that he'd forgotten about the dinner and sent Jonas off on some harebrained vendetta?

He turned sharply to his brother. "Where have you sent him?"

"Nowhere. I haven't spoken to him since yesterday." Publius shot his steward an annoyed frown. "Why wasn't I informed that Jonas had gone out?"

"I wasn't aware of it until you asked for him, sir."

If Publius hadn't sent Jonas on an errand, and the steward hadn't known Jonas was out, something was very wrong.

"Excuse me." Avitus rose from his dining couch and headed for the kitchen to talk to the cook, Jonas's oldest friend. He'd know why Jonas wasn't here.

Publius caught up with Avitus halfway across the peristyle. "Where do you think you're going? You can't go running off in the middle of dinner."

"Jonas has been waiting weeks to meet Livia. If he's not here, I want to know why, and I'm starting with your cook."

"And you wonder why no one invites you to dinner." Publius gave an exasperated sigh. "You may not annoy my cook while he's busy. Come back to the dining room and we'll talk to him after dinner."

"No." Avitus crossed his arms. "I'm not dawdling through two more courses when my friend and mentor is not here when he promised. If you can't tell me where he is, then I'm going to find someone who can." He pushed past his brother.

Publius grabbed his arm. "Be reasonable, will you?" He turned to the steward, who had followed them from the dining room. "Where has Jonas gone?"

"No one seems to know, sir."

"When was he last seen?"

"Yesterday. The doorkeeper said he left the house midafternoon and expected to back before dark, but no one has seen him since."

The hair on the back of Avitus's neck prickled. Jonas had been missing since yesterday afternoon?

The steward flicked a nervous glance at Publius. "There's one more thing, sir. Jonas didn't ask anyone to look after his dog before he left."

"Jupiter's thunderbolts." Publius face reddened. "Go fetch the cook and send him to my study at once."

CHAPTER 3

Livia stared after her husband. What was so important about Jonas that Avitus had gone taut and then gotten up in the middle of dinner? Clearly there was more to this story.

She turned to her sister-in-law. "I hope nothing serious has happened?"

Hortensia gave a forced laugh. "Just a miscommunication. Publius probably forgot to tell Jonas that you were coming tonight and sent him on an errand instead."

That didn't match the men's reactions. "Avitus said something on the way here about Jonas wanting to meet me. Why would Avitus care about the opinion of his brother's freedman?"

Hortensia's lips compressed. "I don't know. I never understood why Avitus was so fond of the old grouch."

"Tell me more about Jonas."

"He served as bodyguard to Publius's father. He was *manumitted* when Old Memmius died."

Which would mean Jonas had been granted his freedom eleven years ago. "So, he's a freedman, but he still resides in your house?"

"Yes. Publius pays him to gather information and keep an eye on certain adversaries. Jonas comes and goes at odd hours, and he's often gone for days. I wouldn't worry about him."

"Then why are the men so upset?"

"I have no idea." Hortensia's tone made it clear she would say no more about it.

Livia tried a different angle. "Are there other slaves in the household that Avitus is fond of?"

Hortensia arched an eyebrow. "My brother-in-law does not confide his personal attachments to me."

And the oh-so-refined Hortensia would never deign to listen to slaves' gossip about family members. Well, snooty snoot, snoot. Apparently Livia wouldn't be wheedling juicy family stories from her sister-in-law.

Hopefully Roxana was having better success. The maid had a knack for getting other slaves to talk about their masters.

The room settled into silence. Livia pretended to sip her wine while she studied Hortensia over the rim of her cup. Publius had welcomed Livia with genuine warmth, but his wife had been frostily polite all evening, sending Livia sour looks when she thought no one was watching.

Why? Was she insulted at being forced to dine with someone of Livia's provincial origins, or was there another reason? Was it possible she viewed Livia as a threat?

"I hope you are settled into your new home?" Hortensia said into the silence.

And what did that question mean? Did her sister-in-law care two figs whether Livia had been welcomed into Avitus's household? Hardly. More likely, Hortensia was fishing for an opportunity to dispense unwanted advice on home improvements. Time to change the subject.

"I hear congratulations are in order," Livia said brightly. "Avitus tells me your son has begun to read."

Hortensia had produced two daughters before finally giving Publius a son. The boy was now five, and an apt pupil. She obligingly began a lengthy monologue about her children's latest accomplishments.

When would the men return?

Publius stalked to his study and dropped into a chair.

Avitus followed. "Now do you agree something is wrong?"

"Obviously. Jonas dotes on that dog like it's his child. He'd never leave it overnight without making sure someone tended to it."

Which implied that Jonas hadn't planned on being gone this long.

"And you're sure you don't know where he went?"

"I thought he was in bed, recuperating from a fight."

A fight! This was getting more alarming by the moment. Before Avitus could ask about the fight, the cook appeared at the door, wiping his hands on a rag.

Publius waved him into the room. "We've been informed Jonas is missing. What can you tell me?"

"Nothing sir. I didn't realize he was gone until this morning, when his dog whined to be let out."

"Why didn't you tell someone he was missing?" Publius asked.

The cook twisted the rag nervously. "Everyone assumed he was away on your orders, sir. If he wasn't home by tonight, I was going to tell you about it."

"When did you last talk to him?" Avitus asked.

"Yesterday."

"Any idea where he went?"

"No, sir. Jonas never gossiped to the rest of us about his assignments." He darted a worried glance at Publius. "Is he in trouble, do you think, sir?"

"We don't know. Return to your duties, but inform me if you learn anything."

The brothers exchanged looks. The most dependable man they knew was missing, and even his closest friend had no idea where he'd gone. Or why.

The knot in Avitus's gut turned leaden. First Gracchus had cheated them of victory, and now Publius's most loyal freedman was mysteriously missing. Logic said the two might be related. "Are your sure this has nothing to do with the trial?"

Publius rubbed his temples. "If Gracchus is responsible for Jonas's disappearance, it's not today's trial that's to blame."

"Oh?" Avitus crooked an eyebrow and waited for his brother to explain.

"In the last three months Gracchus has acquired five new clientes. All wealthy provincials who recently moved to Rome. I've been trying to figure out how Gracchus is drawing them into his web. He must hold *something* over them. Therefore, I sent Jonas to investigate Gracchus's most recent *cliens*, Lucius Cornelius Scaevola. Jonas spent days poking around Scaevola's neighborhood, but he never found a connection to Gracchus. Three nights ago Jonas came home with a black eye and bruised ribs. He told me he'd been warned to stay away from the area, but he claimed it had nothing to do with Gracchus."

Publius stood. "Come, we should return to our dinner before the women begin to worry."

"We can't return to our food as if nothing has happened. We need to question the rest of your staff."

Publius looked annoyed. "I will. After our dinner is over. A Memmius always acts with honor and decorum. He must never allow his household to see he is worried. Come with me, and don't forget to smile."

They returned to the dining room. Publius kept the conversation going. Avitus fidgeted. Despite Publius's assurances, deep in his gut Avitus feared Gracchus was behind this mystery. If so, Jonas was in grave danger.

On the journey home, Avitus alternated between castigating himself for allowing Jonas's absence to worry him and imagining ever more sinister scenarios to explain the freedman's disappearance.

Halfway home Livia laid a hand on his arm. "Are you going to tell me what's bothering you?"

Avitus blinked. "Sorry. Publius was furious at the steward for allowing him to be caught unawares like that. He wanted to make a good impression."

A pathetic excuse, but the best he could come up with.

"So, you're not worried about Jonas?"

He gave her a confident smile. "Jonas is as tough as they come. Publius isn't worried."

But Avitus was.

CHAPTER 4

Avitus slept poorly, last night's conversation still swirling in his head. He wouldn't be able to concentrate on anything else until he'd talked the issue out with his brother.

He met briefly with his clientes, accepted their condolences on yesterday's travesty of a trial, and bid them good day. Then he summoned Timon, his secretary.

Timon was in his late twenties, with a long face and intelligent eyes that missed nothing. His straight hair fell low across his forehead, partly hiding an ugly brand: an F that marked him as *fugitivus*—a runaway slave. He'd fled his former master and settled in Gaul, where he'd enjoyed a comfortable life working as a scribe-for-hire until he was finally caught and hauled back to Rome. He'd been Avitus's secretary for five years.

Timon entered the study and dipped his head. "You wanted me, sir?"

"Do I have any appointments today?"

"No, sir."

"Good. I have business with my brother. I want you to deliver the contract I drafted for Labeo and get his approval."

"Very good, sir. Anything else?"

Avitus shook his head. "You're free to see to your own business."

Everyone had warned Avitus he was wasting his money on a runaway, but Timon had proven capable, hardworking, and loyal. In return, Avitus allowed Timon to pursue business ventures on the side, no questions asked. Both men were happy with the arrangement.

With the day's obligations out of the way, Avitus summoned Sorex and headed for his brother's house.

"I thought you might turn up this morning," Publius said. "Still no word from Jonas, but I've had the household questioned. Jonas received a message yesterday morning. A boy came to the back door and handed the cook's assistant a shard of pottery with a brief message scratched on it. The slave gave the potsherd to Jonas and promptly forgot about it until the steward questioned him."

So. A message delivered to the slave's entrance rather than the front door. Why? "Was Jonas in the habit of receiving messages that way?"

"I've no idea. Jonas did his job. I never inquired into his methods. For all I know he had dozens of acquaintances who only communicated through the slave's entrance. Maybe one of them asked Jonas for help."

A reasonable explanation. Avitus's chest relaxed slightly. Maybe Jonas's disappearance had nothing to do with Gracchus after all. But he had to be sure.

"You're certain Jonas didn't get wind of Gracchus's plans to bribe the judge and try to stop him before the trial?"

Publius shook his head. "First of all, he wouldn't have gone after Gracchus without telling me about it. Secondly, if he suspected Gracchus's bribery plan, he would have warned me. Thirdly, he was injured in that fight and wasn't up to strenuous activity."

"So tell me about this fight. It happened while he was investigating someone. Scaevola, was it? Could that be to blame?"

"I doubt it. He said the fight had nothing to do with my interests, and he'd found nothing suspicious that might connect Gracchus to Scaevola. It was a dead end."

So Gracchus wasn't to blame. Excellent news.

"Then we may assume the message is the reason for his disappearance, and that when he left the house he didn't anticipate being gone for long."

"I agree."

"You need to find out who sent that message and what it said."

Publius blew a frustrated breath. "It might not be possible. I'll have the steward question my slaves again, but I doubt I'll learn anything new."

He rubbed his temples, sighed, then looked up at Avitus. "I know how much you admired Jonas, but he's been missing for a day-and-a-half. We must consider the possibility that he's been killed by random footpads. Maybe you should check with the *vigiles*."

The vigiles were tasked with extinguishing fires, an ever-present threat in a large and crowded city. Since they served at night, the vigiles also acted as a night watch, apprehending thieves, tracking down fugitive slaves, and otherwise keeping the peace. If Jonas had been killed, somebody may have reported it to the vigiles.

"I'll go at once."

After their first awkward morning together, Livia found it easier to pretend she was asleep until Avitus was dressed and out of the room, which avoided both of them trying to dress with the other's servant there to watch.

Today she waited impatiently for him to leave so she could hear what juicy stories Roxana had collected about Avitus and his family. The maid entered the room with an eager smile.

An excellent sign.

"What did you learn about your master last night? I want every detail."

"Not much." Roxana made a wry face. "I heard a few stories about how he and his brother teased their tutors and stole sweets from the kitchen. The usual stuff. Then the rumor came through that Jonas was missing, so that was all anyone talked about." The maid raised her eyebrows. "And guess what I overheard."

"Tell me."

"Jonas has a sister who lives in Rome, but for some reason it's a big secret. The master and mistress don't know the woman lives here, or that Jonas goes to see her."

That made no sense. "If Jonas is a freedman, he can do as he likes. Why would he need to keep his visits a secret?"

Roxana shrugged. "I wasn't supposed to have heard them talking about her, so I couldn't ask for details, could I?"

"Did you hear where she lived?"

"Sadly not."

Too bad. "What else did you learn about Jonas?"

"Everyone was stumped about what happened. They say Jonas is always coming and going on the master's business, but he isn't one to up and disappear."

Intriguing. First a missing freedman, and now a sister who needed to remain hidden. It was time to learn the whole story behind Jonas.

And there was only one way to get the information.

"I feel like hiking to the Viminal Baths today, to see my old friends."

Roxana grinned, eyes alight with mischief. "You mean the one that's a few blocks from your sister-in-law's house?"

Livia grinned back. "My, isn't that convenient? While I visit my dear sister-in-law, you can learn everything you can about Jonas and his mysterious sister."

"I was hoping you'd say that."

"Get the bathing things ready while I check on Brisa and Nissa."

In his bachelor days, Avitus had made do with Brisa to keep house and provide his meals. She was an excellent housekeeper, but she was getting on in years, and Avitus decided she needed an assistant to help her deal with the added demands a wife would bring to his household. So, he'd purchased Nissa to do household chores. Unfortunately, within a day of her arrival, Nissa had landed firmly on Brisa's bad side. By the time Livia took over the domestic arrangements of the household, the two were sworn enemies.

This morning Livia found Brisa in the kitchen, screeching at Nissa. "Stupid girl. That's not the way I told you to clean those lentils."

Nissa worked placidly on, as if she hadn't heard. Brisa had strong opinions about the correct way to do any task. It drove her to apoplexy when Nissa employed a different method.

So Nissa chose a different method as often as possible.

However, as far as Livia could tell, Nissa's lentil-shelling technique was perfectly adequate. To keep the peace, Livia gave Brisa a list of items to purchase and sent her out to the markets. Nissa watched the older woman leave with a look that clearly said, *good riddance*. Livia sighed. The feud between the women was exasperating, but the problem required more patience than she had at the moment, so she left Nissa to her lentils.

Roxana was waiting with the basket of bathing things: thick sandals to protect her feet from the heated floors, clean towels, scented oils to rub on her skin, and an ivory-handled *strigil* to scrape off the dirt and sweat.

Mistress and maid headed to the atrium to collect Momus. Since Sorex generally accompanied Avitus, it fell to Momus to serve as escort whenever Livia went out. Avitus didn't want his wife walking the streets of Rome without a trustworthy male to watch over her. Fortunately, Momus was a cheerful man, so Livia didn't mind him tagging along.

After a pleasant hour catching up with friends in the bath complex, Livia headed for Hortensia's house. On the short walk there, she considered her strategy. What excuse could she give for an unannounced visit?

Unfortunately, only one thing came to mind—asking her sister-in-law's advice on decorating. The idea stuck in Livia's craw, but it was the price she must pay for satisfying her curiosity about Jonas.

"This is a surprise," Hortensia said frostily when Livia arrived. "What brings you here today?"

"Forgive me for coming unannounced, but in all the uproar last night I completely forgot to ask for your advice on painters. I'm planning to redo the dining room, and Avitus assures me you are the perfect person to ask."

That brought a definite thawing of Hortensia's features. "I am something of an expert. Friends consult me for advice from time to time."

Livia did her best to sound eager. "Then I've come to the right person."

"Indeed, you have," Hortensia said smugly. "I've been telling Avitus for years that he must remedy the deplorable state of his home. When I despaired of him ever marrying, I attempted to guide him myself, but he couldn't be bothered. I think he neglected his house on purpose so he had an excuse not to invite people to dinner."

"The same thought crossed my mind," Livia said, adding a silent apology to her husband for slandering him. "I can't in good conscience invite guests to dine in a room with flaking frescoes and lumpy cushions the color of congealed porridge."

Hortensia clicked her tongue. "I should think not. I'm glad you see things my way. I believe you and I may get along just fine."

Translation: They'd be friends so long as Livia agreed with everything her sister-in-law said. Like that was going to happen.

"Fortunately for you, I've compiled detailed plans for each room, which I will be happy to share." Hortensia beckoned a slave with a languid flick of her fingers. "Fetch my scrolls on redecorating Avitus's house."

Hortensia kept scrolls on how Avitus should decorate his house? The gall of the woman!

CHAPTER 5

An interminable hour later, Livia escaped her sister-in-law's house laden with two scrolls containing sketches and detailed instructions for improving every room of Avitus's house. In addition, Hortensia had magnanimously added a list of suitable painters, annotated with the names of friends who had hired them so Livia could view a sample of their work.

One of the women on the list lived nearby, so Livia directed Momus to find the house. While he was occupied with asking directions, Livia beckoned Roxana to her side. "What did you learn?" she whispered.

"Avitus's nurse is still alive," Roxana whispered back. "She agreed to tell us more about Jonas. I've arranged to meet her at Pansa's bakery at the seventh hour."

Which meant the nurse would show up an hour after midday, and it was only midmorning now. Enough time to visit several of the names on her list. An hour later Livia bid goodbye to friend number three, mentally crossing another name from the list.

She checked the time. The shadow at her feet said it was just before midday. Her stomach said it was lunchtime.

"I'm ready for a snack. Do either of you know where to find something to eat?"

"I do." Momus led them to a bakery selling pastry-wrapped sausages. Crisp, flaky dough around a succulent sausage seasoned with cumin, rue, and fiery black peppercorns. Delicious.

They continued down the street as they munched. When her sausage roll was finished, Livia stopped at a public fountain to rinse the grease from her fingers. A man in a plaster-splattered tunic strode up beside her and filled two wooden buckets with water. His hands were smudged with red, black, and yellow.

Hmm. Wet plaster plus pigments meant freshly painted frescoes. Why not take a look?

"Excuse me, are you a fresco painter?"

The man gave an incoherent grunt and trudged away. He entered a doorway halfway down the block. Livia shook the water from her hands and went for a closer look. The door was propped open to reveal a large atrium piled with tarps, baskets, tools, and white-rimmed buckets. There were no workers in sight.

"Hello?"

Momus was instantly at her shoulder. "Are you acquainted with the residents of this home, my lady?"

"No, but I think there's a painter working here. I want to see if he's any good."

"But Mistress—"

"Hello?" Livia called again. Nobody answered. "The residents must not be home, or we'd have been accosted by the door slave by now. So no one will object if I take a quick look."

"But Mistress—"

"Be quiet and follow. This will only take a minute."

She picked her way through the cluttered atrium, following the footprints tracked across the dust-covered floor. The tracks led to a large peristyle dotted with an unimaginative collection of statues and shrubbery. One end was dominated by a large fountain, currently dry and silent because workmen were installing a colorful marble facade around the basin.

That would explain why the workman had been forced to fill his buckets outside. Running water was a luxury only the wealthiest Romans enjoyed. The rest of the city's residents relied on fountains like the one Livia had just used.

She sniffed, detecting the tang of fresh plaster. "The painters are that way." She pointed. "I'll take a quick peek, and we'll be away before anyone knows we're here."

Momus opened his mouth to protest. Livia shushed him with a hand. "Shh. We don't want them to hear us."

She tiptoed to the room. The upper section of the walls had been painted to look like fanciful architecture intertwined with ivy. The painters were now working on the larger middle section. One man ground pigment with a mortar and pestle while another painted a panel of fresh plaster. An older man used string and a compass to mark the outline of a decorative pillar.

Livia studied the finished upper section. It seemed these painters specialized in faux architecture rather than the realistic garden scenes she wanted. Oh well, it had been worth a look. She turned and almost smacked into Momus. He jerked backward, stumbled on his bad leg, and bumped a broom leaning against the wall. It teetered. He grabbed for it. Missed. Cursed under his breath.

The broom clattered to the floor.

All three workers turned at the noise. Surprise quickly hardened into suspicion.

"How'd you get in here?" said the oldest. "This is a private house."

Livia drew herself up. "Sorry, no one answered my call."

One of the workers cursed. "That bum Nikko must be sleeping again. I told Nepos to find us a better door guard." He gave a sharp whistle.

Immediately a clatter of footsteps sounded behind Livia. More workmen formed a loose circle, blocking her exit. One of them looked her up and down, a stony expression on his face.

Livia raised her chin and stared back. "Who's in charge here?"

"I am," said the staring man. He was as brawny as the others, but his tunic was free of plaster stains. The foreman, presumably. "If you're looking for the olive oil merchant, he's staying with friends across the river in the Trans Tiberim district until the house is done. Won't move in for at least a month."

Livia pulled Hortensia's list of painters from her belt and glanced through the names. "Actually, I am looking for a painter called Theodotus, but it seems we were directed to the wrong house. Forgive us for intruding."

The older painter gave her a suspicious look. "Last I heard, Theodotus was on a job over on the Caelian Hill."

Livia adopted an indignant frown. "Are you saying I have been lied to?"

"What do you want with him, anyway?" the painter said. "He's the worst painter in Rome."

"That wasn't what I was told," said Livia huffily. "He came highly recommended."

The painter's eyes narrowed. "By whom?"

"Of course, it was some years ago, so …" Livia shrugged, then gave the painter a bright smile. "I'm looking for a painter to refinish my dining room. When might you be available?"

"You'll have to ask the boss," he replied.

Livia turned to the foreman and raised a peremptory eyebrow. "When will he be free?"

"A month. Maybe longer."

"Pity, I was hoping for someone sooner. Forgive me for bothering you. Good day." With an imperious wave she beckoned her slaves and strode to the door as if nothing untoward had happened. She could feel hostile gazes on her back, but no one followed them.

The moment she passed through the door into the street she whispered a prayer of thanks. Her impulsiveness had almost gotten her into trouble. When would she learn to stop and seek the Lord's guidance before following her every whim?

Behind her, Roxana muttered to Momus. "Lucky for you the mistress fooled those painters with her quick thinking."

"Do not make light of this, you foolish girl." Momus's voice was tight with anxiety. "Those workmen had the look of thugs. Something fishy's going on there and no mistake."

Livia turned to face them. "Momus is right. We shouldn't have entered the house uninvited. Please don't mention the incident to Avitus. It would only upset him needlessly."

CHAPTER 6

After her run-in with the painters, Livia headed directly for Pansa's bakery, which was located next door to her childhood home. Pansa and his wife, Placida, were more than mere neighbors. Livia had grown up playing with their daughters, and their home had been a sanctuary, a place where Livia found the love and understanding she lacked under her father's roof.

More recently Pansa and Placida had become her spiritual mentors, sharing their new faith in Jesus the Christ. Unfortunately, since her marriage Livia was too far away to gather with her fellow believers for prayers or meals. She especially missed talking through her problems with Placida. She hoped her dear mentor would have time for a chat before Avitus's nurse arrived.

Pansa was the best baker around, so the shop was always busy. Livia left Roxana and Momus to purchase some *must cakes*, then she slipped around the queue of customers to peek into the workroom where the dough was prepared. Placida was bent over the worktable, shaping dough into must cakes and other pastries.

"Welcome, my dear girl." Placida enveloped her in a floury hug. "We've missed you. Tell me how you've been."

Livia spent a few minutes talking about her new house and her improvements to the peristyle. Then she brought up the situation with Brisa and Nissa. "They fight over every little thing. The only thing they agree on is their resentment of me as their mistress."

Which bothered Livia more than she liked to admit. In her parents' house, all the servants had liked and respected her.

"Maybe they resent you because they've been mistreated in the past, and they assume you will be no different. Have patience. In time they'll see that you're a good mistress who genuinely cares for them and runs an efficient household."

Patience! Why did Placida always counsel Livia to have the one virtue she found most difficult?

"And how are you getting on with Avitus's family?"

Livia related last night's dinner with her in-laws and her impressions of them. "While Avitus and I dined with Senator Publius and his wife, Roxana made the acquaintance of Avitus's old nurse, who agreed to meet me here today. May we talk in your apartment?"

Placida arched an eyebrow. "You may, so long as you're not prying into your husband without his consent."

"This is about a different matter. Someone is missing and I'm helping Avitus search for him." Which was true, even if her husband wasn't aware of it.

"I hope you're not hiding things from your husband," Placida said. "A marriage must be built on trust and love."

"So you keep telling me."

Actually, a marriage based on love was a foreign concept to many Romans. It was more of a business contract than a relationship. Avitus was better than most men Livia might have married, but she hadn't entered into marriage with an expectation of love. Avitus preferred an existence with as little emotion as possible. The deep, abiding love Pansa and Placida shared seemed more than he was capable of.

"Speaking of trust," Placida said, "have you told Avitus about your faith in our Lord Jesus?"

"I'm waiting for the right moment."

To Avitus, her faith in Jesus would look like Judaism, and Romans viewed Jews with suspicion because they refused to participate in the traditional rites or acknowledge the emperor as a god. She'd been trying to learn about her husband's beliefs so she could paint her faith in the best possible light, lest he forbid her from meeting with her fellow believers.

"The longer you wait, the harder it will be. Don't put it off."

"I'll tell him soon, I promise."

But not until the missing Jonas had been found and Avitus was in a better frame of mind.

Avitus's nurse was a stocky woman with graying hair and a spry step. She had the no-nonsense look of a woman capable of handling rambunctious boys.

After introductions, she studied Livia like a housewife inspecting vegetables. "So this is the young lady that finally caught Avitus's eyes. Why did he pick you?"

Livia wasn't sure whether to slap the woman for her impertinence, or burst into laughter. She'd been expecting a nurse who clucked maternally over her babes, but this woman was the iron-spined variety. Wheedling information from this formidable woman would be a challenge.

No problem. Livia loved a challenge. She met the nurse's stern gaze and adopted an enigmatic smile. "He tells me it's because I wasn't like all the others."

"Obviously."

Hmm. The old woman liked to be blunt, did she? Fine with Livia. "My brother says I intrigued Avitus by debating with him at our first meeting. Apparently well-brought-up ladies don't challenge their guest's legal tactics."

"Then you admit you're not a well-brought-up lady?"

"Not according to Hortensia's standards."

That earned a raised eyebrow and the hint of a smile. Aha. Perhaps the nurse and Hortensia weren't on the warmest of terms. Not surprising. Hortensia would not condone any other strong women in her household. The nurse must be a thorn in her sister-in-law's side. How delicious!

And useful for Livia's goal. "Hortensia was scandalized that I helped Avitus track down the man who killed my father a few months ago. Very unladylike."

The nurse clicked her tongue, but her eyes were smiling. "Avitus would find a headstrong woman intriguing." She poked a finger in Livia's chest. "But don't you dare betray him!"

Livia held the nurse's gaze. "I promise you I will remain loyal. I know how fortunate I am to be his wife."

"See you don't forget it." The nurse gave a sharp nod and her demeanor relaxed. "Now then, your maid said you wanted to know about Damaris?"

That must be Jonas's mysterious sister. "Yes."

"Damaris was a maidservant to Avitus's mother. She was a sweet girl, thoughtful and hardworking. Jonas was her half brother. He was a dozen years older, but he doted on her. He did his best to protect her, but Damaris was a nice-looking girl and the master noticed her, if you get my meaning."

Livia did. Warming the master's bed, willing or not, was one of the harsher realities of slavery.

"One day Jonas saved the master's life. The old man offered Jonas his freedom, but Jonas requested Damaris be freed instead. Old Memmius agreed, which surprised a few people—he wasn't prone to kindness." The nurse gave a cynical snort. "Made perfect sense to me. A trained bodyguard costs more to replace than a maidservant."

That fit with what Livia had heard about Avitus's father, a tough, pragmatic man.

"When Damaris was freed, Jonas arranged for her to be married to a weaver who lived near Pompeii—or so he let everyone believe. In reality he found her a job with a weaver named Hermas who's kept her safe ever since."

"Why all the subterfuge?"

"Jonas wanted to make sure the master never touched Damaris again."

"But you knew Damaris was in Rome this whole time?"

She nodded. "A few of us did. Old Memmius was a hard master, and it cheered us to think Jonas had outwitted him."

Livia made sympathetic noises. "It must have been difficult for Jonas to serve his master, given the . . . circumstances."

"It was." The nurse's tone made it clear it was all she would say on that subject.

"Thank you for explaining the story. Will you tell me where to find Damaris?"

"Only if you promise not to tell Publius or his wife."

"I promise."

After explaining where Hermas's shop was located, the old nurse turned her steely gaze on Livia. "If you want a word of advice, young lady, you'll remember that although Avitus doesn't show his emotions, he still has them. He feels things more keenly than he lets on. So watch your tongue."

A few inquiries led Livia to Hermas's shop, nestled along a street that boasted several other weavers as well as embroiderers and other clothing-related trades. Through the wide shop entrance, she saw two young women sitting at looms while an older one spun thread on a spindle. Another loom sat empty. The two young women were so alike they must be sisters. Nearer to Livia, a man tidied a shelf displaying neatly folded lengths of finely woven fabric in several hues. She might actually find something worth purchasing here. But first, to business.

"Wait here with the basket," Livia ordered Momus, "while we talk to the weaver."

He dipped his head and settled into a bit of shade. Livia crossed the threshold and the man stepped forward with a bow. "Welcome to my humble shop. How may I help you?"

"Are you Hermas?"

"I am." He was at least forty, with a round, pleasant face much like the younger weavers. A family business, apparently.

"I'm looking for Damaris," Livia said. "I was told she works here?"

A brief look of surprise crossed his face, quickly replaced by mild concern. "Damaris is not here at the moment. Perhaps I can help you?"

"When will she return?"

"I don't know." The weaver's demeanor grew wary.

Interesting. Was Damaris missing too? That was an unexpected wrinkle.

"Is she with Jonas?"

"Who is Jonas?"

Hermas was a terrible liar.

"Jonas has disappeared." Livia said. "Everyone in Senator Publius's household is troubled."

The women gave up all pretense of working. They must know something. Good. She would keep pressing. "His friends thought he might have come here. Did he?"

Hermas briefly closed his eyes, the answer obvious on his open face.

Aha. Jonas had been here, and now both he and Damaris were missing. What did that mean? Nothing good, surely.

The oldest woman rose and joined Hermas. "It's as we feared. Dear Lord, protect them under the shadow of your wings."

That sounded familiar. An idea whispered in Livia's heart. Could the weaver and his wife be fellow believers? Livia hummed one of the songs they often sang during prayer meetings.

She was rewarded with recognition on both faces. Praise God! She'd found a way to gain their trust. She quietly sang the next few words then stopped.

Hermas and the woman exchanged looks. He turned to Livia. "You are a follower of the Way?"

She nodded.

"You belong to a group of believers?"

"The one led by Pansa, the baker."

The woman drew an excited breath. "My dream. The bread."

Hermas nodded as if she'd said something profound. Livia looked from one to the other, hoping for an explanation.

"My wife, Judith, often receives words from the Lord through dreams," Hermas said. "Last night she saw Damaris holding a loaf of bread. We weren't sure what it meant."

"Now we are," Judith said. "It's a sign God sent you to help us."

"Possibly." Hermas searched Livia's face. "Why are you involved in this affair, my lady?"

"My husband is Publius's brother. He considers Jonas a mentor and wishes to find him. Can you tell me anything that will help us?"

The weaver closed his eyes, raised his face to the ceiling, and stood silently for a long moment. Praying?

When he dropped his head, he looked less anxious. "Two nights ago, Damaris returned from a delivery. Something had frightened her, but she refused to tell us what had happened. Instead, she sent for her brother. He came the next day, and they left the shop together. We haven't heard from them since."

"Have you checked her dwelling? Asked her friends or neighbors?"

"I checked her apartment when she didn't come to work yesterday. She hasn't been there. We'd hoped she was safely with Jonas, but if he's missing too..." He covered his face with his hands. "I should have gone yesterday to check for messages."

Judith laid a hand on his shoulder. "You didn't know."

"What messages?" Livia asked.

"When Jonas first brought Damaris to us, he was worried Old Memmius or his sons might discover she was in the city. He arranged a system to exchange messages."

Hermas's eyes roved the shop. Livia recognized his expression—a man concerned for the safety of those under his care.

"Perhaps I could check for you?"

Hermas shook his head. "We promised them we would keep their secrets."

Judith tsked and nudged him. "What if they're in danger? The Lord has sent this lady to help us. I'm sure Damaris would want us to accept her help."

The weaver looked from his anxious wife to Livia, then gave a sharp nod. "You're right. Jonas selected three shops run by men he could trust to keep his secret. When he or Damaris wanted to send a message, they left it with one of the shopkeepers and marked the shop with their secret symbol. To seek for a message, you must go to all three shops. At each one, look near the doorway for a drawing of a one-eyed snake curled around some other animal. When you find it, enter the shop and tell the proprietor you want to purchase whatever animal the drawing portrays."

"A very ingenious system."

"Jonas was an ingenious man."

"The more I hear about Jonas, the more I hope I'll have a chance to meet him."

CHAPTER 7

"Wait till Momus hears we're looking for secret messages." Roxana's eyes glowed with eagerness.

Livia waved a warning finger at her maid. "He's still tense after the incident with the painters. Better to let him think we're just shopping." She felt a twinge of guilt for deceiving him, but the day was getting on and she didn't have time to deal with a recalcitrant escort. A little half-truth was more expedient.

"Your secret is safe with me, Mistress."

"Then I suggest you hide that smirk."

The maid's face was instantly blank. "As my lady wishes," she intoned obsequiously.

"Don't take it too far. Momus is no fool."

Roxana's lips twitched. "Where do we head first, my lady?"

"The coppersmith."

Livia emerged from Hermas's shop and beckoned to Momus. "They weave beautiful cloth. I'll have to return later with measurements. In the meantime, we're off to the shops near the forum."

Momus heaved a sigh and fell into step beside Roxana. "I

thought we were finished for the day," he muttered. "Can't she wait and go to the forum tomorrow?"

"Get used to it," Roxana said. "The mistress is always in a hurry to get things done."

That wasn't true. Slaves hurried in order to please their masters. Livia didn't hurry; she was impelled with purpose. She saw no reason to let moss grow under her feet when there was something worth doing.

They did not find a one-eyed snake at the coppersmith's, but Livia did find a very nice serving tray with a decorative rim. Nor did they find one at the basket maker's shop, where Livia purchased a circular storage basket with a snug lid.

Finally, they headed for the shop belonging to Parmashta, the spice merchant. The pungent aroma of cumin, cloves, and other spices wafted down the street to greet them. The open shop front was filled with baskets containing bright mountains of spices in an array of yellows, oranges, and browns. A man stood in the doorway, keeping an eye over the colorful wares. Parmashta, presumably.

Livia pretended to study the spices, bending to inhale their aromas while her eyes searched for drawings of animals. There it was. Scrawled on the wall in charcoal was a drawing of a one-eyed snake curving sinuously around a—Livia tilted her head, squinting at the image.

Momus drew closer. "Is something wrong, Mistress?"

"No. Just a silly drawing that caught my eye. What does that drawing look like to you?"

"An eagle," Momus said.

Roxana snorted. "You're going blind, old man. That's a chicken."

"My eyes are better than yours if you think that's a chicken. Look at the curved beak. And chickens have combs on their heads."

"Who draws an eagle without outstretched wings?"

"Who draws a chicken with talons?"

"Stop your bickering." Livia pondered the drawing. The bird's beak *was* curved, but a chicken seemed more likely. However, she needed an excuse to get the merchant inside his shop before asking about it. She approached him. "Do you have cinnamon?"

"Does Parmashta have cinnamon? Bah! I have the finest cinnamon, straight from Arabia. Come, I will show you."

Livia followed the merchant into his shop. Parmashta sent a shallow wooden scoop into a round basket filled with curled strips of reddish bark. "Can you smell it? Nobody has better. You will buy some?"

Livia motioned for Roxana to handle the purchase. "My mistress would like one scoop of cinnamon sticks, please. And she would also like to buy a chicken."

The merchant looked askance at Roxana. "This is a spice shop, not a butcher shop."

Fish pickle! Had they guessed wrong?

Roxana hung her head. "Forgive me sir, I seem to be confused." She turned to Livia. "Apologies, Mistress. Were you looking for a chicken or an eagle?"

The merchant blinked when Roxana mentioned the eagle. Aha.

"An eagle," Livia said.

The shopkeeper crossed his arms. "Do you wish to buy cinnamon or not?"

Uh oh. Time to try a different tactic. "Hermas, the weaver, sent us. We saw the one-eyed snake and we're here for the message."

The merchant's face lost its wariness. "Wait here." He returned a moment later with a palm-sized shard from a broken amphora with words scratched into the wine-stained inner surface. "Is this what you are looking for?"

"Yes. And we'll take a scoop of cinnamon as well."

Roxana held out the small market basket she carried. The merchant poured the cinnamon sticks into it and dropped the shard on top. Success!

Halfway home Livia realized she'd forgotten to ask the merchant how long he'd held the message. For all she knew it had been waiting for days. It wouldn't do to show the message to Avitus only to discover it had nothing to do with Jonas's disappearance.

She'd better study it before telling him what she'd learned. At least she'd caught her mistake before making a fool of herself. Avitus already thought she was too impulsive. Best not to strengthen that thinking.

By late afternoon Avitus and Sorex had checked with all fifteen *vigile* regions. Across the city of Rome, there had been three unidentified male bodies reported since Jonas went missing. None of them bore any resemblance to Jonas.

Avitus headed home in a foul mood. The lack of a body didn't calm his fears. If Gracchus was behind Jonas's death, his body wouldn't be found.

"Sir?" Sorex's voice intruded into his brooding. "I propose a duel. In honor of Jonas."

A duel? Exactly what he needed. It had been too long since he and his slave had enjoyed a fight. Focused exercise helped him clear his head and burn off unwanted emotions. "Good idea."

They wasted no time donning old tunics and stretching tired muscles. Sorex was a full head taller than Avitus and a handspan broader in the shoulders. He'd been a gladiator before Avitus acquired him. But Jonas had taught Avitus every gladiator's trick, so their bouts weren't as one-sided as they looked.

Sorex pulled two old swords from a chest and tossed one to Avitus. He caught the *gladius* and strode to the middle of the peristyle. Hmm. Livia's improvements created a new challenge. "Watch your feet. I won't defend you from your mistress's fury if you trample her flowers."

Sorex grinned. "It's you who should be worried. Last time I forced you off balance twice."

The big slave took up a position facing Avitus, sword held carelessly, his gaze wandering the flower beds. Avitus wasn't fooled. The ex-gladiator was a crafty fighter who used any ruse he could to mislead his opponent.

Jonas's gruff voice sounded in Avitus's head. *Keep your knees loose. Never drop your guard. Watch your opponent's eyes…*

Jonas had pushed him hard, coaxing and challenging, but never belittling. Jonas's gruff praise had meant more to Avitus than he liked to admit, especially since he never won praise from his father. This fight would indeed honor Jonas, wherever he was.

Avitus gripped the wooden hilt of the gladius, took up a fighting stance, and centered his body. "On my word . . . Begin."

The world and its frustrations disappeared as he focused on his opponent. Sorex got first touch, but Avitus scored the next two. Then Sorex put on an attack that forced Avitus into a corner. His foot brushed against a clump of flowers. Oh, Pollux!

Sorex's blade flicked low then high, trying to force Avitus off balance. When the next thrust came, he leaped sideways. He cleared the plant, but his foot came down on a single low-hanging stem. Uh oh.

"Stop!"

Was that Livia's voice?

"How dare you!"

Avitus darted a quick glance. Livia stood at the edge of the garden, hands on her hips. Her furious gaze was locked on Sorex. "Lower your sword this instant."

The big slave ignored her, his blade still poised to strike. It would be just like the wily fighter to use Livia's distraction to score another touch. Eyes firmly on Sorex's blade, Avitus sidestepped away from the incriminating plant.

"Are you deaf? I said lower your sword." Livia grabbed a vase, raised it to her shoulder and advanced on Sorex.

Hercules, she actually meant to attack him.

"Swords down." Avitus spoke gruffly to conceal his amusement at the ludicrous notion of his wife assailing a man twice her size. Sorex could swat her across the room if he chose.

The big German lowered his blade. A twitch of his lip showed he was amused as well.

Avitus turned to his wife and offered a conciliatory smile. "Don't be alarmed, my dear. We were only sparring."

"Sparring? With real swords?"

He ran a thumb along the blade. "These are dull, not dangerous at all."

"Oh really?"

"We didn't mean to frighten you. I never thought how it might look."

Her fierce scowl didn't ease. Pollux. How could he mollify a wife who'd been alarmed to the brink of smashing a vase over her servant's head? Perhaps an appeal to emotion?

"I've had a frustrating day, and I needed to work out my anger. Fighting helps me clear my head."

"Shouldn't grown men practice swordplay somewhere more suitable than a small garden filled with tender plants?" She ran her eyes over the flower beds. They narrowed when she saw the trampled flower.

"It was my fault, my lady. I suggested we duel to honor Jonas." Sorex gave her his best remorseful look. (Instant penitence was an act all slaves perfected, although on Sorex's scarred face it came off more like a glower.)

Livia turned to Avitus, her anger softened by curiosity. "How does a duel honor him?"

"He was our bodyguard and sword master. As a young boy I admired him and thought him invincible."

"There must be more to the story, the way you've been acting over his disappearance."

"Nothing important."

She scowled again. "Why do you keep everything a secret?"

"Don't accuse me of keeping secrets when you keep your own!"

He regretted his sharp words immediately. He looked away and caught Sorex giving him a pointed stare, one eyebrow cocked in silent scolding. Hades! Why had the gods cursed him with a slave who dared to comment on his morals?

He looked at Livia and saw the hurt. On their wedding day, Avitus had vowed to himself that he would not treat his wife in the callous way his father had treated his mother. At the moment he was dangerously close to breaking that vow.

"Sorry." He blew out a sigh. "Father hated weakness, but I was small for my age and preferred studying to more manly pursuits. I hated sword drills because I always felt like a failure while Publius made it look easy. Then came the accident." He touched his scarred cheek, and had to swallow back the surge of anger that came with the memory. "I was confined to bed for weeks. Jonas took me away to our villa and forced me to regain the muscles I'd lost. He refused to let me give up or make excuses. He knew exactly how far he could push me without breaking me. He took a wounded boy who was ashamed of himself and transformed him into a man."

Livia closed her eyes, absorbing his pain in a way only a woman could. "Thank you, I understand now."

You see, Sorex's eyes said from across the room.

Which was worse? Owning a slave who acted as his conscience? Or the fact that he was right?

Amazingly, only one plant had been damaged by the men's boisterous activities. Men were strange creatures. How did holding a mock fight in the house help anything?

Then the nurse's final remarks came back to Livia. If Avitus felt emotions more keenly than he let on, perhaps fighting was a way of letting them out? If so, it was yet another indication that Avitus was deeply concerned about the missing Jonas.

Did the message they'd recovered from the spice merchant hold the key to finding him? As soon as they were alone, Livia asked Roxana for the shard. Broken pottery shards like this were a common way to exchange brief messages. They were free, they were sturdy, and they were easy to come by.

Three lines were scratched into the clay of this particular shard. She read them out loud. "Look for the dove. Fountain black nymph. Ask blind Sarai."

Roxana wrinkled her brow. "Is that supposed to make sense?"

"It must to Damaris and Jonas. Let's try to figure it out. *Look for the dove.* What might that mean?"

"The dove could be the name of something, like a tavern or a ship."

Livia nodded. "Or it could refer to a drawing. Maybe that's what the bird inside the one-eyed snake was supposed to be."

"Looked like a chicken to me," Roxana said, "but you could be right. Only, why would the message say to look for a dove after they'd already found the drawing on the wall?"

"Good question. Let's move on. What about *fountain black nymph.* Could that mean a fountain near a statue of a nymph?"

"Or a fountain of black stone, decorated with a nymph?"

"Either way, it doesn't help us much. There must be hundreds of fountains in the city."

"True, my lady. And even if we find the right fountain, who is blind Sarai, and what do we ask her?"

Mistress and maid exchanged rueful looks. "It looks like we'll be paying Hermas another visit in the morning."

CHAPTER 8

Livia rose next morning with a sense of purpose. The series of events that had led her to Hermas couldn't have happened by chance. Just as God had directed her to search for her father's killer last spring, so now she felt compelled to find Damaris and Jonas. Her gut told her they were still alive. If so, they needed to be found soon.

After brief instructions to Brisa about tonight's meal, Livia gathered Momus and Roxana and set out to ask Hermas about the cryptic message. They'd gone a block when Roxana inexplicably stopped in the middle of the street. She pointed to a thin boy with ragged clothes who was kneeling beside a black cat. "What's that boy doing with Nemesis?"

Nemesis was Roxana's cat. More accurately, Nemesis was an independent stray who had chosen to follow Roxana when they moved to Avitus's house. Avitus disliked cats and had made it clear Nemesis was not welcome in his home, so she prowled the neighborhood, appearing now and then to accept attention and treats.

Roxana started toward the cat. "Just wait 'til I show that beggar what happens to boys who abuse animals."

Momus grabbed her arm. "Whoa there, missy. The boy's not hurting the beast. Stop your yapping and watch."

Nemesis sprang onto the boy's back and climbed to his shoulder. He rose slowly to his feet, the cat perched on his shoulder and looking very pleased with herself. The boy remained stock still while Nemesis contemplated the busy street, her tail tucked daintily over her front paws.

"See? No need to get all huffy." Momus gave Roxana an avuncular pat on the shoulder.

"Do you recognize the boy?" Livia asked Momus.

"I do, mistress. A young scamp that lives in the area. Called Dap. Earns his living running messages and doing odd jobs."

Roxana put two fingers in her mouth and whistled. Nemesis leapt from the boy's shoulder and trotted to Roxana. The boy watched the cat leave, disappointment clear on his face.

Livia waved him over. His tunic was too big for his narrow frame, but it was clean and neatly mended. His face was clean as well, and his eyes shone with a cheerful intelligence. "Can I do something for you, my lady?"

"I see you like cats."

He nodded earnestly. "Is that your cat? She's a smart one."

"I hope you haven't been feeding her," Roxana said crossly.

"Hush, Roxana."

Thin as he was, the boy had no food to waste on a cat. A boy to run errands would come in handy, and Livia's heart whispered she could trust this one. "Momus tells me you deliver messages?"

"Yes, miss." He bobbed his head and smiled eagerly. "Anything you like."

"I have an aunt who lives on the Caelian Hill. Is that too far?"

He shook his head.

"Tell her my garden looks wonderful, but I need one more lily." Livia explained how to find her aunt's house and gave the boy a copper *as*. "There's a second coin for you if you bring me a reply."

"Very good, my lady." The boy gave Nemesis a last rub behind her ears and dashed off.

"Waste of money, Mistress," Roxana scolded. "I've seen his type before. Uses those big eyes to wheedle coins from soft-hearted ladies. We'll never see him again."

"Two *sestertii* says he'll be waiting for us when we return," Momus said to Roxana.

"Forget it," Roxana replied. "My mother told me never to accept bets from annoying old men."

"A lame excuse, woman. Admit it, you're afraid I'm right."

Roxana rolled her eyes. "Hardly."

"Enough, you two," Livia said. "Tell me more about the lad, Momus."

"He hangs about the neighborhood. Sometimes he runs with the other boys, sometimes he's alone. Animals seem to like him."

"How old is he? Eight? Ten?"

"No idea, but I'd guess he's older than he looks."

"Where does he live?"

"Must live somewhere near, since I see him regular. I hear his mother is sick with consumption, and the boy works to feed the family."

"Does Avitus ever hire him?"

Momus shook his head. "Important lawyers don't need boys like Dap to do their business."

Maybe not, but Livia did.

It was a short walk to the weaver's shop where Hermas welcomed them with a ready smile. "Greetings and peace to you, my lady. How may I be of service?" In a lower voice he added, "Did you find anything yesterday?"

"Yes." Livia held a finger to her lips and slid her eyes to Momus, standing in the doorway. "I want to order new cushions for my dining couches."

Hermas called Judith to join them, and they spent the next few minutes discussing colors and patterns. If Livia wanted a color Hermas didn't have in stock, he had a cousin who could dye to order. In addition, he could recommend several women who had a deft way with a needle, if Livia desired embroidery to embellish the cushions. "I send as much business to the neighborhood widows as I can," he said. "I have samples of their work if you're interested."

When he showed her a sampler of delicate vines done in pale green and saffron over a dark green background, Livia made up her mind. It would fit nicely with the garden-themed frescoes she planned, and the dark background would hide wine spills nicely.

Judith beamed at her choice. "That's my favorite. The woman who does the work is one of our most talented embroiderers."

Livia and Hermas discussed prices and came to an agreement. By this time Momus was slumped against a doorpost, staring out at the street, oblivious to their discussion. Livia pulled the potsherd from her belt and gave it to Hermas. "We found a message. Can you tell me what it means?"

He read it out loud. "Look for the dove. Fountain black nymph. Ask blind Sarai."

"It's from Damaris," Judith said excitedly. "She's alive."

Livia's heart thumped. "You're sure?"

They both nodded. "They used nicknames. Dove for Damaris, Raven for Jonas."

"And the rest of the message?" Livia pointed to the other phrases.

"I've no idea." Hermas turned to his wife. "Do you understand it?"

"Maybe. Damaris sometimes spoke with a blind beggar. Where was that?" Judith pursed her lips.

"The message was left at Parmashta's spice shop, if that helps."

Her face brightened. "That's it! We would pass a blind woman when we went to the spice merchant. Damaris often gave her a coin."

"Did the beggar sit near a fountain with a black stone or a nymph?"

"I don't recall a fountain, but then who pays attention to fountains?"

True. Livia had passed several on her way here, yet she couldn't recall a single detail about any of them. "At least we've narrowed our search to a few streets. That will help. My slaves and I will go at once and search for her."

Hermas gave her a probing look. "Why are you so eager to help us?"

"I can't stop thinking about Damaris. Our Lord calls us to help those in need. Some, like Placida, delight in bringing food to the sick, but I long for challenge and adventure. That's when I feel most alive."

"The mistress rescued me from a rubble pile," Roxana added. "I was trapped and would have died if she hadn't found me. She's clever and brave and she has a big heart."

"I can see that." Judith laid a hand on her husband's arm. "Who are we to reject the one our Lord sent to help us? Have you forgotten my dream?"

She turned to Livia. "Forgive him for being wary. He's very protective of us all."

"As he should be. That's why I'm offering to search while you remain here."

"Your husband doesn't object?" Hermas asked.

"My husband is anxious to find Jonas, and he'll be grateful for any help we can give him."

"Then you have convinced me."

Finally.

"Since I've never met Damaris, you'll need to tell me what she looks like."

Hermas provided a description. "And you'll want this as well." He handed her a small wooden dove. "This token will prove to her that you come from us. May the Lord protect you, and grant you success."

Amen.

"What do we tell Momus?" Roxana whispered as she and Livia exited the shop. "We could say you heard about a painter who is working near a fountain shaped like a nymph, or maybe..."

Livia shushed her. "No more stories. It's time to tell Momus what we're up to."

After walking for a block or two, Livia asked Momus, "What can you tell me about Jonas?"

"Doesn't say any more than necessary and has a stare that would intimidate a lion. But he's fond of the master. And don't take this wrong, my lady, because I would never say a word to dishonor Master Avitus, but sometimes he seeks out Jonas's approval, as if he were still a boy trying to please his tutor."

Very enlightening. "It sounds like Jonas is important to my husband. What if we could help find him?"

Momus shot her a wary look. "How?"

Livia gave him a brief explanation of Damaris and the message system. "I'm sorry to have deceived you, but I felt foolish admitting I was looking for secret messages."

"I wondered why you were so interested in that sketch of an eagle," Momus said.

"It was a chicken," Roxana retorted.

Livia gave her a stern look. "As I recall, when you asked for a chicken, the spice merchant tried to send us on our way."

Momus hooted. "See that, girlie? When will you learn to listen to your elders?"

"It wasn't an eagle either," Roxana said tartly.

"Hush, both of you. The point is, we know Damaris is alive, but we need to find her."

He was silent for a few paces. "Does the master know about this?"

"Not yet. I don't want to raise his hopes until we actually find her." She paused. Now for the clincher. "I'm afraid Damaris might be hurt. If so, every moment we waste increases her suffering."

He straightened his shoulders. "Then lead on, my lady."

They started at Parmashta's spice shop and worked their way five blocks down one street and five blocks back on the next one.

No fountains with black stones. No nymphs. No blind beggars. They returned to their starting place and walked the streets in the other direction. Three streets later Momus pointed down a side street where a fountain of dark stone was set into a wall.

"Good work, Momus. We would have missed it if not for your sharp eyes."

He preened while Roxana rubbed at the faded relief on the fountain's mildewed stones. "I don't see anything that looks like a nymph."

"Nevertheless, let's assume this is the fountain."

There were no beggars in sight, so they continued past the fountain, peering into doorways and anywhere else a beggar might hide.

Nothing.

When they reached the end of the block Livia sent Roxana to ask around for a beggar. The first two women she asked shook their heads, but the third told them of a blind woman who often begged nearby.

Sure enough, they found a woman wearing a badly mended tunic and tattered shawl sitting beside a fountain topped by a large black stone bearing a carved relief of a nymph. "Alms for the blind," she said in a sing-song voice.

They stopped in front of her. Her head swung toward them, eyes aimed disconcertingly in two different directions. "Alms for the blind."

At Livia's nod, Roxana dropped several copper *asses* in the beggar's palm.

"I'm looking for a woman named Sarai," Livia said. "Do you know her?"

"I might. Who wants to know?"

"A friend."

Roxana dropped another coin into the still-upraised hand.

"Why do you seek Sarai?"

"I am looking for a dove who has lost her way," Livia said. "Can you tell me if she is well?"

"Who are you to speak of doves?"

"The one who found this." Livia placed the clay message in the woman's hand.

The beggar searched the shard with nimble fingers before nodding. "I am Sarai. I will lead you to the one you seek."

She scrambled to her feet and held a staff out in front of her, one ear cocked as if listening her way along. The streets grew shabbier and the buildings more crowded and run down. Momus grew tense and hovered closer, but he didn't object until Sarai approached a tunnel-like hallway leading into a rundown tenement building with chipped plaster and missing roof tiles.

Momus stepped in front of the entrance, blocking Livia's way. "I cannot allow you to continue, my lady."

Sarai snorted. "Don't fuss, old man. Only the destitute live here and they don't want trouble. They won't bother you so long as you leave them alone."

"It is his duty to protect me," Livia said. "I'll wait here while you check the building, Momus."

Grumbling, he stomped into the courtyard. He poked at shuttered doorways, ducked under ropes of laundry, and prodded piles of rubbish with his toes. He returned with a happier face. "You may proceed, my lady."

Sarai led them into the courtyard and up a flight of stairs to a balcony running around the second floor. The stairs were steep and the railing so wobbly Livia was afraid to touch it.

The beggar stopped in front of a door that hung askew. "The one you seek is inside, but I must warn you, something has terrified her. She may not be willing to talk with you."

"I understand."

Sarai made a sound like a cooing dove. It was answered from inside by a similar call. Sarai cooed again then said, "I bring friends. They carry your message."

CHAPTER 9

Once Avitus had finished his *patronus-clientes* meetings for the morning, he hiked across the valley to ask Livia's brother, Curio, for his assistance in finding Jonas. After a brief wait, Avitus was ushered into Curio's study.

"Greetings, my friend." Curio flashed his crooked grin, which somehow communicated innocent charm and cynical watchfulness at the same time. He was four years older than Livia, and shared her slim build, expressive eyes, and vibrant personality.

"Please have a seat."

Avitus settled into an ornate chair of dark wood with red cushions. "Nice chair. It's a lot more comfortable than the rickety stools at your old apartment."

Curio laughed. "Everything in this house is more comfortable than my old apartment." Curio had led a wild youth before settling down to take over his late father's role of respectable landlord. "Who would have guessed, when we first met, that I would take my father's place as head of this household or that you would become my brother-in-law?"

"I hope your new aura of respectability hasn't severed your connection to certain useful contacts?"

Curio had a knack for making friends with everyone from poor craftsmen to tough vigiles. He had friends in places a senator's son would never be welcome.

"Never fear," Curio said. "I know the value of maintaining friends in low places."

A servant appeared bearing a tray. When they had been served, Curio sat back and took a sip of well-watered wine. "What brings you here? I hope my sister isn't giving you problems."

Avitus shook his head. "Livia has been commendably industrious. She's transformed the peristyle, and now she plans to redecorate the dining room."

"That's my girl, always ready to conquer the next problem. How do you like her improvements?"

"The flower beds are lovely. Unfortunately, she's ruined the peristyle as a suitable space for sword practice."

"Do I detect a hint of matrimonial disharmony?"

Avitus huffed a laugh. "No, but it was a near thing. She discovered us in the middle of a fight and thought Sorex was attacking me. She threatened to smash a vase over his head. It reminded me of a scrawny cat protecting her kittens from a large, hungry dog."

Curio nodded. "I can imagine her doing that. I've seen her chase boys twice her size to protect an animal or child that was being abused. She's always been fiercely protective of anyone she cares about."

A tickle of warmth fluttered in Avitus's stomach. When was the last time anyone other than his slaves had cared enough to be protective of him? But he hadn't come to talk about his wife.

"I need your help. A freedman named Jonas is missing."

Avitus explained the situation. "Publius is convinced Gracchus isn't to blame, but the whole thing reeks of underhand activities. I was hoping you could check with your resources. I want Jonas found, along with whoever is behind this."

"I'll see what I can learn. Any idea which part of the city he was heading to when he disappeared?"

"No one knows, but I'd start with Scaevola. I did some asking yesterday afternoon and discovered he's recently purchased a house somewhere near the Viminal Gate."

"I'll see what I can learn."

"Thank you."

Avitus left his brother-in-law's house feeling hopeful. A few minutes' walk brought Avitus to Publius's house. He was standing in his study, palms flat on the desk. He didn't look up when Avitus entered.

"You look ready to throttle someone."

Publius's jaw twitched. "My slaves have conspired to keep secrets from me."

"This surprises you?" All slaves were adept at concealing their thoughts from their masters. It was a basic survival skill.

"You won't find it amusing when you hear my news. Early this morning my body slave had a fit of conscience and revealed a fact the rest of the household has apparently been keeping secret for years. Do you remember Damaris?"

How could Avitus forget his mother's kindhearted and infinitely patient maid, who had tended him during the worst days after the accident?

"What about her?"

"It seems she's been living in Rome all these years. Right under our noses."

Interesting. Avitus had always wondered why Jonas never talked about his younger sister after he'd arranged her manumission.

"This brings Jonas's loyalty into question," Publius said.

"Nonsense. Can you blame Jonas for wanting to protect her after how she'd been treated?" Their father had been fond of young slave girls, and his attentions had not been gentle.

"That's not the point. If Jonas has secretly kept his sister nearby all these years, who knows what other deceptions he is capable of."

"Don't be absurd. His service to our family has been commendable."

"Has it? Think of all the times he must have lied to my face to conceal visits to his sister."

"Perhaps it was his way of taking revenge for your callous treatment of her."

Publius's head snapped up. "What are you implying?"

"I wasn't too young to see what was going on," Avitus said levelly. "Father may not have been aware that Jonas and Damaris shared a mother, but you knew. Jonas was hurt and furious that you could use her so selfishly."

"I was young. She was pretty. She never complained."

"Of course she didn't. She was too well trained to complain. But enough about your past sins. If Damaris is in Rome, then she may know what happened to Jonas."

"Which is why I sent a slave to find her. He just returned with the news that Damaris is also missing. Do you see what this means?"

"It's no coincidence."

"Precisely. Damaris must have sent Jonas the message. She's in some sort of trouble and Jonas has gone to help her."

"That doesn't explain why we haven't heard from him," Avitus said.

"Yes, it does. He doesn't want to reveal his secret."

"I see another way to interpret the facts. Gracchus."

"On what evidence?"

"You sent Jonas to snoop into Gracchus's newest cliens. What if Jonas discovered something that Gracchus didn't want known, so he threatened Damaris to force Jonas to stay quiet?"

The idea made Avitus's blood run cold, but he had to be sure.

Publius shook his head. "We both have reason to hate Gracchus, but we mustn't blame him for this. If your theory has any credence, the blame lies with Scaevola."

Publius may think so, but Avitus wasn't convinced. The more he considered Damaris's disappearance, the more he was sure foul play was behind it.

When they left the house, he turned to Sorex. "Find out where Scaevola lives and see what you can learn about him."

Livia followed Sarai into the apartment. The room was cramped, stuffy, and lit by a single oil lamp. A woman sat on a straw pallet against the far wall, her knees drawn to her chin. Despite the haggard face and disheveled hair, Livia could see it was Damaris.

The woman pressed herself against the wall. "Who are you? I don't know you."

"Don't be frightened." Sarai shuffled forward. "Look. She brought the message you left with the spice merchant."

Sarai handed the shard to Damaris, who held it to the lamp. Then she turned to Livia. "Who are you?"

"My name is Livia. I come from Hermas. He and Judith have been praying for your safety. I have a token to prove I tell you the truth." Livia handed her the dove.

The moment Damaris saw it, she relaxed. "Why did they send you?"

"I'm the wife of Avitus. He's very worried about Jonas. We're hoping you can help us find him."

Damaris buried her face in her hands. "Jonas is dead," she moaned. "And it's all my fault."

Livia knelt beside her. "Shh. How can it be your fault?"

"I begged him to come. I was afraid they would find me."

"Who?"

"The bad men."

"Do you mean the men who frightened you on your way home from the delivery?"

Damaris nodded.

"What were you delivering?"

"An order of cloth to a customer who lives on the Esquiline Hill. She kept me waiting a long time, and then I took a wrong turn on the way home. By the time I realized I'd made a mistake it was getting dark. I didn't want to waste time backtracking, so I decided to keep going. If only I'd turned around and gone the other way, none of this would have happened."

"I would have done the same thing." Livia soothed. "What happened next?"

"I noticed a short man coming toward me who kept looking over his shoulder. He made me nervous, so I ducked into an alley to wait until he passed by. Only he stopped at a fountain. He knelt down and sloshed water over his face. That's when I noticed the other man following him. That man gave a shrill whistle and two more men ran out onto the street. The attackers shouted at the short man to give them something. When he refused, they grabbed him and dragged him toward the alley.

"I should have fled right then. But the alley was dark, and I didn't want to trip over something nasty. So I hadn't gotten very far before they barged into the alley. All I could do was crouch low and hope they wouldn't notice me."

The poor woman! No wonder she was so frightened.

"They threw the short man to the ground and said, 'Tell us. We'll beat the location out of you eventually.' Their victim didn't talk so they kicked him. I hid my eyes, but I could still hear the poor man's cries of pain and the sickening thuds. I realized they were going to beat him to death, and I couldn't stay and listen to that, so I ran.

"One of the men chased after me. I made it to the other end of the alley and kept running. I have no idea where I went. I took one turn after another, until I no longer heard him chasing me. Then I found my way home."

"You were very brave."

"No, I wasn't," Damaris said. "I was terrified. That night I didn't sleep a wink, and in the morning I sent for Jonas. When he arrived I told him what had happened. He insisted I show him where I'd seen the crime. I didn't want to go back there, but he said he needed to be sure before he talked with the authorities. So I led my brother to that evil street. And now he's dead."

Damaris broke into quiet sobs. Livia put an arm around her shoulders and held her close.

"It's not your fault," she murmured. "You did as he asked."

"I should have refused. Then he'd still be alive."

"We don't know he's dead."

Damaris wiped the tears from her cheeks. "Yes, we do. While Jonas and I were standing there, four men raced into the street. Jonas grabbed my arm and pushed me into the alley. He told me to run away, and he'd meet me later at the Temple of Castor. He made me promise not to stop or look back no matter what I heard. Then he turned to face them."

So that's what had happened. Jonas had sacrificed his life to protect Damaris—but from what? Who? And why? What crime was worth murdering innocent bystanders?

"Jonas sounds like a very brave man."

"He was." Damaris took a ragged breath and wiped her face with the tail of her shawl. "My heart was on fire, but I kept on running, until I tripped and twisted my ankle. No more running after that. I could barely walk. I didn't think I could make it as far as the Temple of Castor before dark. But I wasn't too far from where Sarai often sits. I hobbled my way to her and she led me here."

"The next morning, she let me borrow her staff so I could limp my way to the Temple of Castor, but Jonas wasn't there. So, I left the message with the spice merchant and came back here to wait."

Most women would be a sobbing wreck after half of what Damaris had endured. Livia was very impressed.

"You must be exhausted. Let me hire a litter and get you home."

Damaris shook her head violently. "I can't go back. What if they're watching for me?"

Uh oh. She was closer to hysterics than Livia thought. "Shh. Don't be frightened. If you don't want to return to Hermas's shop, we'll take you somewhere else. Would you like to come to my house?"

"No! Avitus and Publius will blame me for what happened to Jonas."

Strange what the mind will believe when a person has been traumatized. Livia took Damaris's hand and stroked it.

"Then we'll take you somewhere else. I have a friend named Placida, a kind and generous woman. She'll feed you fresh bread and wash your scrapes and wrap your injured ankle. You'll be safe there. How does that sound?"

Damaris sniffled and wiped her face. "Why would she want to help me?"

"Because she's my friend, and because she and her husband are followers of Jesus, like Hermas and Judith. They consider it a service to God to help those who are hurting."

"Then I agree."

CHAPTER 10

Avitus arrived home midafternoon to find his wife still out. Was this usual? He had no idea women spent so much time away from home. He hoped Livia hadn't been out shopping the entire day.

He gathered a snack and sat down to jot notes on the case he'd discussed with a client he'd met in the forum. He was interrupted by Sorex's special knock.

"Enter."

Sorex padded into the room, chewing on an olive. The big slave was eternally hungry. He was also an expert at ferreting out information.

"What have you learned?"

"Found Scaevola's house. Under renovations, so he's not staying there, but he shows up to inspect. The place is well guarded. His men chase everyone away from the door. No gawkers. No curious visitors. Door kept shut at all times."

Pilfering construction supplies was a perennial problem, but that level of security seemed excessive. "What's in that house that's so valuable?"

"Nobody knows. And nobody asks, because Scaevola's henchmen have made it clear their boss doesn't like nosy questions. That's why they picked a fight with Jonas."

It was Scaevola's guards who had attacked Jonas? Now they were getting somewhere. "So Scaevola is obsessed about security, and his henchmen attacked Jonas for asking too many questions?"

"Right."

What was Scaevola hiding? Was Gracchus involved, or not? And how did Scaevola's secrets relate to Jonas's disappearance three days later?

As so often happened, finding the answer to one question raised three others in its place. And where were they going to find answers to those?

Livia had forgotten about the messenger boy until she spotted him trotting toward her. "Good afternoon, my lady. Your aunt sends her greetings and says she'll have someone bring you another lily tomorrow."

"See that, girlie?" Momus said to Roxana. "You'd be paying me two sestertii if you'd had the guts to accept my bet."

"Just shows who's smarter," Roxana replied.

Livia hushed her slaves with a stern look then turned to the boy. "Do you have time to take another message?"

He nodded.

"There's a weaver's shop near the base of the hill, run by a man named Hermas. Do you know it?"

"Yes, ma'am."

"Tell him the dove has been found and is resting at a safe place."

"The dove has been found. Right, miss."

"Roxana, pay him one as for bringing me Auntie's reply and

another for delivering the message to Hermas."

Dap grinned as the coins were placed in his hand. "Thank you, my lady."

That would ease Hermas's worries. Now to share the good news with her husband.

Only Avitus was shut in his study, so Livia didn't have a chance to talk until they met for dinner. She settled into place and tried to gauge his mood—always a challenge. "Good evening. I hope your day went well?"

He replied with a monosyllable she interpreted as affirmative.

"I found a weaver to make new cushions for the dining couches."

Another grunt. More like a growl, actually. Was that anger smoldering behind his eyes? Uh oh.

"Is something wrong?"

"I don't want to talk about it." Avitus stuffed an olive in his mouth and looked away.

Clearly, he was not in the proper mood to learn his wife had been tracking down missing persons. Well, she would wait until after the meal and hope the food cheered him into a better mood.

Brisa arrived with a steaming platter of fried sardines and a bowl of minted cucumbers. The old woman was an exceptional housekeeper but only barely adequate in the kitchen. Since Avitus was used to having his meals brought in from hot food shops, Brisa's lack of cooking skills hadn't been a problem. He didn't seem to mind the bland pottages and greasy stews he was served, but Livia was accustomed to tastier fare. Tonight's meal was her second attempt at broadening Brisa's culinary skills.

But Avitus stared at the platter as if it contained a pile of squirming maggots. "What's this?"

"One of my brother's favorites. Fried sardines with herb sauce."

Livia plucked a small fish from the platter and took a bite. The fish were overcooked, but the sauce was almost as tasty as Cook's. Not bad for a first try.

Avitus gingerly picked up a sardine, took a bite, and chewed. His expression remained unreadable. Drat the man.

"What do you think?"

"Not bad." He reached for another.

Did that mean he liked them, or was he merely hungry? Sigh.

She nibbled another sardine and allowed her eyes to go unfocused, so she could imagine the dining room filled with new paintings. Would it be better to be surrounded by a serene and beautiful garden or an untamed forest filled with exotic animals? The exotic animals would be more interesting, but perhaps the calmer scenery would be more amenable for digestion?

Something moved at the edge of her vision. Livia shifted her gaze and almost choked.

The furry black form of Nemesis slunk into view. The stealthy beast was approaching from behind Avitus, so he had yet to notice her. Livia glared at the cat, but Nemesis's gaze was fixed on the platter of sardines. She crept closer, whiskers quivering.

Livia crooked a finger at her maid.

"More wine, my lady?" Roxana murmured in her best obsequious dining room attendant voice.

"Nemesis," Livia whispered.

Roxana stifled a gasp and returned the wine pitcher to the serving tray. She sidled past the tray, edging closer to the cat. She was two paces away when Nemesis leaped onto Avitus's dining couch, placed her front paws on the table, and sunk her teeth into a sardine.

Avitus jerked in surprise, sending wine sloshing from his cup. Then he shot to his feet with a loud curse just as Roxana lunged for the cat. Nemesis scrambled away from the shouting humans, tipping the platter of fish to the floor in the process. Avitus threw his cup after the fleeing cat, then stormed from the room.

For two heartbeats, Roxana and Livia stared at each other in horrified shock. Then Roxana said, "I'm sorry, my lady. I'll catch her and take her out."

"No. Call Nissa to clear the mess first. Then deal with the cat."

Roxana curtsied and hurried to the kitchen. Livia took three deep breaths and went to face Avitus. She found him in the garden plucking leaves from her newly planted rose bush and ripping them to bits.

"Avitus. I'm sorry. I've made it clear to all the slaves that Nemesis isn't allowed in the house."

"It isn't the cat." Avitus plucked another leaf. Ripped it in two. "Publius gave me some unsettling news."

Rip.

"About Jonas?" Livia asked.

Rip. Rip.

"Yes."

Could Livia be given a more opportune moment to share her news? "I found a woman named Damaris who knows what happened to him."

Avitus spun to face her. "You found her?"

"Yes, and she said—"

"Hold it." He fixed her with his powerful stare, the one he used to intimidate witnesses during a trial. "How did you find out about Damaris? Have you been prying into my brother's household?"

"Roxana heard about Damaris from Hortensia's slaves and told me. I thought you'd want to talk to her, so I found her."

All perfectly true, even if she omitted a few details.

But Avitus's face darkened. "I hope you weren't wandering the city searching for her?"

"I didn't do anything dangerous, if that's what you're implying."

"I'm not sure I trust your estimation of danger. I once found you in a smoky tavern in the *Subura* slums."

He would bring that up. "There were extenuating circumstances. I was searching for my father's killer."

"Who held a knife to your throat and would have taken you away if I hadn't come to your rescue."

That act of bravery had opened Livia's eyes to Avitus's true character. She would never forget his steady gaze, calming her panic while he challenged her captor and eventually freed her.

She'd learned two things that night: that her first impression of Avitus had been wrong, and that seedy taverns were more dangerous than she'd realized.

"My search for Damaris didn't involve any taverns. I remained safe and decorous at all times."

He scowled. "I don't think decorous is an acceptable term for a wife who goes behind her husband's back."

Anger warmed Livia's face. "I thought finding Damaris would please you, but apparently aristocrats think it beneath their honor to receive help from anyone as lowly as a wife."

He flinched as if she'd slapped him. It served him right, accusing her of going behind his back!

A heartbeat later his shock vanished, replaced by a mask of cold dignity. "We are both upset and not thinking clearly."

Livia was thinking with perfect clarity. If Avitus didn't want to hear what she'd learned from Damaris, then fine. She'd keep the news to herself.

"I can see you aren't interested. Forgive me for bothering you." She stalked back to the dining room to see what was left of their dinner.

Later that evening, after the cat had been put out and the mess had been cleaned up, Livia sat in the bedroom while her maid brushed out her hair.

She was still miffed at Avitus. Had he learned anything useful about Jonas in the past four days?

No. Only Livia had.

Yet when she tried to share her discoveries, he got upset. "Why did I think Avitus would be more reasonable than other men?" she grumbled.

"You can't blame the master for reacting like that, my lady." Roxana said. "It's only natural he would be alarmed to find out his wife was talking with beggars and so forth. It's a sign he cares about you."

"About me, or about his *dignitas*?"

Dignitas was the sum of a Roman man: his honor, prestige, influence, and reputation. It wouldn't reflect well on Avitus if his wife was discovered visiting blind beggars.

Roxana clicked her tongue. "Of course it's you he cares about, my lady. The master thinks less of his honor than any aristocrat I've ever heard of. No arrogant man would keep the slaves he's chosen."

Livia couldn't argue. Avitus filled his household with slaves no one else wanted, like Timon the runaway, and Momus, who'd been sold off because he'd been injured, and he was too old and slow. Avitus was a good man, even though his overprotective tendencies exasperated her. If only she could convince him not to be alarmed when she took initiative.

"We need to talk," Avitus's deep voice rumbled behind her. He came around and sat on the bed facing her.

"I wish to—" Avitus cleared his throat and stared at a spot above her left shoulder. "I didn't mean to sound harsh. My temper was already thin, and the cat eroded what control was left." His eyes shifted to meet hers then veered away again. "Now that we are both calmer, perhaps we can discuss what you learned from Damaris?"

An apology?

Her indignation crumbled. Followed by guilt. She hadn't exactly been a model of patience herself. "I'm sorry for chasing after Damaris without telling you. You were worried over Jonas, and I wanted to help."

She gave him a full account of all that Damaris had said about Jonas and the mysterious thugs. He listened in rapt silence, his eyes glued to her face.

"So Damaris witnessed a crime?" he said when she'd finished her tale. "Where did this take place?"

"I don't know. Damaris was so upset I didn't press her for details."

"A wise decision. You did well to learn as much as you did."

Was that a compliment? "Thank you."

"I'd like to talk with her. Where is she?"

"She was too frightened to return home, so I took her to stay with Pansa and Placida."

He rubbed his chin. "That's next door to your brother's house, correct? Is there a place where we can talk with Damaris?"

"Yes."

"I have several small matters to attend to tomorrow morning, but I could meet you there at midday. Would you be willing to arrange it?"

"I'm sure Pansa won't mind."

"Excellent."

"See there, my lady?" Roxana said when he was gone. "He does appreciate your work."

And it filled Livia with warmth.

CHAPTER 11

Avitus found his wife standing at the entrance to Pansa's bakery, nibbling an almond pastry. She greeted him with a smile. "Damaris is waiting for you in Pansa's apartment. I thought it would be nicer to lead you there myself."

"Thank you."

Avitus left Sorex outside with Momus. If Damaris was as frightened as Livia had described, Sorex's battle-scarred face wouldn't help matters. His wife led them into a workroom filled with flour-covered tables, flanked at one end by two large ovens.

The baker saw them and hurried over. "Greetings, sir. I am glad to see you again. We pray God's blessing on you and your house."

"Thank you."

They exchanged handshakes. Pansa was in his mid-forties, but he had the eyes of an ancient sage: deep, wise and serene. Avitus could see why Livia and Curio held Pansa in high regard. Someday Avitus would have to sit down with this man and talk philosophy. But not now.

"Thank you for allowing me to use your home."

"You are welcome." The baker turned to Timon. "And greetings to you as well. I am Pansa."

Timon hid his surprise and took the proffered arm. "I am Timon. My lord Avitus's secretary."

Many of Avitus's class would be offended by a man who extended the same respect to a slave as he had shown to the master. And yet Pansa did it with a sincerity and dignity that felt entirely right.

"I won't keep you," the baker said. "May God prosper your discussions." He dipped his head and returned to his tasks.

Livia ushered Avitus into a tidy apartment, blessedly cooler than the sweltering workroom. Roxana and an older woman rose when he entered. It had been sixteen years since Avitus had last seen his mother's former maid, but he recognized Damaris at once. Her hair showed hints of gray, but otherwise she looked just the same—caring face, serious eyes, slow and graceful movements. Those gentle hands that had salved his burned skin and cooled his forehead after the accident.

He shoved the memories away. He must remain clearheaded.

She gave him a deep curtsy. "You are looking well, my lord."

"Thank you."

Her voice brought a fresh flood of memories: the agony of damaged skin and the humiliation of his father's callous rejection. From that day on, whenever Father looked at his younger son, all he ever saw was a weak boy who had ruined both his face and his future—a disgrace to the family honor.

Stop!

He stuffed the painful memories away before they unraveled his composure. "I assume Livia told you why I wanted to talk with you?"

"Yes, my lord. I will do whatever I can to help you."

He gave her an encouraging smile. "I know you will. Let's sit down and you can tell me what happened."

Livia, Damaris, and Avitus each took a stool. Roxana stood behind her mistress while Timon positioned himself in a corner where he could record details without being obvious.

When Damaris finished her account, Avitus said, "I know it's difficult, but I must ask a few questions to clarify the details. I'm sorry."

She swallowed and nodded.

"After witnessing the crime, you sent a message asking Jonas to come. Why?"

"I didn't know what to do. I was afraid the men would find me. What if they came to my apartment or attacked Hermas's shop?"

The panic in her voice was like a punch to his gut. He would find the men who terrified this sweet woman and make them pay!

"I'm confident you will be safe. Those men don't know where you live, and the weaver hasn't seen any sign of trouble."

Livia thanked him with her eyes and squeezed Damaris's hand. "You see, God is protecting them, just like he protected you."

Damaris nodded and seemed to relax slightly.

Avitus paused to get his thoughts in order. "Where did the attack happen? How do I find the alley where you witnessed the crime?"

"It's somewhere near the Viminal Gate. The alley runs beside a tavern called the Triton. I don't remember any other landmarks. I'm sorry."

"You don't need to apologize. You're doing an excellent job of remembering the details. Can you describe the man who was being attacked?"

"He looked perhaps twenty. Very short, with a narrow face, protruding teeth, and straight black hair that hung down over his eyes. He was poorly dressed."

"Anything else that could distinguish him?"

"His voice was high and had a Greek accent."

He smiled at her. "You always had a good ear for accents."

"Thank you, my lord."

"I'm not your lord anymore. I'm a concerned friend."

That brought the response he'd hoped it would. A hint of color to her face. Both embarrassed and touched.

"So, a short young man, probably Greek, possibly a slave. Good. What about the attackers? Describe them, please."

"They were all large men. I only got a good look at two of them. One was mostly bald. He walked with a limp and had a whiny voice. The one who chased me was short, with wide shoulders, long unkempt hair, and a gruff voice."

Avitus now had sufficient descriptions to begin searching for the criminals. Now to fill in the details.

"Why did Jonas take you back to the alley? What was he looking for?"

"He never told me exactly, but he wanted to know if the attackers said anything about the fountain."

"Did they?"

"No. The only thing I heard them say was, 'Where is it?' The poor young man kept saying he didn't have it, but they didn't believe him."

A single sob escaped. He'd pushed her far enough.

"Thank you for being so brave. We're almost finished. Just one more question. Why do you think the men attacked you?"

"Because they recognized me."

"You're sure it was you they recognized?"

She nodded. "When they ran after us, I heard the gruff one say, 'It's the woman. Kill them both.'" Her voice broke and she started crying. "He's dead, isn't he?"

Livia put an arm around her shoulders. "We do not know that. Don't lose hope."

Avitus forced optimism into his voice. "Jonas is a tough old bird. We may find him, especially now that we know where to look."

"And if he's dead?"

"Then I promise you I'll find your attackers and bring them to justice."

Avitus left the bakery pondering Damaris's story. It was clear Jonas's disappearance was a result of the crime she'd witnessed, which meant they needed more information about the crime. Who was the victim? What did he have that his attackers wanted? Who wanted it so badly they were willing to murder innocent bystanders?

At least they knew where the attack had occurred, so they knew which vigiles' office to visit for more information. If Avitus remembered correctly, there had been a death reported in the Viminal region. He hoped the victim matched the description of the man Damaris saw.

It was a short walk from Pansa's bakery to the Region Six vigiles' barracks. The young squaddie on duty jumped to attention when Avitus appeared, flanked by his two slaves. "Good afternoon, sir. How may I help you?"

"I'm looking for a missing slave. I understand you may have found him."

A strange look came over the young vigilis's face. "Why is everyone so interested in that stupid slave?"

Avitus's pulse quickened. "Others were asking about a slave?"

"Yesterday some pompous servant of a rich foreigner was here asking about runaways."

"Did he claim the body?"

"No. It had already been claimed."

Interesting. "Did the foreigner leave a name?"

The squaddie consulted a wax record tablet. "Babak, a silk trader from Palmyra. Lives on the other side of the Tiber River, near the Aemilius Bridge."

A Palmyran silk merchant. That would bear looking into.

"Was the dead slave a short male with protruding teeth and longish hair?"

The young man shrugged. "Don't know. Never saw him."

"Then look it up in the records."

"Right, sir. Sorry, sir." The squaddie obediently fetched the pertinent record tablet. "Here you are, sir."

Avitus scanned the entries. And there it was, an exact match of the man Damaris described. Avitus read the relevant details out loud so Timon could copy them down. "Body discovered in a refuse heap near a sandal maker's shop . . . identified by his foreman, Prochoros, as a member of the water commission work gang. Name: Zeno. Occupation: plasterer. According to Prochoros, the deceased slave stole a large sum of money and ran away. Body discovered following night. No sign of the stolen coins. Presumed beaten to death by thieves."

Avitus returned the record tablet. "Can you tell me anything else about this crime?"

The vigilis shook his head. "Like I said, I wasn't involved, but I heard Prochoros was furious when he heard the money was gone. He insisted on searching the body himself. Not that it did him any good, but then Prochoros isn't the brightest of men. More brawn than brain, as they say."

"What does Prochoros look like?"

"Big man, rough face, and a nasty temper. Hair cropped short and eyes always popping out of his head like you just insulted him."

"Thank you for your help."

Back on the street, Avitus considered what they'd learned. "Our victim is a runaway slave who stole money from his foreman. What does that tell us?"

"His attackers were after the money." Sorex said. "Must have been a lot, if they killed him over it."

That much seemed obvious. "But if the attackers were merely thieves, why were they still around the next day to attack Damaris and Jonas?"

Killing a slave wasn't so terrible a crime. Not worth murdering innocent bystanders over. The facts weren't yet making sense. "There must be more to this story. Any thoughts?"

"Why would a silk merchant who lives on the opposite side of the city be searching for a runaway in this area?" Sorex said. "Sounds fishy."

"I agree," Timon said. "Maybe the silk merchant is lying about having a runaway slave. Maybe he was really after the money? Maybe he's the one who sent the two attackers?"

Intriguing possibilities. Avitus checked the shadows. Not much past midday. Plenty of time to trek across the city.

"Timon, go to Publius's and report everything we've learned. While you do that, Sorex and I will hike across the river to see what we can discover about the silk merchant."

After the meeting, Livia hired a litter and escorted Damaris back to her house. Hermas and Judith welcomed her home with hugs and tears. Then they insisted on putting her to bed with a promise of hot soup.

"Is there anything else I can do for you before I go?" Livia asked Damaris.

"You've done so much already," Damaris said.

"But . . . ?" Livia raised both eyebrows.

"I know it's unlikely after all this time, but if Jonas is alive. . ." her voice faltered. She swallowed and tried again. "Would you check for messages again? Just in case?"

"I'll be happy to. I'll go at once."

Livia gathered her slaves and set off for the nearest shop. They scrutinized each one in turn. No one-eyed snakes. Just to be thorough, they swung by the forum and checked the Temple of Castor as well.

Nothing.

They left the forum with heavy hearts.

"At least we can tell Damaris we've done all we could," Roxana said.

Or had they? What if Jonas was badly injured? Wouldn't it be terrible if he were hiding near the alley, unable to walk, with no way to contact Damaris? Shouldn't somebody check to see if he'd left a message at the scene of the attack?

Yes, somebody should.

And that somebody might as well be her. She paused at the next intersection to get her bearings.

"I want to look for a glass maker's shop Hortensia told me about. It's up near the Viminal Gate, somewhere near a tavern called the Triton."

Livia ignored the twinge of guilt at her little fib. A mistress had no obligation to disclose all she knew to her slaves. In fact, it was frequently expedient to limit what they were told. Momus gave a long-suffering sigh and obediently followed as Livia led them up-hill to the street atop the Viminal ridge.

"Are you sure this is a good idea, my lady?" Roxana whispered as Momus lagged behind. "What if the dangerous men are still there?"

"I promised Damaris I'd look for messages. What if Jonas is injured and hasn't been able to get a message to the usual places? We'll only take a quick look and then we'll leave. Nothing will happen."

CHAPTER 12

By the time they arrived at Babak's street, Avitus was sweltering in his toga. Sorex gave the unwieldy woolen garment a few tugs in a vain attempt to improve the drape. He eyed Avitus critically. "You wouldn't want to argue a case looking so rumpled, but it will do for now."

They approached Babak's door. A burly doorkeeper straightened to attention at the sight of a man wearing a toga with the broad stripe that indicated the highest social class.

"Is this the house of Babak, the silk merchant?" Sorex asked.

The doorkeeper gave them an obsequious bow. "It is indeed. How may I help you?"

"My master desires to speak with the merchant."

Another deep bow. "I will inform him of your desire, my lord. Please follow me." The doorkeeper sent a boy scurrying to inform the merchant, then led them with grave dignity through a small but opulently furnished reception room and into a garden that stretched for miles in all directions.

Except that was impossible.

Actually the garden only *seemed* immense, because the peristyle walls were painted with scenes that fooled the eye into thinking it was much larger than it actually was. An impressive feat. Livia would be delighted to see this colorful peristyle that seemed to stretch to far horizons.

Hercules! Married less than a month and already Avitus was thinking about what might please his wife. His brother was right, marriage truly did alter a man.

Several slaves appeared. In moments a portable table had been brought in and laid with a small feast. The slaves melted into the shadows. Finally, a lone figure glided into the garden. His black hair and beard glistened with oil and his fingers glinted with gold rings. He wore a voluminous garment in the eastern style that had the sheen of silk.

"Welcome to my humble home. I am Babak, purveyor of silks and luxury goods. Please be seated, noble sir, and partake of this simple fare."

Avitus took a seat on a marble bench. Babak sat opposite, his dark eyes bright with curiosity. "I do not believe I have had the pleasure of meeting you, sir?"

"I am Aulus Memmius Avitus."

The merchant clapped his hands in delight. "But this is wonderful. You must be the brilliant advocate who defended my good friend Cornelius Labeo."

It seemed the goddess *Fortuna* was blessing Avitus with good fortune today. He'd defended Labeo in an ugly lawsuit case. The man had been extremely grateful. "Labeo is a good man. I was glad to help him obtain justice."

"The gods be praised for bringing you to my door today. A matter has arisen that vexes me. It is my hope that a man as knowledgeable as you could guide me in this matter."

"And what is that?"

"A customer claims I did not fulfill my promised delivery, and thus he does not need to pay what he owes. I would not bother so esteemed an advocate as you, sir, except that the customer has friends in high places. He threatened to have me ejected from the city if I caused him trouble."

Avitus clenched his jaw. Wealthy Romans sometimes tried to renege on contracts, hoping foreigners wouldn't have the legal knowledge to fight them in court. It was the sort of case Avitus excelled at. Few of his station cared enough to fight for the rights of foreigners, but Avitus had experienced injustice firsthand, and he'd devoted his life to fighting it.

"I'll be happy to look at the contract. If the document is valid and your records are in order, I'll consider undertaking the suit for you."

Babak clapped again, a delighted smile filling his face. "Excellent! This is just what my friend Labeo informed me. The fine advocate did not share the snobbery so common among the Roman elite. I am honored to make your acquaintance, noble sir, and I am eager to know what business brought you to my door."

Avitus sipped his wine and nibbled a date stuffed with pistachios. He was tempted to get to the point, but he guessed the wily merchant would be more cooperative if he bided his time. He waved a hand at the colonnaded garden with its painted walls. "This peristyle is a marvel. I feel I've been transported to a vast garden."

The merchant beamed. "My wife is fond of flowering things, and this was done to please her."

"My wife is fond of gardens as well. She has been searching for a painter. Would it be possible to learn who painted this?"

"I can do better than that. The painter is still here. I will introduce him to you." Babak gave Avitus a shrewd look. "But I do not think my garden has become so famous that you came to view its delights."

Avitus bit into another date, letting Babak's curiosity simmer. The merchant's eyes darted from Avitus to Sorex, standing silently behind his master. Avitus's visit had made the merchant nervous, but only mildly so. Nothing in his manner indicated he was trying to cover up a murder. But some men were excellent liars. Time to try a new tactic.

"I was told you were making inquiries about a missing slave."

The merchant blew out a dismissive breath. "How did such a trifling matter come to your worthy attention?"

"An acquaintance of mine has gone missing. When I was told you had been making inquiries, I thought you and I might be able to help each other."

"I will be delighted to share what I know, but I fear it is not much. The naughty boy stole one of my wife's bracelets and ran off. I was most eager to find both slave and jewelry, so I sent inquiries to every branch of the local authorities. As is so often the case, it was in the last barracks to be questioned that we found the delinquent."

"You found him?"

"Alas, only his body."

"And the jewelry?"

"Gone. Stolen by whomever stabbed the unfortunate boy."

"I'm sorry for your loss."

Babak could tell him nothing else of value, so after being introduced to the painter, Avitus took his leave.

Livia and her slaves arrived outside the Triton tired and sweaty. She could see why Damaris remembered it. The tavern stood out on the dingy street with its bold painting of the sea god arcing over the doorway. The lower half of Triton's body sported a rather plump dolphin's tail in pale blue, and the conch shell he used as a trumpet was painted a garish orange.

Now that Livia knew the Roman gods were nothing but myths, she thought Triton looked ridiculous. Why did otherwise intelligent people believe such fantastical creatures existed?

"Strange name for a tavern," Roxana said.

"No, it's not," Momus said, still puffing from the walk. "I can think of dozens of taverns named in honor of the lesser gods."

"I meant a strange name for this location. Shouldn't a tavern named after a sea god be located near the docks rather than here on the opposite side of the city?"

Momus rolled his eyes. "You ask too many questions, girl."

"Humph." Roxana turned to Livia. "Mind if I get a drink?" She pointed to a nearby fountain.

"It was a thirsty walk. Go ahead."

Roxana knelt and plunged her whole arm into the basin. Was she hoping to find a clue to explain why Jonas had been interested in the fountain? While Roxana examined it, Livia surveyed the street. If Jonas had been injured, where might he have left a message? The more she looked, the more she realized how ridiculous it was to expect Jonas had left a doodle of a one-eyed snake for her to find. The real reason she'd come had been to satisfy her curiosity. Not the wisest of motives.

"I don't see a glassmaker on this block, my lady." Momus said.

"Neither do I. We'll go two blocks farther and if we don't see anything, we'll start asking. Come along, Roxana."

They passed the tavern and the alley came into view. Livia wrinkled her nose at the acrid smell of urine emanating from the narrow thoroughfare.

"Mistress?" Momus said sheepishly. "If you'll forgive me, my lady, but we haven't passed a latrine lately, and. . ."

Double fish pickle! Livia tried to think up a reason to stop him, but nothing came to mind. "Be quick about it."

Momus disappeared into the shadows. Livia hadn't intended to go near the alley, but since they were here, she might as well take a look. She edged closer, scrutinizing the mouth of the alley while staying out of Momus's line of sight.

Roxana tugged her sleeve. "My lady. Behind us."

Livia turned to find two brawny men approaching. One had shoulders like an ox, stubbly cheeks, and a mane of wild black hair. The other was balding, with pale skin. He lifted his knee in an odd manner when he walked.

A jolt of fear churned her stomach. Lord protect them! The killers!

Don't be pathetic, she told herself sternly. Even if they were the men who'd attacked Jonas, they weren't going to accost her in broad daylight in a public street. And anyway, they couldn't possibly suspect she knew about Jonas. Absolutely nothing to be afraid of.

"Are those—?" Roxana whispered.

"Maybe. Stay calm and pretend we're lost."

"Looking for someone?" asked the hairy one. He had a low, growling voice, a flattened nose, and small eyes that glittered menacingly.

Roxana adopted an I'm-just-a-brainless-girl face and batted her eyelashes at them. "We're looking for a glassmaker named Alexander. Someone told me he lives on this street, but we can't find him."

"No glassmakers around here," the hairy one said.

Roxana nodded eagerly. "That's just what I was telling my lady. I said, 'My lady, I don't seen a single glass shop, and—'"

"Enough talk, girl. We don't like strangers hanging around our street. You and your lady had better move on." He crossed his arms and glared at them.

"We can't go just yet." Roxana giggled. "Our escort couldn't wait until we found a latrine, so he slipped in there." She pointed at the alley.

Both men's faces turned hard. They stepped closer.

"You there! Leave my lady alone." Momus charged from the alley and went nose to nose with the thugs. "Back off, both of you, if you know what's good for you."

"Take your women and go if you don't want trouble," the bald man said.

"How rude," Livia said in her most imperious tone. "Let us leave this unsavory street at once."

Head held high, she strode away. She could feel their eyes boring into her back, but she kept her stately, unhurried pace for two blocks before turning onto a side street.

"Are they following us?" she asked Momus.

"No."

She stopped and waited for her pulse to return to normal.

Momus gave her a dark look. "Why did you pretend we were looking for a glassmaker? Why didn't you tell me you were looking for Jonas?"

"I wasn't."

"No? Then why did I find his club in that alley?"

He pulled a club from his belt and held it out. It was a knobby piece of polished thorn wood, with a crosshatched handle and a rearing lion carved into the face.

"See that carving? I'd recognize it anywhere. And see here?" He pointed to dark, reddish-black smudges. "Do you know what that is, my lady?"

Her stomach lurched. "Blood?"

"Yes."

Heaven help her! What kind of clue had she thought they would find at the scene of a violent crime?

CHAPTER 13

Avitus arrived home from Babak's tired, sweaty, and frustrated. He yearned for a cool drink and a chance to sit down and close his eyes. Instead, he found Livia pacing the peristyle.

"You're home. Thank goodness. We need to talk."

Jupiter help him. He wasn't ready to face an emotional female just now. He settled slowly onto a bench and dabbed the sweat on his face, all the while studying his wife. He read a confusing array of emotions in her face: fear, guilt, grief, anger. What had happened? How could he defuse the situation as painlessly as possible?

He was still formulating a response when she blurted, "I think we met Jonas's killers."

Avitus was suddenly glad he was sitting down.

"I was only looking for messages," Livia continued breathlessly. "I would never have considered looking in the alley, but Momus needed to relieve himself and he went in before I could stop him, and then the men approached us and tried to scare us away, so Momus argued with them, and then he showed me Jonas's club and it had blood stains on it and—"

He halted her rush of words, alarm surging through his veins.

He'd never seen Livia so close to hysteria, even when he'd rescued her from an angry, knife-wielding ex-suitor.

"Shh. You're safe now. Why don't you sit down and we'll talk this through."

"I can't possibly sit."

He hoped that meant she wasn't as close to fainting as she looked. "Let's start from the beginning. Are you telling me you went to the alley behind the Triton?"

Even after she explained the entire story, he still couldn't fathom by what logic she'd thought it made sense to look for messages near the Triton. Assuming logic was involved at all. He was beginning to suspect Livia never operated via logic. Nor, it was becoming evident, was she capable of leaving a mystery unsolved once she'd gotten the scent of it in her nostrils.

"I hope this teaches you why you shouldn't go traipsing to crime scenes. The next time you're tempted to go searching some-place you shouldn't, please come tell me instead."

She nodded without a word of argument. Maybe the fright had gotten through to her. He gentled his face. "You must be hot and tired after your busy day. Why don't you wash the dust from your face, and I'll send Brisa with something cool to drink."

He motioned to Roxana, who obediently guided her mistress to the bedroom. Then he shut himself in his study and marshaled his thoughts. Livia's safety first. He should have realized Momus was too old and too easily manipulated to keep his wife out of trouble. She needed a younger guard who could curb her reckless tendencies. That must be remedied at once.

He called for Timon. "I want you to find a bodyguard for my wife. You know the kind of man we need to watch over her."

"I'm not sure I do, sir."

"Someone younger and less garrulous than Momus. A man who can keep up with her boundless energies and who won't be bamboozled into allowing her to go where she should not."

"Very well, sir. I will explore the slave markets."

"I want someone in place by tomorrow morning."

"Tomorrow? I don't think it's pos—" Timon cleared his throat. "That may prove expensive."

"I don't care how much it costs. Scour every slave market and gladiator's barracks if you have to. Don't come back until you've found someone."

"As you wish, sir."

One problem solved. Now to deal with the next issue. Avitus called for Momus.

The doorkeeper arrived with a hangdog expression. "Sir?"

"Your mistress says you found Jonas's cudgel?"

Momus nodded miserably. "Forgive me, Master. I ought to have suspected when the mistress suddenly decided to look for a glassmaker so far away. And when we didn't find one, I should have known better than to leave her out of my sight for an instant." He hung his head. "Forgive me for failing you."

"You didn't fail. You kept her from harm and brought her safely home."

The doorkeeper nodded, still staring morosely at the floor.

"However, the past few days have shown me that my wife needs her own attendant instead of expecting you to escort her on top of your usual duties. Therefore, I've asked Timon to purchase a guard for her."

The doorkeeper's shoulders sagged in relief.

Avitus excused Momus and whistled the three-note signal he used to summon Sorex. The big slave appeared in the doorway, a dangerous light in his hard face. "Is it time to hunt for the killers?"

"Yes."

It was midafternoon when Avitus and Sorex arrived outside the Triton and discovered their mistake: The Triton tavern was half a block from Scaevola's residence. If Avitus had realized that fact earlier, he wouldn't have wasted half the day trekking out to interview Babak.

But Sorex hadn't mentioned the tavern by name in his report on Scaevola, and he'd not been present when Damaris related her story. Therefore, neither had realized the connection between the attack in the alley and Scaevola until now.

Sorex shook his head and muttered invective in Germanic.

"Nothing we can do about it," Avitus said. "Let's get to work."

They'd agreed to start with a little quiet snooping to see what they could learn about the thugs or what might have happened to Jonas. If he was dead, his body might be hidden somewhere nearby.

Sorex headed into the Triton while Avitus strolled the street. First he wandered to the fountain. It seemed an ordinary fountain. Why had Jonas asked about it?

After so many days, any clues the victim might have left had been erased by foot traffic and sloshing buckets. Avitus moved on, pretending to browse shop displays. He worked his way down a block then turned and headed back to the Triton.

No sign of the thugs Damaris had described. No sign of anyone watching the alley. The only person who paid him any notice was a beggar. Avitus wandered to the man and dropped a coin in his lap.

"I'm looking for a couple of miscreants who robbed my sister earlier today." Avitus described the men. "Sound familiar?"

"Maybe."

Avitus dropped another coin.

"I remember now. The bald one who limps is called Gimpy. The other one is called Hairy."

"Do they live around here?"

"They're staying at a house undergoing renovations just over there." The beggar pointed to a door with an ox cart parked beside it. Scaevola's house.

"Are they friends of the owner?"

"They work for him. They guard the door and hassle anyone who comes near."

If Gimpy and Hairy were Scaevola's door guards, that meant they were the same men who had attacked Jonas the first time. Were the crimes related after all?

"What else can you tell me about Gimpy and Hairy?" Avitus dropped two more coins into the man's lap.

"Prochoros hired them to find a missing slave."

"Oh?"

"Prochoros works for the water commission. One of the public water slaves ran off with his money bag. Prochoros hired Gimpy and Hairy to chase the slave down."

"Did they catch him?"

"They found him, but he was already dead, and the money was gone. Or so they claim." The beggar dropped his voice. "Some of us think Gimpy and Hairy stole the money."

That was an interesting wrinkle. Prochoros hires the two thugs to retrieve the runaway, but instead they beat him to death and take the money for themselves. Or, since they worked for Scaevola, maybe he'd bribed them to steal the money?

"Thanks for your time." Avitus dropped a final coin and strolled away.

The beggar drifted off to the tavern just as Sorex emerged. As usual, he was munching on something. He crossed to Avitus and offered a handful of toasted almonds. "Hungry?"

"No thanks. What did you learn?"

"Scaevola was here to check on his house six days ago."

Which meant he'd been here the day Damaris witnessed the slave being attacked. Very suspicious. Avitus told Sorex what he'd learned from the beggar.

Sorex tossed the last of the nuts into his mouth, chewed twice, and swallowed. "So it looks like Scaevola is behind Jonas's death?"

"That's what I'm thinking. Same thugs in every attack."

It also explained why the thugs were nearby the next day when Damaris returned with Jonas. But how were the attacks connected?

"It's time to draw out his henchmen and see what we can learn."

They headed for the alley. The buildings on either side rose three stories, throwing the alley in deep shadow. They searched its length in the dim light, picking their way past a pile of smashed amphoras, puddles of night soil, a broken sandal, and other debris.

Sorex prodded a pile of moldy straw with his toe. "Have we given them long enough? This alley stinks."

"Let's find out."

Avitus loosened the dagger sheathed in his boot. Although it was illegal for anyone but the Praetorian Guards to carry a blade on the streets of Rome, prudent men carried a concealed dagger when they anticipated danger. Sorex didn't need a knife. He was lethal with his bare hands.

No one waited at the mouth of the alley to attack them, but when they emerged, a man lounging outside the tavern walked to Scaevola's door and was admitted.

"Somebody has noticed us," Avitus said.

The man exited the house, glanced in their direction and hurried away. No shrill whistles or rushing men. Hmm. It appeared the killers weren't interested in confronting Avitus and his formidable bodyguard.

Now what? Avitus studied Scaevola's house, mulling over his options. Aha!

"If you were working for a house under renovations, where would you hide a body you wanted to get rid of?"

"In a rubbish cart." Sorex said.

"Exactly."

They strolled to the ox cart and peered inside. A thick layer of plaster dust covered the bottom of the cart. Splintered boards lay atop the dust, along with a couple of empty sacks, and a handful of loose mosaic tiles.

"I'd say this cart's been emptied recently."

"Uh huh." Sorex knelt and peered underneath. "I see blood between the floorboards. Lots of it. Not too old, either."

The pieces added up to one conclusion: Gimpy and Hairy had thrown Jonas's body in their employer's cart and hauled him outside the city. Probably to the nearest dump.

"Time to tell Publius. We'll need his men to help us search for the body."

After resting for a few minutes to cool down and relax, Livia wandered to the peristyle to think. A saying of Placida's ran through her head: "When you sow lies, you reap problems."

So true. How was she ever going to convince Avitus to trust her when she'd intentionally misled Momus in order to go someplace she should never have gone? The fact that she'd been forced to lie about her destination should have alerted her to the idiocy of the idea. And now Avitus was more convinced than ever that she was a foolish girl who couldn't be trusted to stay out of trouble.

Sigh.

Roxana arrived with a tray. "I hope you're feeling better, Mistress. I've brought you some dinner."

"Thank you."

When she'd finished eating, Roxana drew an object from her belt, eyes shining with excitement. "I found something. When we were at the Triton, I remembered that Jonas had asked Damaris about the fountain. Why was he interested in it? I wondered. Did he think the victim stopped there to hide something before his attacker caught up with him? So I searched it and I found this." She held up a palm-sized shard.

"What does it say?"

Livia had been teaching her maid to read. She smiled encouragingly while Roxana sounded out the words.

"The altar of Marcus Aulius at the Temple of Sancus." Roxana looked up expectantly. "Is that right?"

"Yes, very good."

"Do you think it's a clue?"

"Maybe."

It sounded more like a note for a lovers' rendezvous, but it wouldn't hurt to check. The Temple of Sancus wasn't far from their house, so it would be easy to stop in and look around.

"I also learned something from Timon earlier. He told me the victim was a slave who stole money. I bet the money was what his attackers were after. Right?"

Livia nodded.

"If I was a runaway desperate to hide a bag of coins on short notice, where better than a temple?"

Suddenly Roxana's clue looked more promising. People feared the wrath of the gods and would never steal anything from a temple, which is why temples were used as storehouses for valuables and important documents. The victim could have left the stolen bag of coins near the altar erected by Marcus Aulius (whoever that was) with reasonable assurance that no one would steal it.

"An interesting theory," Livia said. "Tomorrow morning, we'll stop by the temple and see what we can find."

That earned a big grin. "Thank you, my lady."

Maybe they'd find nothing, but maybe they'd discover a bag of stolen coins. And Avitus couldn't possibly object to his wife visiting a temple.

CHAPTER 14

They found Jonas's body just before sunset in a refuse dump under a pile of broken roof tiles.

Avitus thanked Publius's men for helping with the search and left them to deal with the body. On his way home, he stopped at the weaver's shop to tell Damaris the sad news.

Jupiter Best and Greatest, that was difficult.

Avitus arrived home wanting only to lock himself in his study and grieve. Instead, he found Timon waiting in the atrium. "I've purchased a bodyguard."

Ah yes, the new bodyguard. One more thing to deal with before he could face the emotions churning in his gut.

"Tell me about him."

"Ex-gladiator, sold off when he was injured. Served as bodyguard to a spice merchant's wife the last four years. The lady got rid of him after her husband died."

"What was her reason for rejecting him?"

"Too coarse. Too sullen. Too proud."

"And is he?"

Timon shrugged. "Sure, for someone who wants a slave that grovels like lapdog."

Avitus smiled to himself. An obsequious slave could never handle a mistress as headstrong as Livia.

"Good work. Send him to my study."

The slave was of average build, with skin a few shades darker than a typical Roman and ropes of sinewy muscle on his arms and legs. He looked young and healthy. Remarkably unscathed for a gladiator, no visible scars other than his right hand, where three fingers were missing below the second knuckle. He stood straight and still, his face devoid of emotion except for a smoldering resentment behind his dutifully lowered eyes.

"Your name?"

"Pyriphlegethon."

The name of one of the five rivers of the underworld. The fiery one. A suitable name for a gladiator, one supposed, although it seemed a trifle grandiose, especially given the unprepossessing figure standing in front of him.

"Are you as fiery as your name suggests?"

The fighter shook his head. "The trainer bought five of us on the same day. Assigned us the names on the spot. I was the best-looking of the bunch, so he gave me the longest name."

Even considering the lack of facial scars, the man was no beauty. Avitus could only imagine how battered the others must have been.

"How many bouts did you win before your injury?"

"Fourteen."

Not a bad record for a young man. It showed he could think on his feet. All to the good.

"You served as a bodyguard since the loss of your fingers?"

"Yes, sir."

"Your previous owner was not pleased with you. Why?"

The slave's posture remained as subservient as before, but his nostrils flared. "The lady wanted a bodyguard who could fetch and carry. I was too clumsy." He moved the thumb and forefinger of his damaged hand like pincers.

"Were you born a slave?"

"No, sir."

"I'm glad to hear it. I cannot use a slave who is too servile."

That got a reaction. The man's eyes flicked up, confused.

"You've been purchased to protect my wife. Your new mistress is independent and impulsive. I need a man who is capable of keeping her from straying into unsuitable places. She is kindhearted to a fault, but determined to accomplish whatever she sets her mind on doing. You will need to be vigilant at all times."

Another reaction, this one a scowl. Which meant he understood the challenges of the assignment. A good sign.

"Your mistress will not appreciate your interference, but neither will she mistreat you for it. I'll introduce you in the morning."

After sending Timon to find the new slave a place to sleep, Avitus raised an eyebrow at Sorex. "What do you think?"

"Good choice. Looks capable."

"I hope so."

Sorex dipped his head and was gone, leaving Avitus to face his grief over losing the man who had taught him to believe in himself when no one else did.

Avitus awoke with a headache. Yesterday had been a long and trying day that ended in private grief. Today would be worse.

He was due in the forum by the second hour to get on the docket of the *urban praetor* for a preliminary hearing. Later he would join Publius's household for Jonas's funeral rites. And before any of that, he must inform his wife he'd purchased her a bodyguard.

She would not be pleased.

As her husband, he had every right to dictate her behavior, but it wasn't a task he wished to face on an empty stomach. So he dressed, ate breakfast, and invited his clientes to Jonas's funeral.

Finally, he could delay no longer. Livia was still in their bedroom while Roxana fussed with her hair. He gave her a brief account of finding Jonas.

"Poor Damaris," Livia said. "She's been through so much: losing her brother, being chased through the streets, witnessing a brutal crime. Have you learned anything about the man who was killed?"

"Why does that matter?"

"It might help Damaris make peace with the situation if she knew who he was."

Avitus didn't see how that would help, but he didn't understand the workings of the female mind. "He was a public slave named Zeno who stole his foreman's money and ran away."

"Thank you."

Wait a moment! He's seen that glint in her eyes before. Pollux, he'd been taken in. He gave her a stern look. "The killers are still at large. Until they are apprehended, I worry for your safety. I slept poorly thinking about what might have happened yesterday if the gods had not seen fit to protect you."

"I'm sorry. I should never have gone near the Triton."

At least she admitted it. Progress.

"Yesterday's events have made me realize that Momus is too old and slow to keep up with you, so I've purchased you an escort slave. An ex-gladiator."

Her face grew stony. "I don't want a new escort."

"And I don't want my wife accosted by murderers. So in addition to your new guard, you will promise that you'll desist from asking about the killers or about Zeno's death."

"I promise," she said through tight jaws.

"Your new slave is waiting in the kitchen. I'll leave you to get acquainted."

He left before the storm brewing in her eyes erupted into angry torrents. Hades, marriage was more treacherous than he'd thought.

Livia stared at the closed door for several heartbeats, too furious to move.

It was her own fault, a voice niggled in the back of her head. She should have known better than to go near the Triton. If she'd thought things through before charging off to search the scene of the crime, then Avitus wouldn't have panicked and purchased her a bodyguard.

But if she hadn't gone to the Triton, they wouldn't have found Jonas's body. Had her husband considered that? No. A curse on overprotective men and their precious dignitas.

She brooded over Avitus's decision while Roxana finished her hair. "Avitus doesn't have any idea what I want in a slave. Did it occur to him I would have liked a say in the matter? We could at least have discussed it before he acted."

"Cheer up, Mistress. You'll soon win the new guard over, like you did Momus. Any slave with half an ounce of sense will quickly realize how lucky he is to have you as his mistress."

Humph.

She was still brooding when Avitus left for the forum, attended by Sorex and Timon. She did not wish him good fortune.

When they were gone, Livia asked Roxana to fetch the slave. He marched into her presence and stood at attention, back stiff, jaw clenched, as if expecting trouble. He looked to be in his late twenties, although the scowl creasing his forehead made him appear twice that age. Under the scowl were broad shoulders, a trim waist, and sturdy legs. The only obvious deformity was a mangled right hand.

"What's your name?"

"Pyriphlegethon."

She would have accused him of joking if he hadn't said it with such resignation. No wonder he was morose with a name as preposterous as that. "We'll need something shorter. By the time I utter all those syllables a thief can have taken my purse and gotten away."

Did she imagine a flicker of relief in his stiff face?

"What were you called before someone gave you that ridiculous name?"

"Grim."

An apt name, but hardly suitable for the slave of an upper-class lady.

"Grim is not the most cheerful of appellations. What was your birth name?"

His jaw twitched. "Grim is the only name I know, my lady."

"Oh, really?" So he wanted to be difficult?

"I think Grim's a perfect name for him, my lady." Roxana's eyes twinkled with mischief. "Imagine how it will shock your mother."

"For shame, Roxana."

But Livia's mother would find the name appalling—a wickedly delightful thought. If she was to be stuck with the man, she might as well get some benefit out of it.

"Very well, I shall call you Grim."

A few minutes later Livia strode from the house, formulating a plan to test her new slave. If she was to be stuck with the infernal man, she wanted to know from the start how much of an annoyance he would be.

They were barely out the door before an opportunity presented itself. Dap jogged toward her, waving eagerly. "Good morning, my lady. Nemesis learned a new trick. Would you like to see it?"

"Scram, boy." Grim inserted himself between Livia and Dap, arms akimbo.

"Let the boy be."

Instead of obeying her, Grim stayed put, scowling more fiercely than ever. "What's your name, boy?"

"Dap." He copied Grim's stance and gave him an impudent stare. "What's yours?"

"He's called Grim," Roxana said. "He's been assigned to protect us from scruffy boys like you who pester fine ladies."

Was everyone in the household intent on testing Livia's patience today? "Peace, Roxana. And move aside, Grim. The boy is not a threat."

Grim obeyed, but he continued to glower at Dap.

"Go ahead, Dap."

The boy whistled. Nemesis raced from the shadows, trotted up to them, and rubbed against Roxana's legs. Grim eyed the cat like a senator might eye a leprous beggar. Hmm, that didn't bode well.

"Time for introductions," Livia said. "This is Nemesis. She's not allowed in the house, but I expect you to treat her with respect."

Grim glowered at the cat. Nemesis regarded the man with disdain. As if they'd exchanged some unseen signal, man and cat turned their backs on each other. Nemesis sat down to lick a toe. Grim scanned the street, body taut and head swiveling as if the neighborhood was a hotbed of criminality. Oh joy. Her new escort was a cat-hating, sullen pessimist with no sense of humor. Just what she wanted.

Livia took a cue from Nemesis and decided to ignore Grim as well. She beckoned Dap closer. "Show us your trick."

The boy held up a little ball made out of rags. "Ready, girl?"

He tossed the ball back and forth between his hands, then put his arms behind his back. A moment later he knelt and held out two fists. Nemesis walked up to him, sniffed both fists and then licked one.

"Good girl." His hand opened to reveal the ball. Then he tossed it down the street. Nemesis raced after it, pounced, batted the ball into the air, and pounced again. Then she sat down with one paw draped protectively over the ball and looked at them, clearly pleased with herself.

Roxana scooped Nemesis into her arms. "Aren't you a clever one." She stroked the cat, who purred loudly.

Livia glanced at Grim. His gaze roved the busy street, jaw clenched and arms folded, studiously ignoring the cat and her antics. Why had Avitus chosen this sour dolt of a man to guard her? Livia needed slaves who saw humor and hope in the world around them, not just danger and corruption.

A bucket of rancid fish pickle!

She bid goodbye to the grinning boy, called her glowering guard, and moved on. The Temple of Sancus was an ancient structure a short walk from the house. They entered the temple precinct, which included the large columned temple on its raised platform, along with outbuildings used by the priests. Unlike most temples, this one featured an opening in the roof, which had something to do with needing open air to swear oaths. Whatever. She wasn't here to visit the temple.

They were the only early morning visitors, so Grim should have relaxed. Instead, he grew tauter than ever. He radiated hostility, as if his mistress had forced him to do something utterly vile. But she wasn't going to let Grim ruin her attitude.

She clasped her hands and started a slow circuit of the grounds. Grim followed, a pace behind her, watching her like a hawk. The area surrounding the temple was dotted with engraved stone altars that resembled short pillars with a decorative capital. Each altar bore an inscription, generally the abbreviated form of the donor's name, followed by VSLM, the usual abbreviation for *has fulfilled his vow willingly and deservedly*. These votive altars had been erected by people hoping to earn the god's favor.

Now that she was a follower of Jesus, she saw the folly of leaving an offering to please the gods. What good did these engraved hunks of rock do, except to proclaim the piety of the men who had installed them?

She wandered past the altars, silently reading each inscription. Some of them were so old she could barely make out the letters. She was beginning to fear she'd missed the correct one when she found the inscription she'd been seeking: M AVL, short for Marcus Aulius.

She stopped and studied the pile of small objects that had been left atop the altar by worshipers. Mostly clay figurines and some jewelry. No bulging bag of coins. No shards bearing cryptic messages. Based on the layer of shriveled leaves, it didn't look like anyone had added an object to this particular altar in months.

She searched the ground near the pillar's base. Nothing.

It appeared Roxana's clue had been nothing more than a lover's rendezvous after all. Ah well. She felt a brief pang of guilt for the poor man or woman who'd left the message and then waited in vain for their lover to arrive. "Sorry," she whispered.

She hoped the lovers would be able to make it up.

CHAPTER 15

After an uneventful visit to the baths (where the water was warm and her hostile escort was blissfully out of sight), Livia headed for Pansa's bakery to relay the sad news about Jonas. While they walked, Roxana chattered to Grim about Livia's childhood home and her long friendship with Pansa and his family. The dour slave neither spoke nor looked at Roxana as she talked, his eyes constantly roving the streets.

He was just doing his job, Livia reminded herself.

Sigh.

At least he agreed to wait in the street while Livia entered the bakery. She found Pansa and Placida bent over a tray of risen dough. Placida gave Livia her usual hug and Pansa gave her a kiss on the cheek. "Welcome, my child. What can we do for you today?"

Livia told them the sad news. Pansa led them in a prayer of comfort for Damaris. Then he said, "Damaris told us that Hermas and his household share our faith. They worship with Asyncritus."

Asyncritus, better known as Brother Titus, led a house church somewhere near Livia's home. Pansa had counseled Livia to join his gatherings.

"I haven't had a chance to meet him yet."

"Don't put it off," Placida said. "Marriage is a big adjustment for a woman. You need friends you can trust to advise you and pray with you."

"I know, but I've been too busy."

"It will ease our hearts knowing you have someone nearby to guide you in the faith," Pansa said gravely.

"I'll talk to him soon. I promise."

"Good." Pansa excused himself to check on a batch of bread being pulled from the ovens.

Placida turned to Livia. "How are you feeling about Jonas's death?"

The question caught Livia by surprise. "I am ... disappointed. Sorry we couldn't find him. And angry that an innocent man was killed by criminals."

"Is that why you're so uptight today?"

"No! My husband decided Momus is too old and slow, so he's saddled me with a grumpy ex-gladiator who hates cats and never smiles."

"And this angers you?" Placida said.

"Yes. There was nothing wrong with Momus."

"That's not why you're angry."

Livia huffed a sigh. How did Placida always know the truth in her heart?

"I'm angry because Avitus didn't give me any say in the matter. How am I supposed to feel when he announces he's bought me a slave without any input from me? I'd thought he was more considerate, but it turns out he's just as uncaring as Father was."

"Don't say that, my child. It's not true and you know it."

"That's how it feels right now."

Placida clicked her tongue. "Your husband is grieving the death of a good friend. He's hurting and angry, and he's trying to bring his world back into control in any way he can. The first thing he thought of was his wife's safety."

In Livia's opinion, he thought entirely too much about her safety.

"Why does the new slave upset you?" Placida said.

"He's sullen and hostile. He hates me, although I've done nothing to deserve it."

"Nothing?" Placida raised a reproachful eyebrow. "I suspect you were angry at Avitus before you met the man. Am I right?"

Livia nodded.

"And have you allowed that anger to color your attitude? Did you meet him with an open mind, or were you inclined to resent him before you set eyes on him?"

Ouch.

"I may have been a bit prickly," Livia admitted. "But that doesn't explain his hostility. I haven't criticized him, punished him, or threatened him, so why is he taut with simmering anger?"

"Think how frightened he must be."

"Frightened? He watches the world like an eagle eyeing up prey."

"Yes, frightened. He just faced the humiliation of a slave market. He's in a new household. He knows nothing about you or Avitus. He can only assume you'll treat him as poorly as others before you. And then he observes your displeasure from the first moment he meets you. If I were in his sandals, I'd be convinced I was doomed to a life of misery."

As usual, Placida's wisdom gave Livia a new way of looking at the situation. It hadn't occurred to her to consider his point of view. Maybe she'd been too quick to notice his faults and ignore the rest.

"You can either continue to resent him, or you can see him as an ally and a sign of your husband's care. The choice is yours."

Avitus emerged from the urban praetor's court into the hum of activity that filled the Forum of Augustus. Clumps of advocates, litigants and their supporters milled about, awaiting their slot on the docket, discussing strategies, or listening to other cases. He'd been fortunate to get an early slot on the praetor's schedule, so he had time to talk with Curio before attending the funeral. But first he must escape the bustling forum.

The colonnaded side aisles looked too crowded, best to work his way through the middle of the vast rectangular forum and head for one of the southern exits. He was almost to the exit when a voice said, "Greetings, Advocate."

Pollux. Avitus turned to find Babak, the silk merchant, hurrying toward him.

"What a fortuitous meeting," Babak said.

Was it? Avitus doubted all "chance" meetings involving hopeful prospective clients. But he forced a smile. "Good day. What legal business brings you to this busy forum?"

"I was here to support a friend."

"I hope the case went as planned?"

"Indeed, yes. Our gods favored us with a happy outcome, but the day is even better now that fortune has brought us together. Permit me to remind you that we eagerly await a visit from you and your esteemed wife."

Ah yes. The merchant had invited him to bring Livia to view the paintings. "I'm afraid important business will occupy me for the next several days."

Babak's face fell. "I am sorry to hear it. My wife has grown tired of having workmen in the house and has decided to send the painters away after they finish their current room. Perhaps your wife would accept my wife's humble invitation to visit?"

Hmm. Sending Livia to see Babak's paintings would keep her mind off Jonas and the search for his killers. "We'll discuss it."

Babak's smile returned. "My wife will be most delighted. We are eager to be of assistance to the advocate who did so much for our good friend Labeo."

And there it was, the true reason for the "fortuitous" meeting. "I haven't forgotten the contract issue you mentioned."

"I am honored you are willing to consider it, Advocate. Would your schedule allow me to come to you next week?"

Avitus nodded his assent.

"Excellent. I look forward to our meeting. May the favor of your gods rest upon you in the meantime."

"I don't trust that man," Sorex said when they were finally free of the crowds and striding down a street. "He's hiding something."

"Most people are," Timon said, amused.

Sorex muttered something scathing in Germanic. Timon rolled his eyes, but Avitus could see Sorex was worried. A prudent man heeded the concerns of his bodyguard. "I agree we should find out more about the merchant, especially if I'm going to allow Livia to visit him. Timon, see what you can learn. Start by finding out if he's really a friend of Labeo's."

The secretary bowed. "With pleasure, my lord." Timon cultivated an extensive network of clerks, imperial freedmen, and other functionaries who were willing to part with information for a price. One of many reasons his rogue of a secretary was more valuable than the sedate and obsequious scribes employed by others. The taint of being a runaway didn't diminish his useful qualities one bit.

While Timon departed to wheedle information on Babak, Avitus and Sorex headed to Curio's house. His brother-in-law welcomed them to his study with a weary smile.

"I'm glad you're here. Gives me an excuse to be rid of my apartment manager. I've been stuck with him for the last two hours, listening to the complaints and excuses of my tenants."

Avitus dropped into a chair. "Happy to oblige."

"I see you're dressed for court today. How did it go?" Curio said.

"Productive. I had a hearing with the urban praetor to present a lawsuit. He agreed to our suit and assigned a panel of three judges. The hearing will be next week."

Then he told Curio about retrieving Jonas's body and what they'd learned about his attackers.

"I'm sorry. He was a good man. Have you found his killers?"

"Not yet, and that's the problem." Avitus described Livia's run-in with the thugs.

"Still up to her old tricks, I see," Curio said. "She was always too curious for her own good."

That was an understatement.

"I've been forced to purchase her a young bodyguard who I hope can curb her recklessness better than Momus."

"But you're afraid that won't be enough?"

"For the woman who chased a killer into the Subura?"

Curio winced at the reminder. Despite his best efforts, when she was under his care, Livia had escaped her escort slaves to search for a killer at a tavern deep in the dangerous Subura district. "She won't make that mistake again."

Avitus wasn't so sure. "She needs a project to keep her busy until we can apprehend the killers. What can you tell me about a Palmyran silk merchant named Babak?"

Avitus explained how he had crossed paths with Babak, who had invited Livia to meet the painters. "He seems respectable, but I'm wondering if it's safe for her to accept his invitation."

"I've not met him personally," Curio said, "but I've heard of him. He's been in Rome for years. From what I understand, he comes from a large family that has connections all through the silk caravans. He's a savvy merchant who knows everyone worth knowing in the luxury goods market. He's also an expert in avoiding taxes. Uses every smuggling trick there is to avoid paying import duties."

"So he has connections to the criminal elements in Rome?"

"Smugglers, yes, but I've never heard of him being mixed up in serious crime. So far as I know Babak keeps a low profile and mostly abides by the laws. Seems harmless enough. Just don't let him sell you anything."

"One last question. If I wanted to find out more about a foreman named Prochoros who leads a crew of public slaves near the Viminal Gate, who should I talk to?"

CHAPTER 16

Livia pondered Placida's words while they headed home. Maybe she'd been unfair in her judgment. Could she accept Grim as a loyal servant instead of seeing him as an unwelcome imposition? Was it really as simple as changing her own attitude?

It would make life easier if she could count on Grim as an ally. Roxana seemed confident she could win Grim's loyalty. And, as Pansa often reminded his flock, Jesus taught his followers to extend love and grace, even to those who didn't deserve it.

Well then, she'd give it a try.

They returned home to find the house empty. Perfect. Livia sent Roxana to find her a snack and ordered Grim to accompany her into the peristyle. She settled on her favorite bench. Grim stood stiffly in front of her, his gaze fixed on the ground.

Why did he stand there bracing for a scolding when he'd done nothing to deserve one? How badly had his previous owner treated him? What would it take to break through his mistrust and convince him she was not his enemy?

Lord Jesus, forgive me for judging Grim unfairly. Guide me now.

Livia adopted her most patient, kind tone and addressed him. "In this household slaves are treated fairly. Do your job well and you have nothing to fear. So you can stop acting like a soldier who has been accused of dereliction."

He blinked. Straightened his shoulders a smidgen.

So far, so good. Roxana returned bearing nuts, olives, half a loaf of bread, and a pitcher of water. She set the tray next to Livia. "Brisa is out shopping and Nissa was busy scrubbing the floor, so I gathered what I could."

"Thank you." Livia popped an olive in her mouth and waved Roxana to help herself. The maid took a handful of nuts. Grim stared at her.

"You may eat something, Grim."

Grim remained where he was, watching Roxana with consternation.

"You must be hungry."

He returned his gaze to the floor. "I'm fine, my lady."

Livia sighed inwardly. He was acting as any slave would. She was the one breaking traditions by allowing her slaves to eat with her. She couldn't blame him for refusing.

"This isn't a test to trick you into misbehaving. You've been with me all morning. I'm hungry, so I assume you must be as well. I don't like eating while men stare at every morsel in sullen silence."

He remained still as a statue. Roxana rolled her eyes and ripped a hunk of bread from the loaf. "Let me explain something, you big dolt. In this household slaves aren't expected to act like furniture, silent and still until given an order. When the lady gives you permission to eat, she means it. Here." Roxana tossed the chunk of bread at him.

He caught it and glared daggers at her. "Do you make light of everything, you foolish, babbling woman?"

She marched to him, hands on hips. "Right now, I'm deadly serious. We have the kindest, cleverest mistress in all of Rome. Don't you dare insult her by rejecting her generosity." She emphasized the last words by poking her finger in his chest. Then she snatched the bread from his hand and stuffed it in her mouth.

He stared at her, slack-jawed. Roxana's unorthodox attack had broken through his protective shell. Now to soothe his feelings.

"Mind your manners, Roxana. The poor man is miserable enough without you taunting him."

He blinked. Flicked a glance at Livia then back to Roxana. He'd probably never been defended by his mistress before.

"Did my husband explain what prompted him to purchase you?"

He shook his head.

"I thought not." She gave him a brief account of all that had happened regarding Jonas, Damaris, and Zeno, the slave. He listened in stolid silence until she got to the part about finding the message shard that led them to the Temple of Sancus. Suddenly he jerked his head up. She stopped. "What's wrong?"

"Nothing, my lady."

"Nonsense. Something is bothering you. Spit it out."

"She'll keep after you until you answer," Roxana said. "Save us the trouble and tell us now."

His jaw twitched. "You went to the temple because you were searching for stolen money?"

"That's right."

The angry creases in his forehead relaxed and his jaw unclenched. Livia gave a silent shout of victory. He was thawing.

If only she knew why.

Suddenly Roxana laughed. "Ooh! You thought the mistress was looking for love tokens, didn't you?"

When his face reddened, understanding dawned. The man had assumed Livia had gone to the temple to arrange a liaison with an illicit lover. No wonder he'd gone all hostile.

"Mistress Livia is loyal to her husband," Roxana said. "That's why she's so keen to help the master figure out who killed his friend."

That prompted a snort of disbelief.

Roxana put fists to hips. "For your information, the mistress and I tracked down a murderer."

"It's true," Livia said. "Sorex can tell you about it later." She continued her explanation of all they knew about Jonas, Zeno, and the men who attacked them.

When she finished, he shook his head. "It makes no sense. Why would Zeno steal money and then hide it? If I were running away, I'd take the money and get out of the city as quickly as possible."

"Good point," Livia said, delighted they'd gotten him talking. "Nothing about this crime makes sense, does it? Let's consider all the facts that don't add up."

She listed them on her fingers. "Why would Zeno steal money and hide it? If he was running away, why was he still in the city? Did the attackers find the money, or is it still missing? What else?" She raised an eyebrow at Grim.

"Why were the same attackers still there the next day when Jonas returned?" he replied.

"Excellent question. It seems to me that Jonas's death won't make sense until we know more about Zeno and why he stole that money. I wish Avitus hadn't made me promise not to look into him."

"You could send me, my lady," Roxana said. "I have friends who might know something about Zeno."

"That's not a bad idea."

Livia and Roxana both looked at Grim. "You have a problem with that?" Roxana asked.

He shrugged. "I'm not responsible for what foolish maids do on their own. But try to take this seriously. These men are dangerous. And whatever you do, leave the mistress's name out if it."

Livia and Roxana exchanged raised eyebrows. It seemed Grim wasn't as uncooperative as they'd thought.

Lord be praised!

The funeral for Jonas didn't include a procession featuring the masks of his illustrious ancestors or other trappings typical of an aristocrat's funeral. But Publius had provided plenty of myrrh and frankincense for the pyre, as well as professional mourners to add the proper note of grief.

When the body had been reduced to ashes, Avitus and Sorex trudged back into the city. It had been a long, trying day, and the worst was yet to come. He dreaded facing his angry wife, but when he entered the house, he found the new guard playing dice with Momus and his wife bent over a tablet, helping Roxana with a spelling drill. No ugly rants. No martyred looks.

He didn't understand why, but he wasn't going to complain. After exchanging pleasantries, he dumped his sweaty toga on the floor of the bedroom, pulled a fresh tunic over his head and lay down to release the tension in his neck and shoulders. He was feeling much more himself by the time Timon appeared with a report on Babak.

"Tell me what you learned."

"As you requested, I first checked with Labeo. He and Babak are friends, and he remembers telling Babak about you."

Timon went on to report details about Babak's various business ventures and associates. "In sum, he specializes in silk, but he is happy to deal in any other luxury good that comes from the East. I did hear one other detail you'll find interesting. An imperial clerk told me Babak has been to the palace on more than one occasion to supply the Empress Messalina with silks."

Avitus stored that fascinating tidbit away for later use. One never knew when a fact like that would come in handy. For now, he'd satisfied himself that Babak had been telling the truth, so far as it went. Which meant it would be safe to send Livia to visit him.

He brought it up after dinner. "I met a silk merchant the other day. I was impressed by the paintings in his peristyle and thought you might like them. He's invited you to visit his wife tomorrow."

Livia seemed delighted at the prospect. "How nice of him to extend an invitation to me. And how thoughtful of you to think about my search for painters when you have so much else going on."

Jupiter be praised. His plan had worked.

CHAPTER 17

The silk merchant's invitation was the perfect opportunity to let Roxana look into Zeno. By the next morning Livia had it all planned. She explained it to Roxana as she was getting dressed.

"I'll ask my friend Fabia to go with me to Babak's house. That way propriety will be satisfied and you'll be free to question your friends. What do you think of that?"

"Brilliant idea, my lady." Roxana's voice was brimming with excitement. She loved snooping even more than Livia did. "I won't disappoint you."

When she was dressed and ready to go, Livia explained her plan to Grim. "Any objections?"

He shook his head. "So long as she doesn't do anything stupid!"

Roxana gave him an exasperated humph. "I was born in the Subura; I know how to take care of myself."

He replied with a wordless grunt that eloquently expressed his lack of faith in Roxana's abilities. In return she gave him a sour face.

Well, it was good to see her slaves getting along. If only Brisa and Nissa could do as well. Livia went to check on them before leaving, and found Nissa in the kitchen rearranging the spices.

"Stop that," Livia snapped. "You're only making your life more miserable by annoying Brisa."

She ordered Nissa to put the spices back in order and then to water all the plants in the peristyle. That should keep her out of trouble for an hour or two.

With her domestic staff under control for the moment, Livia gathered her escorts and headed for the home of her longtime friend, Fabia. Growing up, the two girls had spent many happy hours together. Fabia was always ready for an adventure. She'd jump at the chance to meet an intriguing foreign merchant and his wife.

When they reached Fabia's front door, Livia sent Roxana off on her errand. "Be back here by midday, and be careful who you talk to."

"Yes, Mistress."

Fabia was delighted to find Livia at her doorstep. She sported an ornate hairstyle, an expensive tunic with heavy embroidering on the hems, and at least a dozen silver bangles on her slender arms, which clanked as she drew Livia into a hug. "Livia darling! I've missed you so! Tell me all about marriage. How bad is it?"

The friends spent an hour discussing the unfathomable behavior of males, conjugal relations, stubborn slaves, and the challenges of redecorating. Fabia was betrothed to a man even older than Avitus, who was often away for days at a time dealing with business matters in the port of Ostia. Fabia was not particularly upset that her new husband would be away from home so often. "It will mean more freedom for me to visit as I please without concern for his social plans."

"Speaking of plans, I have a proposition for you."

"I'm all ears."

Livia explained her invitation to visit the silk merchant's wife and view the paintings. "Will you join me?"

Fabia waggled her eyebrows. "Would I turn down a chance to meet an exotic gentleman who deals in silk?"

Livia laughed. "That's what I'd hoped you'd say."

"Then let's be off."

When she heard Babak lived in the Trans Tiberim district, Fabia insisted on borrowing her mother's carrying chair rather than walking all the way across town and over the river. The women settled onto the litter while Grim and two of Fabia's attendants followed on foot. While the litter bearers trudged across the city, Livia listened to Fabia prattle on about her latest gladiator crush. There was a new one every few months and Livia was not up to date.

By the time they arrived at their destination, Livia knew every commendable feature of her friend's favored gladiator. She was more than ready for a change of subject when they arrived at a doorway guarded by a brawny man who watched passersby with the same level of hostility one would expect of a cornered bear facing a pack of wild dogs.

The man's fearsome scowl evaporated at Livia's name. He bowed low with folded hands. "Your visit is expected, my lady. Please follow me."

He led them into a large atrium and handed them off to a graceful maid, who also bowed low. "Welcome, ladies. The master and mistress are in the garden. This way, if you please."

True to Avitus's word, the silk merchant's peristyle was stunning. Livia felt she'd been transported to the royal gardens of some far-off eastern potentate. This was exactly the look and feel she wanted in her dining room.

Her awe must have been obvious for when she brought her

gaze to rest on her hosts, their faces shone with delight. "Welcome to our home, Livia Aemilia. I am Babak, humble purveyor of silk, and this is my wife, Nahla."

"Thank you for inviting me. May I introduce my dear friend, Fabia, a fellow connoisseur of beauty. My husband praised your peristyle gardens, but his words were not nearly eloquent enough to capture the reality."

"Your delight is ours, most honored lady. Please take your time to examine the paintings as closely as you wish."

Babak excused himself, leaving the women free to talk. They took a circuit of the colonnade, their hostess stopping at each section to point out her favorite details or comment on the origin of the scene. Nahla was unabashedly pleased with the painters' work, but she was sick and tired of the mess. "I've decided to cancel the remaining two rooms I'd planned on getting redone, so you've come at the perfect time. If you wish to discuss hiring the painters, I'll introduce you."

"They don't have other jobs lined up?"

"I don't think so. They were expecting another month of work here. I imagine they'll be happy to accept your project."

When the tour was completed, a sumptuous snack was laid out for them by silent and efficient servants. While Fabia and Nahla discussed silks and embroideries, Livia studied the garden walls, committing to memory the features and designs that would suit her vision and the confines of her much smaller home. The painters had an excellent eye for details. Their flowers appeared real enough to pick and the animals looked like they were actually moving.

The more she studied the artwork, the more excited Livia became. It was no chance coincidence that her husband met this man just when Livia was looking for a painter. *Thank you, Lord Jesus, for guiding me to a talented painter who respects the beauty in your creation.*

After her prayer, she turned her attention to the conversation. Before long Livia knew the life history of Babak, his wife, their children, and various relatives that lived in Rome or were part of the import business.

When the snacks and anecdotes were depleted, Nahla led Livia to the guest room where the painters were at work. The head painter was young, no more than twenty-five. He was tall and narrow shouldered, with a mop of shaggy brown hair and hands smudged liberally with pigments. When he heard that Livia was interested in hiring him, he was all smiles. He promised to visit the house in three or four days to discuss the project.

After that Livia took her leave. "I thank you for a most enjoyable morning," she told Nahla. "When our dining room is fit for company, I'll have you and your husband to dinner."

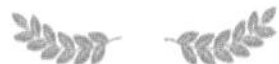

After seeing her mistress safely to Fabia's door, Roxana headed for the Subura, a poor neighborhood filled with overcrowded apartment buildings that spread across the valley between the tip of the Quirinal ridge and the Esquiline Hill. She had many friends there. Some were slaves, others craftsmen and shopkeepers. She headed for the home of one friend in particular, a devious freedman named Cyzicus who had been her family's landlord. If anyone knew something about runaway slaves being beaten to death, it would be him.

For his legitimate income, Cyzicus managed two multistory tenement buildings. He lived in a comfortable first-floor apartment in one of them. Like every other building along the street, the exterior walls were covered in drab plaster encrusted with layers of painted graffiti advertising everything from last year's political candidates to upcoming chariot races.

The interior of Cyzicus's apartment contrasted sharply with the dingy street. His reception room was painted in panels of deep red trimmed with golden scrollwork. One wall was covered by an intricate tapestry from Parthia or some other eastern land. Cyzicus lounged on a couch piled with silken cushions embroidered with silver thread. Beside him was a shiny bowl of roasted almonds sitting atop a delicate table of inlaid wood.

Roxana had always been careful not to inquire how the man had amassed his wealth. It was the kind of thing she was better off not knowing.

Cyzicus plucked an almond from the bowl with pudgy fingers. "Well, if it isn't little Roxana. I haven't seen you in . . . how long has it been?"

"Four years since Mother and I were sold to cover my father's debts."

"What brings you back to these pestilential streets?"

"I'm on an errand for my mistress."

Cyzicus raised an eyebrow. "In the Subura?"

She grinned at him. "I may have taken a detour."

"To visit your dear old landlord?" he scoffed.

"Why not?" Roxana gave him an innocent smile. "I like to come by the neighborhood now and then to see who's still here."

"And here I am." He popped the almond in his mouth. "What is it you want, girl?"

"Information about a public slave who tried to run away and was killed up near the Viminal Gate. Our doorkeeper claimed this slave stole twelve thousand sestertii. I told him he had cheese for brains, so he bet me ten sestertii that he was right."

It was an outrageous story, but it might amuse Cyzicus enough to cooperate.

"Why come to me? The Viminal isn't my territory."

"You know people who can help me."

"Nothing is free, my dear."

As if she didn't know. Roxana placed silver *denarii* on the table, one at a time. When she got to three, Cyzicus swept a hand over the table and the coins disappeared. "Talk to Fullo. He runs a tavern near the Viminal Gate."

She waited. Cyzicus looked pointedly at the table, but there were other ways to earn his help. "A slave of Senator Publius's told me the aediles were planning a crackdown on illegal gambling and unregistered prostitutes."

His eyebrows rose. "That's what I call useful information. Good girl. You haven't lost your knack for listening."

"You taught me well."

"So I see." He winked at her. "The tavern you want is called the Black Bull. It's near the Praetorian barracks, so be on your guard."

She left him chortling over his bad pun. Fortunately, at this hour of the morning, the tavern was empty of Praetorian Guards, or any other customers. A handful of men and women were tidying the floor and getting things ready for another day of business.

Roxana put on her friendliest smile and strolled inside. "Good morning. Which of you is Fullo?"

Everyone glanced at a man pouring wine from an amphora into a series of pitchers. He scowled at Roxana and kept pouring. "Can't you see we're not open? Come back later."

"I haven't come for your wine."

"Must be she's come to enjoy your charm, Fullo," one of the workers said. The others laughed.

Fullo lowered the amphora to the floor with a grunt. "Begone with you; you're disturbing my workers."

Roxana stood her ground. "Cyzicus thought you might be able to answer a question for me. Was he wrong?"

At the mention of Cyzicus, Fullo's scowl disappeared. "Why didn't you say you were a friend of his? How is the old reprobate?"

"Charming as ever, but he's gained another chin since I last saw him."

Fullo chuckled. "One of these days he's going to get so fat he won't fit through his door. What can I do for you?"

"I need information on a public slave named Zeno who stole money and tried to run away last week."

"Heard about that. One of Prochoros's crew, which explains why he was fool enough to make a break for it."

"Because Prochoros is. . . ?"

"Someone a nice girl like you should stay away from. Nasty piece of work, and dishonest as the day is long."

Roxana gave him an appropriately shocked face. "If a friend of mine wanted to find Prochoros, where should he look?"

"Works for the water commission, but I'm warning you, stay away from him."

"What about talking to his crew?"

"You could try the old man with the bum leg," said the woman who'd spoken earlier. "He'll know what's going on."

The tavern keeper shook his head. "Bad idea. You know how riled Prochoros has been since the slave went missing. Worse than a camel with a toothache. Stay away from their barracks. If you're desperate to find someone who knew the dead slave, I'd suggest asking around near the Viminal Baths. The crew's done a lot of work near there. Leaky pipes."

Roxana thanked him and headed for the bath complex perched on the north side of the Viminal Hill. Since Mistress Livia used to live nearby, Roxana was familiar with many of the shops surrounding the bath building. She started with the shopkeepers Livia had visited often. They recognized Roxana and were happy to talk, but no one remembered Zeno.

As one shopkeeper said, "Why would I pay attention to a public slave?"

Why indeed? Roxana glanced at the sun, soaring overhead. She was due back at Fabia's. She'd try one last shopkeeper. Who had she overlooked? Hmm, what about the pushy old man who sold perfumed bath oils?

She approached his cart with an exaggerated swing in her hips and a flirtatious smile on her face. "Good day, old man."

"Well, if it isn't sassy-tongued Roxana," he said. "What mischief are you up to, traipsing about the streets without your mistress?"

"I'm doing a favor for a friend. She's been trying to find a slave named Zeno who works on the crew doing repairs to the water pipes. He's very short, with a long face, black hair, and a Greek accent. Do you remember him?"

The man nodded. "Sad looking chap. Seen him around these past months."

At last!

"Did you ever talk to him?"

"Not much of a talker, that one. Only person I ever saw him talk with was Eleni."

"Who's she?"

He pointed. "Snippy little thing with a tongue sassy as yours. Sells pastries."

Roxana craned her neck to look. Since the mistress always bought baked goods from Pansa, Roxana hadn't paid other pastry sellers much heed. "You mean the girl with the red and gold cart?"

"That's the one. Seen Zeno talking with her more than once. He was sweet on her."

"Thank you." Roxana gave him a copper as and a peck on the cheek, which left him grinning.

She was tempted to question the pastry seller at once, but the girl had a queue of customers and Roxana was already running late. Better to return to the mistress.

At least she had something useful to report.

CHAPTER 18

A message arrived from Publius late morning. Avitus broke the seal and opened the tablet:

I endeavored to have Jonas's killers arrested, but the authorities were unable to find them. The miscreants have disappeared, and the remaining workmen claim not to know where they have gone. We are told the pair were hired recently and are not part of Scaevola's household. To add to my frustration, Scaevola has been out of the city for the past three days and thus was not available to answer questions.

The Prefect of Vigiles has agreed to put the criminals on his watch list, but I suspect we will need to find them ourselves if we wish justice to prevail. I count on you to pursue this matter.

Avitus had been afraid this would happen. He should have insisted Publius deal with the killers as soon as they found Jonas's body. Now the criminals had slipped from their grasp, and Avitus was too busy preparing for a trial to run after them today. He sent Sorex to the Triton to sniff around while he and Timon worked on speeches for the upcoming case. They'd finished one speech and started another when Sorex's knock sounded on the study door.

"Enter."

"Scaevola's house is shut tight. All the workers have been sent away. So I looked into Prochoros instead."

"The foreman of the dead slave, you mean?" Timon asked.

"Right. Prochoros lives near the Triton, but he drinks at a tavern called the Black Bull. Regulars there have seen him with Gimpy and Hairy. Back at least nine months."

So Prochoros knew the thugs? That would explain why he'd hired them to track down his missing slave. And if the killers knew him, then it wasn't likely they were in cahoots with Scaevola to steal the money. Which turned Avitus back to wondering why they'd beaten Zeno to death. Could Prochoros have been so desperate to find the stolen money that he'd ordered the thugs to do so?

"Did you find out how much was stolen?"

"No, but I heard the money is still missing. Prochoros had the whole slave barracks searched. He insists Zeno hid it somewhere. Refuses to believe the money could have been stolen by random thieves."

"What makes him think that?"

Sorex shrugged. "Who knows, but it doesn't sound like Gimpy and Hairy stole it. They were helping him search."

Hmm. It was beginning to sound like Gimpy and Hairy worked for Prochoros. But if so, why had they been guarding Scaevola's door? And if neither Prochoros nor the thugs had the money, where was it? And how was any of this related to Jonas or Damaris? The more they learned, the more confusing things got. Which meant they were missing something important.

If only he knew what it was, or where to look next.

Who would have guessed the search for Zeno would lead Livia to a street she used to travel daily?

"That's the woman we want, my lady." Roxana pointed to a petite woman who stood behind a two-wheeled cart painted a cheery red with yellow accents.

As they approached, the pastry seller was arguing with a large man. "Either buy something or go away," she said with a scowl. "I have no time for loiterers."

"I have as much right to stand in this street as you do," the man replied.

"You can stand there till you rot, but I'm not giving you a crumb unless I see a coin." Small as she was, her voice was loud and fearless. A strong woman. Livia liked her already.

The man reached for a pastry. The pastry seller swatted his hand. He laughed and reached again.

"Keep your paws off my goods!" She moved the cart a few paces away.

Her tormentor followed. He put both hands on the cart and leaned toward her with a nasty laugh. "I'll take whatever I want."

Oh, how Livia hated bullies! She raised her voice. "You there! If you do not intend to purchase the wares, then I suggest you take yourself off."

The man turned and gave her a blank stare.

"My lady means scram," Roxana said. "Or she'll have her bodyguard beat the stuffing out of you. He used to be a gladiator, and he ate oafs like you for breakfast."

Grim obediently crossed his arms and glared, his features hard as granite. "Beat it, scum."

The man muttered a curse and trudged off.

"Good riddance," the pastry seller called after him. Then she gave Livia a deep bow. "Thank you, my lady. He's been bothering me the past two days and I was at my wit's end."

"You're welcome," Livia said. "What's your name?"

"Eleni, miss. May I help you? My master's pastries are the best in the city. The pistachio cakes are his specialty."

A woman who got right to business. Livia would do likewise. "I understand you know Zeno."

The pastry seller hesitated for a heartbeat before shaking her head. "I don't think so."

But the hesitation had given her away.

"You were seen talking to him," Livia said, her tone leaving no room for denials.

Eleni waved a hand at the busy street. "I talk to people all day long. Doesn't mean I know them."

"Zeno was a slave who worked for the water commission. He was short, with a long face and black hair, and he spoke with a Greek accent."

"I see lots of people with dark hair and funny accents."

"Maybe so, but you know who I mean," Livia said. "I can see it in your face."

"What of it? I don't know where to find him, if that's what you're asking."

"I don't need to find him. He's dead."

Eleni turned pale. "Says who?"

"The vigiles. They told my husband that Zeno was killed a week ago. I have reason to believe he was murdered, and I'm trying to figure out who killed him."

The woman's countenance turned from bewildered to hostile. "What does a rich lady like you care about Zeno?"

"The men who killed Zeno also killed a friend of my husband's. He wants to catch the men who did it. Will you help me?"

A flicker of interest. But she shook her head. "I have work to do. The master is angry if I don't sell all my stock."

Was that her price for divulging information? Fine.

"What if I bought everything on your cart? Would you be free to talk then?"

"Maybe."

Livia quoted a generous price. Eleni accepted. She bundled the pastries and handed them to Roxana.

"We may as well eat some of them now," Livia said.

Roxana grinned. "If you insist." She handed one to Livia and offered one to Grim. He shook his head. Roxana shrugged and turned to Eleni. "Would you like one?"

"Why not?" She accepted the proffered treat and ate it with relish.

Livia nibbled her cake. Flaky dough, with a moist filling of ground pistachios and just the right amount of spice. Delicious. "Do you know a more private place where we can talk?"

"Follow me." Eleni grabbed the handles of her cart and led them to a quiet side street. She parked in front of a shuttered shop entrance. "What do you want to know?"

"Tell us about Zeno."

"I met him a year ago when the baths first began to have leakage problems. He was on the crew that came to dig up the pipes. There was more than one leak so they were back and forth to fix things several times. They passed me every day and he caught my eye. He wasn't as rude as the others in his group, and he always walked dejectedly at the back of the line.

"He always looked sad, so one day I smiled at him. The first time, it startled him. He dropped his eyes and hurried past. But the next day he looked at me, so I smiled again. He smiled back. After that we became friends. He would talk with me whenever he could. He was very smart. He knew how to read and he knew all about things like how the water gets from the aqueducts to the fountain in the street, or how a crane lifts heavy blocks up to the top of a building. Sometimes he found a coin while he was working, and he treated me to a bit of cheese or a piece of fruit."

"Sounds like he was a good man. What made him so desperate that he stole the money?"

"Zeno wouldn't steal money."

"According to his foreman, Zeno took money from a strongbox and was running away."

Eleni gave Livia the same ferocious scowl she'd given her unwanted customer. "Prochoros is a thief and a liar! He's a horrible man. Zeno hated him. That's why he took the tablet."

What?

"Are you saying Zeno stole a note tablet?"

"That's right. The kind that folds." Eleni pantomimed folding the two outer leaves of a tri-fold tablet.

"Why would Zeno want a note tablet?"

"He suspected his foreman was up to something illegal and was looking for proof. He discovered that Prochoros had a secret tablet where he recorded his illegal payments. It was his chance to make Prochoros suffer."

"What was Prochoros doing?"

"Zeno never said, exactly. Something to do with the pipes. He was pretty sure some of the others were involved, too. That's why he kept his notes with me, so none of his crew mates would find out."

"He kept notes?"

"Yes, on a different tablet. And he showed his notes to someone important. One of the engineers. That man promised Zeno he could earn his freedom if he found out who else Prochoros was working with. That's why Zeno stole the other tablet."

"When was this?"

"It was, um…" Eleni paused to count on her fingers. "Eight days ago."

The same day Damaris saw Zeno being beaten to death. So that's why Zeno had refused to talk. He'd been protecting Eleni. Zeno the slave had more courage and honor than half the men in the senate.

As gently as she could, Livia explained what Damaris had witnessed. "Zeno died protecting you. If you want his sacrifice to make a difference, please let me see the tablets."

Eleni chewed her lip. "He made me promise not to give them to anyone except the engineer."

"It's been over a week since Zeno died. I don't think the engineer is coming. My husband is an advocate and his brother is a senator. I'll take the tablets to them. They'll know who to talk to."

Eleni gave a decisive nod. "I think Zeno would agree." She knelt and fumbled under her cart. "It was Zeno's idea to hide them here where no one would think to look."

She rose and handed Livia two dusty tablets. "Take them and make sure Prochoros pays for his crimes."

"Thank you. I promise I will do everything in my power to make sure Zeno didn't die in vain."

Avitus leaned his stool against the wall of his study and listened while Timon read the latest draft of his speech for the upcoming case. He closed his eyes, imagining the gestures and delivery he would employ.

The speech came to an end. Avitus opened his eyes. "Not bad for a second draft. The opening statement is solid, but the first two points lack punch and the final point is vague."

His secretary pursed his lips. "Perhaps you should switch the order, sir? Start with point number three?"

"Let's try it."

He and Timon worked through it again, shaping, cutting, refining. The secretary had an excellent ear for rhetoric and a mind twice as devious as Avitus's.

"Read it through again."

Timon's voice lacked the baritone depth and power of his master's, but he had observed Avitus in action long enough to do a fair imitation of his style. Avitus suspected Timon could handle a legal case better than half the hacks who hung around the forums waiting for out-of-town customers in need of legal aid.

Avitus closed his eyes and leaned back on his stool. The pacing was better this draft, and the points flowed logically from one to the next.

"Almost there. One more draft to polish the phrasing ought to do it."

Someone rapped on the door. "Avitus? I must talk with you."

Livia's voice. Of all the infernal nuisances! He hated being interrupted when he was composing a speech, but his wife's voice was brimming with excitement. She wouldn't be put off for long, so may as well get it over with.

"Come in."

His wife burst into the office and thrust two dusty tablets at him. "You'll never guess what we found."

He looked from the tablets to Livia's flushed face while his mind tried to deduce what on earth she was talking about. Why did she always charge into the middle of a topic without giving proper context? Where had she been today? Ah, yes, to visit the silk merchant and view the paintings.

"Did the painter give you sketches? I'm glad you liked his work."

"The painter is wonderful. That's not what I'm talking about." She wiggled the tablets. "We've found Zeno's records."

Zeno? Records? He cleared his throat while his brain tried to decipher what she meant. Nothing came to mind, so he was forced to admit, "I'm not following you."

"Zeno. The slave Damaris saw being attacked. He didn't steal money and run away. He was investigating something illegal with the plumbing. These are his records." She set the tablets on his desk.

Beard of Hercules. Had his wife been questioning suspects despite her promise? But he mustn't jump to conclusions. Best to gather firm proof before making accusations.

"I thought you went to see Babak. How is it you found these?"

"The pastry seller gave them to me."

Right. Clear as mud. "And why were you talking with a pastry seller?"

"Because things weren't adding up. Why would a runaway slave steal money and then hide it and remain in the city? I thought we needed to know more about him."

So she *had* broken her promise! He fought to keep his voice from rising. "You promised you wouldn't ask after the slave."

"I didn't." Livia lifted her chin and met his gaze, her eyes steady. "While Fabia and I visited the silk merchant, Roxana asked some friends of hers for information on Zeno."

Avitus didn't know whether to laugh or cry at her audacity. Once again, his wife had found a loophole. How formidable a lawyer she could have been, if she'd been born a male.

But she was a woman. And his wife.

"You know very well the intent of that promise was for you to desist from investigating these crimes."

She scowled. "I discover information that finally explains the truth about Jonas's death, and you accuse me of breaking a promise?"

"Yes. Sending your maid was a technicality, and—"

"I see what the problem is." She jammed her fists into her hips and glared at him through smoldering eyes. "You aren't willing to accept help from a woman. If Sorex or Timon had brought you the tablets, you would have thanked them, but God forbid your wife uncover evidence for you."

"Don't put words in my mouth. It's my duty to be concerned for your safety—"

"Are you suggesting it isn't safe for me to talk to street vendors?"

"No, but—"

"Are you suggesting Grim isn't capable of protecting me?"

"Stop it! You're twisting my intent. Searching for criminals is not a game."

"I wasn't looking for criminals, and neither was Roxana. We were talking to a friend of the victim. Furthermore, I immediately brought my discoveries to you because I was under the impression that you would find the information useful. But since you haven't bothered to look at it, I begin to suspect you don't really want to find the criminals after all. I'll leave you to your scrolls." She spun on her heel and stomped out, slamming the door behind her.

For a moment Avitus was too stunned to move. In all his experience he'd never dealt with a woman like Livia before. She was the most confounding, unpredictable, fascinating, exasperating, brilliant, bewildering . . . he didn't have a name for all the conflicting emotions she'd stirred up inside him.

He shook his head to clear the red fog from his eyes. Then he picked up the tablets. A quick glance told him one tablet held what looked like accounts, except that none of the entries included a name. Just a jumble of initials. The other was a detailed list in a tiny hand, written in some sort of code. He'd need better light to read it properly.

It wasn't immediately clear that either tablet held proof of Livia's claims, and at the moment he was too frustrated to care. He locked them in his strongbox and went to the baths to work off his anger and calm his thoughts.

Jupiter, Best and Greatest, what was he going to do about his wife?

CHAPTER 19

A sweat, soak, and massage cleared Avitus's head from the onslaught of emotions. Once he could think straight, he left the baths and headed for the vast public garden that filled the valley to the north of the Quirinal Hill. A stroll in the fresh air and serenity of the gardens would help him crystallize his thoughts regarding how to deal with his fractious wife.

He appreciated Livia's independent nature and her sense of justice, but how was he going to get through to her that she must not take matters into her own hands?

How could he protect his wife and his own dignitas if she insisted on flaunting the very reasonable boundaries he set for her?

He turned to Sorex, following silently at his elbow. "I watched her track down her father's murderer despite all our warnings. Why did I think she would be content to stay home and spin wool?"

"She's a woman of action, my lord. Is that a bad thing?"

"Taking action is one thing, but I can't allow her to twist my words so she can do as she pleases. If she refuses to abide within sensible boundaries, I'll have to use more forceful means."

"I'm not sure that will work, sir. She deals with problems in the only way she knows how—head on. The more you try to stop her, the more obstinate she'll become."

"You have a better suggestion?"

"Allow her to help you."

"No."

"Why not? She can gain the cooperation of women and slave girls who would never speak to you or me. Why not use that to your advantage?"

"That's not the point. I've asked her to desist from meddling in the matter, yet she refuses to listen."

"And so you reject what she's learned? I hope you're not making the error of Caepio, my lord."

Caepio was a general from the previous century who was responsible for one of the legion's most inglorious defeats: eighty thousand soldiers lost. "What does an incompetent general have to do with this? Are you implying Livia and I are at war?"

Sorex shook his head. "Caepio lost because he was unwilling to listen to the advice of his subordinates. Is that not the story?"

"What's your point?"

"I hope you aren't rejecting her assistance out of pride."

Pride was not the issue! A willful wife who found loopholes that gave her an appearance of obedience even while she broke her solemn word to her husband—that was the issue.

"A wife must submit to her husband."

"We must all submit to those in authority over us," Sorex said. "No one questions this. But consider the difference between how I submitted to the trainers when I was a gladiator and how I submit to you. In the first case I was compelled through whips and threats, thus I hated them. You I serve willingly. Which choice will you make for your wife?"

"You serve me well because we respect each other. That is exactly what my wife lacks."

"How do you know? Is it possible you have misinterpreted her actions?"

"She blatantly sought out information on Zeno after promising not to. What else am I to conclude?"

Sorex raised an eyebrow. "I thought a lawyer never made conclusions before he questioned the motives of the accused."

Why did Avitus own the only bodyguard in Rome who quoted legal strategy to his master? He could almost hear the gods laughing at him.

But was Sorex correct? Had Avitus made a false assumption? Was it possible Livia's actions were more than selfish disregard for his authority? Did he have the courage to ask her for the truth?

He arrived home to find Livia sweeping the patio with a vengeance. Each fierce swipe sent clouds of dust and bristles flying through the air, while a bug-eyed Brisa watched from a doorway. She was clearly appalled at her mistress. The lady of the house should not be reduced to menial tasks, but Avitus understood. It was Livia's way of working off emotion through physical action.

He approached her, keeping a safe distance from the broom. "I fear I may have been operating under a misconception."

She didn't look at him, but the broom stilled. "About what?"

For a fleeting moment he considered changing the subject. No. That would be cowardly. Delaying the discussion would not solve anything.

"Why are you going to so much trouble over a man you don't know? Jonas means nothing to you."

She swung to face him, gripping the broom as if it were a weapon. "He's important to me because he's important to you.

And Damaris. I refuse to spend my time on trivialities like frescoes and cushions when a man you care about has been unjustly murdered."

Would he ever understand a wife that was led by feelings rather than logic?

His bewilderment must have shown because Livia bristled. "You don't believe me?"

"I do." He held her gaze, trying to communicate with his eyes what fumbling words could not. "It never occurred to me you would care so deeply for a man you've never met."

"Jonas was your family. That makes him my family, too." She emphasized her claim by slamming the broom on the ground and giving him a fierce scowl, as if daring him to disagree.

Her ferocity was touching. "Jonas would have liked you. And he would have boxed my ears for scorning your help. I've been so used to fending for myself that I didn't recognize kindness when I should have."

Her scowl faded. Now to offer an olive branch and see if she would take it.

"Perhaps you would tell me about those tablets you discovered?"

She related what she'd learned from the pastry seller about Zeno, Prochoros, and the suspected illegal activities. Then Avitus retrieved the tablets from the strongbox and laid them on the desk. He studied the one that appeared to be a ledger. Each entry began with a date followed by three letters, possibly the initials of a customer. Next came a figure, always a substantial amount. Then came notations of disbursements. A small sum went to F, a larger sum to P and a sizable sum to N. Avitus did some quick calculations on the first several entries and found the payments were consistent percentages. F received 15 percent, P received 30, and the remaining 65 percent went to N.

The records went back a year and a half, and the most recent entry was dated mid-August. That was only a few weeks ago, so the document was current.

"This is almost certainly a record of accounts," he told Livia. "Except I don't see anything that describes what service or goods the payments were for, and everything is listed only by initials. This document won't help us until we figure out what those letters represent."

Avitus turned his attention to the other tablet. Obviously a list, but of what? The notations meant nothing to him. It was written in an abbreviated shorthand he couldn't decipher.

"I assume this is the tablet where Zeno recorded his observations, but I have no idea what any of it means. Would you return to the pastry seller tomorrow and ask additional questions?"

Livia rewarded him with a delighted smile. "I'll be happy to."

"Ask what jobs Zeno was working on lately. Ask for more information on the engineer who promised Zeno his freedom. And ask about these initials." He tapped an entry in the ledger. "If we assume P stands for Prochoros, it would help to know who F and N are. Especially N. He appears to be the one in charge. But remember," he said sternly, "Prochoros and his thugs killed Zeno to protect their schemes. We mustn't let them suspect we're looking into the matter."

"I won't mention Zeno to anyone but Eleni. Satisfied?"

"Yes."

"Good." She kissed his cheek. And then the woman who had wielded a broom with fury only moments ago skipped away humming a happy tune.

How could she move from rage to joy so easily? Would he ever understand women?

It was a glorious morning. How different it felt knowing her husband had actually requested her help instead of trying to stop her. She wasn't entirely sure what had caused his change of heart—but she wasn't complaining!

"You're in a fine mood this morning, my lady." Roxana said as she wrapped an embroidered cloth belt around Livia's ankle-length tunic.

"Avitus asked us to return to Eleni and ask her more questions."

"Wonderful. Are we going now?"

"Yes."

They headed to the atrium to collect Grim. They found him with Momus, staring at a wooden board leaning against the wall. A small circle was drawn on the board and a handful of pebbles lay on the ground below it.

"Castor and Pollux! I've been swindled," Momus said.

"What's the problem?" Livia asked.

"Grim here made me a wager, best out of ten strikes. I beat him by one. Then he proposed we double the wager, but we throw with our left hands. I agreed. You'd expect that neither of us would do as well with our left, would you not?"

Livia nodded.

"And you'd be wrong." Momus glared at Grim. "The man is deadly as a slinger with his left hand."

The younger man met his gaze calmly, a self-satisfied smile softening the corners of his lips. It was the first time Livia had seen her dour bodyguard smile. Interesting.

Momus turned to Livia. "He misled me on purpose. I shouldn't have to pay a cheater."

Grim's smile vanished. "I didn't cheat. I challenged you to

throw with our left hands. You never asked me which hand was stronger."

"Anyone whose master is a lawyer should know to look for loopholes before agreeing to a bet," Roxana said tartly.

Momus turned to her, jaw thrust forward in indignation.

Time to defuse the situation. "You've been tricked, Momus, but that's no excuse for slandering Grim. Did he lie to you?"

Momus shook his head.

"Then the contest was fair." Livia turned to Grim. "Now you've played your trick, please explain to all of us why you are a deadly shot with your left hand."

"A guard spends a lot of time waiting. Throwing at targets gave me something to fill the hours. When I lost my fingers, I couldn't throw as accurately as I had before, so I decided to practice with my left hand." He cast a sideways glance at Momus. "When I saw how useful the skill was in winning bets, I practiced all the more."

So there was a devious streak to her new slave? How fascinating. What else was he hiding behind that stiff, frowning visage? Livia looked forward to finding out.

"Thank you, Grim. You two can settle your accounts later. I have errands to run. Come along."

Her first stop was a quick visit to introduce herself to Asyncritus, the physician, as she'd promised Pansa. The physician's shop was at the base of the Quirinal Hill. It smelled of pungent medicinal herbs. One wall held shelves crammed with tidy rows of labeled bottles.

A girl of perhaps fourteen was minding the shop. "May I help you?"

"I've come to talk with the doctor."

"I'm sorry, my father is out seeing a patient right now. If it's a simple ailment I might be able to advise you," the girl said.

"I'm not ill. I'm a friend of Pansa, the baker."

"Oh." The girl's face brightened. "Father will be sorry he missed you. You could try tomorrow morning, an hour before dawn."

Livia nodded her understanding. She missed early morning prayer gatherings, but until she broached the subject of her beliefs to her husband, she couldn't leave the house that early without arousing suspicion.

"Thank you. Some other time. Would you tell your father that Livia called?"

"Certainly, miss."

That duty completed, Livia headed across the valley to talk with the pastry seller. Eleni and her cart were in the same place they'd been the day before.

"Good morning, Eleni. My husband is very interested in Zeno's documents, but he sent me back to ask more questions."

"I'll help as much as I can, my lady." Eleni said.

"First of all, who was the engineer Zeno was talking to? Is he Prochoros's supervisor?"

Eleni shook her head. "Prochoros reports to Fornax. Zeno didn't trust him. Zeno suspected Fornax was taking bribes from Prochoros."

Aha. So the F in Prochoros's ledger might be Fornax. So far, so good. "Did Zeno tell you anything about the engineer who promised him his freedom?"

"No, my lady."

"How would you recognize him when he came to ask for the tablets?"

"He would say the password. 'The master plumber is found.'"

"Did Zeno tell you who Prochoros is working for?"

"Sorry, no. He was always so secretive."

"Did he ever mention anyone who had a name starting with an 'n' sound? Like Nasica or Novellus?"

The pastry seller shook her head again. "Mostly Zeno talked about Ozias. He's worked on the water system since forever and knew all about it. He's the one who taught Zeno how everything worked. That's why Zeno got sent to make repairs at the baths so often."

That sounded promising. "Where could we find Ozias?"

"He can barely walk anymore, so he stays near the barracks. Prochoros only keeps him because he knows so much."

"Where would we find the barracks?"

"I don't know exactly, but it's near the *Castellum Marcia*. That's the big water tank where the *Aqua Marcia* comes into the city."

Livia had never paid much heed to the various *castella* that dotted the city. She knew the tanks were part of the water system, but she had no idea what they were for. She also knew the aqueduct called Aqua Marcia entered the city somewhere between the Viminal and Colline Gates. That should be easy enough to find.

Livia thanked Eleni and strolled away.

"Where to next, my lady?" Roxana said. "Are we going to talk with Ozias?"

Ozias was the logical person, but Livia had just won Avitus's trust, and she didn't want to jeopardize it by doing something he would consider inappropriate.

"I can't. Avitus wouldn't like me talking with a public slave, or bumping into his foreman, Prochoros."

"Grim and I could go."

Grim stared at her, pop-eyed. "I can't abandon the mistress to babysit you."

"I didn't mean we'd leave her standing in the middle of the street, you bonehead."

While her slaves glared at each other, Livia considered the idea. It just might work.

"How about this? You two look for Ozias while I stay at my brother's house. I ought to be a dutiful daughter and see how my mother is handling the household now I've moved out. And I've been meaning to ask Cook about some new recipes for Brisa."

A few minutes later, Livia stood in Curio's atrium bidding Grim and Roxana goodbye.

CHAPTER 20

Roxana and Grim headed toward the Castellum Marcia. "The sooner we get this over with, the better," Grim said. "Follow me and don't chatter like a magpie the whole way."

Roxana lengthened her stride to match his. "What has you so mad? Are you afraid the master will scold you for letting the mistress out of your sight?"

He didn't answer.

"Then it's me, isn't it? Admit it, you don't like me. You think I'm too saucy and impertinent."

"I don't know why the mistress puts up with you. You sound more like a fishwife than a respectable servant."

"Well, for your information, I grew up in the Subura, where knowing how to bargain was more important than proper grammar, and knowing how to defend yourself was more important than a graceful bow."

"How'd you become a fancy lady's maid?"

"I had a cousin who taught me to be a hairdresser. I wanted to work in a nice shop like she did."

"But instead you ended up a slave?"

"Yes," Roxana said through clenched teeth. "My dreams were crushed. Does that make you happy?"

He shook his head.

Mollified, Roxana continued. "My father was a freedman. He had a small basket shop. But he got sick with lung fever. Mother and I tried to scrape by, but Papa owed too much money. The day after he died, Mother and I were taken to the slave markets to pay his debts."

"I'm sorry," Grim said.

They walked for a while in silence. "What about you?" she asked.

"What about me?"

"How'd you end up a gladiator?"

He scowled. "I don't want to talk about it."

"I told you my story."

He shrugged. "No one forced you."

If the lummox thought that logic would get him out of talking, he was dead wrong. A girl didn't grow up in the Subura without learning a thing or two about how to manipulate others. She gave him a sugary smile. "If you don't want to answer I can make up my own story. Let's see… Your father ran off with a harpist, leaving your mother and four children. You hated her, so you stole her last sestertius and fell in with a group of brigands who attacked poor travelers until one day—"

"That's not what happened at all!"

"Are you sure? Because you look like a brigand." She gave him a wicked grin.

"I look like my father," Grim said through clenched jaws. "He was a soldier."

Roxana widened her eyes and let her mouth gape open to disguise her glee at provoking him into talking. "Where did he serve?"

"In Syria, with the Tenth Fretensis."

"So you grew up in an army fort?"

Grim gave her a bitter snort. "I grew up in a brothel in the shantytown outside the fort, which is an even more hardscrabble place than the Subura. When I was nine my mother died in childbirth. Since I was always getting into fights, the brothel keeper sent me to become a gladiator. I was sold a few times until I ended up in Rome. I'd have won my freedom if it weren't for this." He held up his damaged right hand. "So we both have plenty of reason to be bitter at the gods."

"No, we don't. Mistress Livia is the nicest mistress ever."

"So you've told me."

"You don't believe it? Has she done anything to make you doubt her kindness?"

"Yes. She sent me on an errand with you."

Olympus! Had the sourpuss made a jest? "You poor man," Roxana said, voice oozing false sympathy. "Stuck with an acid-tongued fishwife on a fool's errand to find a lame slave who probably knows nothing. Such a heartless mistress we have."

His lips twitched.

"Since you didn't want to come anyway, how about you let me do the talking when we find Ozias?"

"Suits me."

Grim led them right to the Castellum Marcia. Roxana might have mistaken the pillar-fronted building for a shrine if it weren't for the continuous rumble of water emanating from inside.

A group of men loitered nearby. "You wait here while I talk to them."

"Fine."

Roxana wandered closer to the castellum, gaping at its decorated facade as if she'd never seen anything like it before. She exaggerated the sway of her hips and smiled at the men. "Hello, boys. I'm looking for Ozias."

"What do you want with him?"

"That's my master's business, isn't it? Do you know him?"

One of them pointed at a man seated on the ground beside the castellum. "Over there."

Roxana approached. "Are you Ozias?"

"Eh? What'd you say?"

"Are you Ozias," she shouted above the thunder of roaring water.

"I am. State your problem."

"Eleni sent me to talk to you. About Zeno."

His face grew wooden. "Zeno's dead. Either state your problem or go away."

"Zeno is my problem. My master wants to find the men who killed him, and he wants to put a stop to the crimes Zeno found, but we need to know more. Can you help us?"

Ozias lifted his head and scanned the area. "Prochoros is gone, so I'll talk, but be quick about it. What do you want to know?"

"What did Zeno find?"

"An illegal water pipe connected to one of the distribution castella. He was going to report it, but I told him to keep his mouth shut. A slave has no business nosing into things like that. It wasn't long until he noticed another suspicious pipe. I warned him to quit looking. I warned him Prochoros was probably making good money installing unauthorized connections, but that only spurred the boy to look harder."

Roxana's heart was pounding. This was exactly the kind of information they needed. "Then what?"

"He got his hands on an old writing tablet and kept records of every illegal connection he could find. I told him the authorities weren't going to listen to a slave, but he found someone who did. Zeno was promised his freedom if he could find out who was paying Prochoros to install the pipes. Wasn't easy. Zeno finally managed to follow Prochoros to a marble dealer. When Prochoros left the marble dealer's shop, he had a bulging bag of coins." Ozias raised both eyebrows, in case Roxana missed the significance of what he'd said.

She widened her eyes and gushed, "Ooh, how suspicious."

"Zeno thought so. A few days later he disappeared and Prochoros was in a fury. Told us Zeno had stolen money and run off. Turned the barracks upside down searching for it. He even made us dredge the castella."

"Did you find anything?"

"No. Now go away before he comes back and finds me talking with you."

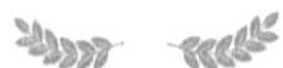

While she was waiting for Roxana and Grim to return, Livia had a brilliant idea. If Zeno had uncovered illegal pipes, then it might be helpful to understand more about the water distribution system. Her Aunt Livilla's husband had been a senator, so Auntie might be able to introduce them to the water commissioner who oversaw the whole system.

Roxana's report on Ozias only reinforced Livia's decision, so they headed south to Auntie's house, on the Caelian Hill. The doorkeeper ushered them inside with a smile. "Always a pleasure to see you, Miss Livia. Go right to the peristlye and I will let the mistress know you've come."

Aunt Livilla's garden was Livia's favorite in all of Rome, filled with a myriad of blooming plants. It had been the inspiration behind her alterations to Avitus's peristyle. She hadn't copied the exact form, but she'd captured the joyful yet peaceful atmosphere.

Auntie appeared from the direction of the kitchen. She was past fifty now, with graying hair and wrinkles around her eyes, but she moved with energy in her step and her eyes sparkled with life. "Livia dear, so good to see you. I hope the plants I sent are doing well?"

"Yes. They're a lovely addition to the space and Avitus has praised the results."

"Glad to hear it." She turned to Roxana. "I trust you have been helping your mistress adjust to her new home?"

Roxana bowed, blushing at the attention. "Of course, my lady."

"Good, good. And who have we here?" Auntie eyed Grim with curiosity.

"This is Grim, my new escort."

"Grim?" Auntie raised an eyebrow in mild reproach. "Is that really the best name?"

"It suits him perfectly," Roxana said, shooting him a wicked grin.

Grim's jaw twitched.

Aunt Livilla gave Roxana a stern look. "It's no wonder he's grim with your acid tongue abusing him. Causing strife among the servants will not help your mistress, girl!"

Roxana paled. "Sorry, my lady."

"You should be. Now mind your manners, show Grim to the kitchen and tell my cook to send us some refreshments."

"Yes, my lady."

Aunt and niece settled onto padded benches. They spent the next few minutes discussing Livia's new flower beds, her vision for the dining room frescoes, and the painter she'd found through Babak, the silk merchant.

"This silk merchant sounds fascinating," Auntie Livilla said. "I'd love to meet him."

"I can arrange that. When our new dining room is completed, you and Babak will be my first guests."

"I'll hold you to that promise, my dear."

They paused while a slave served them fruit nectar in fragile glass cups. Auntie took a long sip then quirked an eyebrow at Livia. "Now then, tell me what else you've been up to."

"I've stumbled onto another crime." Livia explained about Jonas, Damaris, Zeno's death, and the illegal pipes.

"You have been busy! I hope you haven't been interfering in these matters without Avitus's knowledge?"

Livia shook her head, glad she didn't have to evade the truth. "We've come to an understanding. He actually sent me to gather information. I thought I could surprise him with some expert advice. Wasn't Uncle Balbinus acquainted with the water commissioner?"

"Not the current commissioner," Aunt Livilla said. "He knew the previous one, Octavius Laenas. Your uncle had his sudden passions, and aqueducts were one of them. He visited the source of every aqueduct that feeds Rome." Auntie shook her head fondly. Her marriage to Balbinus had been an alliance of wealth and politics, but they had been genuinely fond of each other. Perhaps one day Livia and Avitus would share similar feelings—if Avitus was capable of such things.

"Could you arrange for Avitus to talk with Laenas?"

"Certainly. Why don't I invite you to dinner?"

"That would be fabulous, Auntie. It's so kind of you to offer."

"An old soul like me gets lonely, and I'm happy for an excuse to enjoy the company of a few friends. I'll send word to Laenas immediately, to see if he and his wife can join us tomorrow evening. Will Avitus be available then?"

"Of course. He never goes anywhere."

Auntie clicked her tongue. "Your husband is a busy advocate. You're sure he doesn't have a trial or an appointment with a legal client tomorrow?"

"He hasn't mentioned any."

Aunt Livilla took a sip, then looked at Livia over the rim of her cup. "You haven't been following your husband's legal career, have you?"

Livia shook her head. "He doesn't talk about his cases."

"I assume you at least know about Senator Gracchus bribing the judge to defeat Publius?"

Gracchus was a name Livia recognized. Avitus and his brother despised him. And they despised it when men cheated the law, too. Odd that Avitus hadn't said anything.

"When was this?"

"A week ago. It was the talk of the forum."

"I haven't been listening to gossip lately."

Livia hadn't spent time wandering the forum. Nor had she yet made friends with any of the women who patronized the bath complex near Avitus's house, so she'd been making quick trips and not paying attention to other women's conversations.

Aunt Livilla filled Livia in on the trial and the unexpected verdict. "I'm sure Avitus was as furious as Publius at seeing justice subverted so blatantly. I'm surprised he didn't mention it."

"I remember now. He said he didn't want to talk about it."

"Maybe it's because he thinks you don't care."

Ouch.

"If you'll take a piece of advice from your old aunt, a relationship must be reciprocated. If you want your husband to trust, respect, and admire you, you must give him trust, respect, and admiration in return. And the best way to demonstrate your respect and admiration is by showing an interest in his legal activities."

"I see. I'll keep it in mind."

Livia pondered her aunt's advice on the way home. She hadn't realized her disinterest in legal matters might give Avitus the idea she didn't care about him. She was proud of how he helped unimportant clients stand up to the elite in court. He believed justice was every citizen's right, not just reserved for the wealthy. From now on she would pay more attention to his work.

And she'd have to ask him about Senator Gracchus.

CHAPTER 21

Livia found Avitus in his study, as usual. He beckoned her into the room with an eager smile. "You're back. Did the pastry seller tell you what we needed to know?"

"Some of it." She explained all that they had learned from Eleni and Ozias.

"Well done. Now let me show you what Timon and I have deduced."

Timon laid the two tablets in front of her. "From what I can make out, Zeno's tablet is a list of pipe sizes and locations. There are thirty-four entries, which implies a large and organized fraud."

"So the tablet confirms what Eleni and Ozias have told us?" Livia said.

"It would appear so, my lady. I also studied the ledger." He flipped it open. "I believe these initials in the ledger represent customers, so I copied them into a list. I started with the most recent entries, since we believe they will be the easiest to identify." Timon handed her a tablet with a column of initials written in his tidy hand:

G U O

L C S

M F A

M D F

S P R

L P M

. . . and so on.

Roxana peeked over Livia's shoulder "How do you know these letters stand for customer names? Couldn't they mean something else?"

"See how the first initials match up with the most common first names?"

Roxana ran her finger down the list. "Oh, I see. M. for Marcus, G. for Gaius, L. for Lucius, and so on."

"Very good. The remaining initials also fit the more common names, and no group of letters is repeated, so each one represents a unique customer."

"That's a lot of information from a list of letters," Roxana said, giving Timon a look of awe.

"Now let us consider what it tells us." Avitus gestured to Timon, who opened a fresh tablet and poised his stylus over the smooth wax, ready to record his master's thoughts.

"Zeno was recording illegal connections," Avitus began. "He showed his information to a water engineer, who was impressed enough to offer the slave his freedom if he could find out who was behind the fraud. Eventually Zeno followed his foreman to a marble dealer and observed that Prochoros returned from that visit with a bulging coin purse. Combining that fact with the ledger, we can deduce the marble dealer's name begins with the letter N. We presume he is the mastermind behind the scheme, and therefore the one who is ultimately responsible for Jonas's murder."

"So our next goal is to find the marble dealer?" Livia said.

"Ultimately, but we don't yet have sufficient information to locate him. I propose we begin by attempting to identify one or more of Prochoros's customers, to find out which class of men we're dealing with. It may also give us an avenue to discover who N is. Alternatively, we could attempt to find which engineer was working with Zeno."

"Maybe this will help," Livia said. "Aunt Livilla's late husband was a friend of the old water commissioner, Octavius Laenas. When I asked her about him, Auntie promised she'd invite him to dinner so we can talk with him. She's hoping Laenas will be available tomorrow night. I promised her we were free."

Avitus looked impressed. "Excellent idea."

"We can ask him about Zeno's findings and see if he knows about the engineer."

"That might not be wise," Avitus said in his let's-be-cautious tone. "For all we know, Laenas was happily taking bribes during his time as commissioner. We don't want him to learn about our suspicions until we have the proof we need."

Why did her husband always imagine the worst? But Livia had to concede it was a valid point. "I'll trust you to ask whatever questions you think best."

Hopefully it would be enough to lead them in the right direction.

Timon suddenly picked up the ledger. "Excuse me, sir. I have an idea."

"Yes?"

"Look at this entry. L. C. S. Could that refer to Lucius Cornelius Scaevola?"

Avitus's eyebrows rose, as if the name was significant, but Livia didn't recognize it. "Who is Scaevola?"

As Avitus explained who Scaveola was, she fought to hide her annoyance. Why hadn't he bothered to tell her this before? Anyone with half a brain could see Scaevola was involved in the attacks. But she kept the annoyance from her voice. "So Scaevola might be a customer?"

Avitus nodded. "It would explain why he was so anxious to keep nosy neighbors out of his house and also why the guards he hired were connected to Prochoros."

It made sense to Livia. "So our next step is to find out whether Scaevola has an illegal water connection. How can I help?"

"You've already done more than I could have asked. We'd still be thinking Zeno was killed over stolen money if not for your discoveries."

His compliment filled her with warmth.

"However, this is a job for Timon. He can check with his contacts about whether Scaevola has a water license. We may need you to question the pastry seller again at some point, but in the meantime, you are free to get back to the household projects you've been planning."

Livia wanted to protest, but Aunt Livilla's advice came back to her. It was time to show her respect by agreeing to her husband's plan instead of arguing. And since the painters weren't free yet, she knew just what project to work on.

It was time to take Brisa for a cooking lesson.

The following morning, Avitus sent Timon to verify their theory about Scaevola. The secretary returned before midday, grinning like a cat who'd just discovered an unguarded butcher's shop. (Hades. He was thinking in cat metaphors. Was there no facet of life immune from the influence of his wife?)

"You confirmed our theory."

"Yes, sir. First I checked the water commission records. The house has been piped with running water for years, but since water rights are granted to individuals rather than properties, the water was disconnected when Scaevola purchased the building. According to a clerk, Scaevola hasn't renewed the water license." Timon paused in fine orator's fashion, allowing Avitus's tension to grow. "Yet somehow he has water running in his peristyle fountain."

"I thought the house was closed. How did you get inside?"

"I paid a resident of the neighboring building to let me look out her fourth-story window."

"Very clever."

"Do you think Jonas could have found out Scaevola had illegal water, sir? Maybe that's what he meant when he asked Damaris about a fountain?"

"A possibility. Let's go see what Publius can make of our discoveries."

Publius listened with growing interest to all Avitus told him about the water fraud and the link to Scaevola. "We suspect Jonas discovered the water issue," Avitus said. "Did he say anything to you about it?"

"He never mentioned anything about water," Publius said, "but your theory makes sense to me. Did you bring the stolen ledger?"

Avitus handed the tablet to his brother.

Publius looked down the list, his eyebrows rising higher with each line. When he'd finished he raised the tablet in triumph. "This is brilliant! We have him at last."

There was a hard edge to Publius's voice that set a prickle up Avitus's spine. "Who? Scaevola?"

"Gracchus."

Huh? How did the tablet incriminate Gracchus? "I don't see a connection."

"Gracchus is the mastermind behind the scheme."

In Publius's mind, Gracchus was the mastermind behind every suspicious event in Rome. "Sorry to disappoint you, but the mastermind is a marble dealer whose name begins with N."

"Wrong. Let me explain." Publius ran his finger down the ledger, supplying a name for eleven of the most recent entries. "You see? These initials match men of new wealth who recently became clientes of Gracchus. I've been searching high and low to discover how he's collected them. It never occurred to me he might be winning supporters by providing a commodity they lacked in an underhand way. Devilishly clever."

"You still haven't explained how Gracchus is connected to the fraud."

Publius adopted his pedantic older brother voice that set Avitus's teeth on edge. "Let us suppose a cliens of Gracchus was denied a water license. He goes to his patronus asking for help. Instead of petitioning the water commissioner like an honest man, Gracchus has a more devious scheme. He finds an engineer who could be bribed to look the other way while an illegal water line was installed."

"I thought this was about Gracchus gaining new clientes, not helping those he already has."

"I'm getting to that," Publius said with exaggerated patience. "Let us further suppose Gracchus sniffed an opportunity. Are there not plenty of other residents in this city who wish to enjoy the luxury of running water, but who lack the social standing to be granted a license? If Gracchus were to offer them an alternative that promised water without the bureaucracy or the yearly fees, many would gleefully accept."

It sounded plausible, but they still had no evidence. "Are you implying the N in Prochoros's ledger stands for Gracchus?"

"Jupiter, no! Gracchus is much too devious to be involved directly. He employs a middleman, this marble dealer presumably. What's his name?"

"We don't know."

"Pity. Anyway, this is how I envision it. Gracchus whispers a name in his new friend's ear—so-and-so, the marble dealer. And then the marble dealer handles the rest, collecting payment, arranging for the plumbers, and so forth while Gracchus goes back to drinking wine, composing satirical poetry, and admiring young slave girls."

Hades! The more Publius explained his theory, the more plausible it sounded. If Gracchus was behind all this, and he discovered Livia had been asking questions that uncovered his lucrative scam…

She must be stopped at once!

"On top of that," Publius went on blithely, "Gracchus now has leverage over his new clientes. If they grow lax in their support, he can threaten them with exposing their illegal water connection. It's brilliant, really."

Publius banged a fist on his thigh. "I say the gods have given us a chance to avenge ourselves against Gracchus for all the pain he's caused us."

The feverish excitement in Publius's eyes set Avitus's neck prickling worse than before. "Slow down. You just said yourself there's nothing linking Gracchus to the pipes."

"We'll get to that. First we need proof the men I suspect are guilty. Let me check with some of them, see if we're right about the water."

"Even if you prove that the men you suspect have unauthorized water supplies, it won't give you the leverage you want to punish Gracchus. We could shut down the whole scheme and he'd walk away unscathed."

"Not if we can find the mysterious marble dealer and get him to talk."

"I don't think that's likely."

"You don't sound happy about this discovery. What's wrong?"

Reluctantly, Avitus told his brother about Livia's encounter with the killers. "The men who killed Jonas have seen her. If they find out she's been asking questions and Gracchus learns who she is…"

He didn't need to tell Publius what dangers that might lead to.

His brother grimaced. "I warned you about choosing an independent-minded wife. Tell her about Gracchus and force her to stop."

It wasn't that simple, but there was no point trying to explain it to Publius. Instead, he urged his brother to caution.

"Promise me you'll be careful. We don't want Gracchus or his underlings to know we suspect him and have a chance to destroy any evidence before we can find it."

"I'm a politician. I know how to make discreet inquiries." Publius gave him a wolfish smile. "Did I tell you I have a new slave who's captured the heart of one of Gracchus's kitchen maids? I encourage his amorous liaisons. It's amazing what information passes through a senator's kitchen."

All the more reason to worry!

On his way home, Avitus considered and rejected a dozen scenarios for convincing Livia to give up the investigation. By the time he arrived at the house he had a pounding headache and no idea what to tell his wife. No matter what he said, she would ask why he'd decided to back off—and he couldn't explain that without telling her about Gracchus.

Which he couldn't do, because Livia would go after Gracchus just as she'd charged at Sorex the other day, with no thought to her safety. He could not allow that!

Curse the man to Hades and back. On top of everything else, Gracchus threatened the peace of Avitus's marriage.

CHAPTER 22

Avitus arrived home and discovered that Livia had gone to her brother's house for the day.

"She arranged for Brisa to have a cooking lesson," Momus said with a grin. "You should have seen the old woman's face when they left. Ready to skewer someone, she was."

Thank the gods for a reprieve. Avitus shut himself in his study. The best thing to restore equilibrium was to get busy on productive work. As he focused on precedents, counter arguments, and the finer points of rhetoric, his worries over Livia faded away.

A tap on the study door dragged him back to the present. "A merchant to see you, sir. Says his name is Babak."

Ah, Babak and his contract dispute. "Thank you, Momus. I'll meet him in the peristyle, and we'll need a snack. Something nice."

After exchanging greetings, Babak ran his eyes over the peristyle. "You have a lovely garden. Am I right in guessing it is the handiwork of your wife?"

"Yes," Avitus said. "The first of many home-improvement projects she plans to undertake. The house has been in need of a woman's touch for far too long and she has much work to do."

Babak chuckled. "Better to let our wives redecorate than to risk them becoming bored and find other ways to amuse themselves, eh? I will send you the painter in two days. He is almost finished with the winter dining room."

Excellent! Something to keep Livia busy at home. Just what they needed. "My wife will be delighted to hear it."

He was rescued from further small talk by Nissa, who brought a bowl of toasted almonds, a platter of sliced meat drizzled with chopped egg and *garum* sauce, and a plate of must cakes.

Babak bit into a cake and hummed in pleasure. "These are excellent." He popped the remainder in his mouth, took a sip of wine, set down his cup, and snapped his fingers. His attendant stepped forward with a leather scroll case.

"At our previous meeting, I mentioned the troubles I am having with a recalcitrant customer. Here is the contract that pertains to the dispute."

His attendant undid the clasp, drew a scroll from the case, and handed it to Avitus. The document detailed the purchase and delivery of a quantity of silk cloth. It was properly dated, stated the complete names of both parties with sufficient clarity to avoid misunderstanding, and was duly signed by witnesses.

"This contract looks to be in good order. Are these witnesses citizens?"

"Yes. I have dealt with enough Romans to know their propensity for ignoring the rights of noncitizens. I am careful to arrange my business in such a way that I will have legal recourse if necessary."

"A pity not all noncitizens are as careful as you. What are the specifics of your complaint?"

"The buyer claims that half the shipment was damaged and thus he only paid half the agreed-upon price."

"You're certain his claim is untrue?"

Babak placed a hand on his chest. "I would never damage my reputation by selling inferior goods."

"You have witnesses to verify the silk was good?"

Babak shrugged. "Myself and the slaves who loaded the shipment into his cart."

That meant the case could come down to Babak's word against his customer's. Not ideal, but still worth considering. "I'll need to collect testimonies from character witnesses to prove your honest reputation."

"Of course. I will supply names."

So far, so good. "Who is the buyer? Have you worked with him before?"

"No, Advocate, and to my shame, I did not check him as thoroughly as I should have. Only when he refused to pay did I scrutinize him. What I learned does not please me. This man has often used the threat of powerful friends to cheat honest merchants. He is a freedman who once served Senator Saturninus."

Not a close crony of Gracchus. That was fortunate. Avitus wanted to stay away from Gracchus's notice until they got to the bottom of the water fraud. He rerolled the scroll and handed it back. "I hate to see greedy senators and their followers flaunt the law so blatantly. It appears you have a strong case, but I'd like to talk to the men who handled the shipment, and I'll need to see some further documents."

"Perhaps Your Excellency would care to visit my warehouse tomorrow to look at the manifests?"

Hmm. Visiting Babak's warehouse would give Avitus and his attendants an opportunity to search the warehouse district for marble dealers without Livia knowing about it.

"I have a trial tomorrow. Will the day after work?"

"Of course, Advocate. Shall we say the third hour?"

"Agreed."

On the litter ride to her aunt's house that evening, Livia tried to engage Avitus in conversation. After the third monosyllabic answer, she gave up. Did he really dread social events so much?

They arrived at the house to discover that in addition to Laenas and his wife, Auntie Livilla had invited Curio, plus another couple and their widowed daughter, bringing the guest list to the ideal nine, three per dining couch. If anyone had wondered at the purpose of the evening, they might have suspected Livilla was attempting to play matchmaker between Curio and the widowed daughter.

Auntie had thoughtfully placed Livia and Avitus where they could converse with Laenas. Since small talk was not her husband's forte, Livia kept the conversation going, exchanging polite pleasantries. She paused at opportune moments to allow Avitus to bring up the aqueducts, but he failed to get the hint.

By the end of the first course her husband had yet to say anything useful, so Livia took charge. "What is your opinion about the new aqueducts the emperor is building?"

Laenas's face brightened at the question. "We can use the water, at the rate the city is growing, but I have grave concerns about how the project is being handled."

"How so?"

"Emperor Claudius is in a hurry to complete the aqueducts, and nothing good ever came of rushing a construction project."

"You foresee problems?" she said.

Laenas nodded gravely. "Gallus, our esteemed commissioner, doesn't pay enough attention to the details and his underlings know it. As long as he sees progress, he's satisfied. He doesn't dirty himself climbing into half-finished channels to check the quality of the bricks or inspect the plasterwork."

"As a consequence, the engineers in charge of the project are free to cut corners and pocket the extra. Every dishonest building supplier in Rome is lining up to get a share of the take. Mark my words, the new aqueducts will be springing leaks before the project is complete."

Livia felt Avitus draw a breath and paused, hoping he would take over the conversation.

He didn't.

Would every dinner party be like this? Ah well, she wasn't shy about talking to people, even ex-consuls. She adopted her best innocent-but-curious look. "I've always wondered how water gets from a spring miles away to a fountain in a house like this."

His face lit up like a child offered a tray of sweets. "It's a very complicated system of tunnels, arches, basins, and pipes. Aqueducts must be designed to a consistent slope from start to finish. Too shallow and the water won't flow. Too steep and the water flows too fast and the force of it destroys the channel. Thus, the main challenge in building an aqueduct is to ensure the correct gradient for its entire length. Whenever possible, the aqueduct is buried in the ground, but when it crosses a valley or stream, we build arches to maintain the channel at the proper level."

"Hush, dear," Laenas's wife murmured. "You're boring them with your talk of gradients and flow."

"Not at all," Avitus said. "I would rather listen to a man talk with passion about a subject he knows well than waste the evening talking about inconsequential subjects."

At last! Livia sent him a quick smile of thanks.

He gave her an odd look, but—wonder of wonders—he asked Laenas a question. "Is the gradient still critical once the water reaches the city?"

Laenas gave him a delighted smile. "Yes and no. When the water reaches the city, it is emptied into a castellum, a large settling basin, which traps silt and debris that might have been swept along. That way the smaller pipes downstream don't become clogged. The main castellum also divides the water into separate branches of the system that take it to the various regions of the city. These branches carry the water to smaller distribution castella. From there water flows through small-diameter lead pipes to its destination."

Now they were getting somewhere. "What keeps people from tapping into the water lines without purchasing a license?"

"A good question, young lady. All pipes connecting to a castella must be stamped with the proper authorizations. However, there are over one hundred fifty castella in the city, maintained mainly by gangs of public slaves. Who will notice when a few pipes do not bear the official stamps, or are larger than the size listed in the tax records? There is always a temptation to make money selling unauthorized water rights."

Livia's heart thrummed. The consul had described exactly what Zeno had discovered. "Don't the water engineers notice illegal pipes?"

"In theory the engineers and foremen should notice and plug any unauthorized connections, but many are neither as conscientious nor as honest as they should be. Especially now when everyone's attention is focused on the new construction. It isn't just the new aqueducts, you see. An additional sixty castella are needed to distribute the water, along with the associated piping."

She was about to ask how private citizens might report suspicious water connections when Avitus said, "What do you hear from the frontier?"

She was tempted to kick him!

The rest of the evening was spent discussing the fighting in the troublesome region of Thrace. Every time Livia tried to steer the conversation back to the water system, Avitus changed the subject. She'd gone to the trouble of arranging a meeting with Laenas and Avitus was squandering it. What was wrong with him?

CHAPTER 23

Finally, the evening came to an end. Avitus had succeeded in keeping Livia from telling Laenas about their water fraud suspicions, but now he was trapped in the carrying chair with an irate wife. Would it be cowardly if he got out and walked beside Sorex instead? Maybe he could claim his stomach was upset and the swaying of the litter made him nauseous? Or maybe…

"I thought you liked my Aunt Livilla."

Huh?

He studied his wife's face in the wavering torchlight. What was she asking? He'd been expecting a complaint about how he'd avoided the subject of water theft. He didn't see where her question was leading. Best to play it safe and interpret it literally. "I find your aunt delightful. An exemplary hostess."

"Really. Because tonight you acted like you didn't want to be there."

Uh oh.

He gave her an apologetic smile. "That wasn't my intention. I enjoyed the dinner and Laenas was pleasant company. For an ex-consul, I found him exceedingly palatable."

"You make it sound like ex-consuls are normally dreadful."

"Most of them are. Hidebound, self-important, and full of bombast." The kind of people both he and his wife disliked on principle.

"Laenas wasn't bombastic," Livia replied. "I found him enthusiastic and informative. Do you think he'll help us expose the fraud?"

Curse it, she'd circled back to the topic he'd been trying to avoid all evening. Fortunately, Laenas had given him an excuse. "I don't think so. Water is no longer Laenas's responsibility, and the current commissioner is only concerned with getting the new aqueducts finished. He isn't likely to care about a few suspicious pipes. Based on what Laenas told us, I've come to the conclusion that there's no point trying to fix the corruption. Besides, it's not our responsibility."

Livia turned to face him. "After all our work, you suddenly think we should drop the matter because one stuffy old man doesn't think it's important?"

Avitus adopted a conciliatory tone. "I know your sense of justice urges you to finish what Zeno started, but in doing so you've lost sight of our objective. Exposing systematic corruption within the water system was never our goal. For all we know, the corruption reaches to the commissioner himself, or someone just as powerful. Men like that are untouchable."

She made a disgusted face. "I thought you cared about justice."

"Justice for innocent citizens, yes. Battling governmental corruption, no."

"If we don't expose them, the criminals will continue to make a profit at the expense of honest men. Do you want that on your conscience?"

"Those who go up against corruption generally suffer for it—along with their families. *That* is not a fate I want on my conscience."

Her eyes searched his face in a most uncomfortable manner. "The man I married upholds justice, no matter what. He doesn't give up because things grow complicated. I believe you are still that man, so there must be another explanation. Why won't you tell me?"

Because explaining the long feud with Gracchus and the reasons they should fear him would only upset her all the more, and a righteously indignant wife was the last thing he needed.

"I've told you all you need to know."

"No you have not! You've intentionally been keeping things from me."

That sounded ominous. "Such as?"

"Just the other day I was embarrassed because I didn't know about Publius's treacherous defeat at the hands of your rival, Gracchus. You must have been outraged, yet you said nothing to me."

Hades. Could she have chosen a worse time to mention that trial? "It happened the day we went to dine with Publius. I saw no reason to ruin your evening with depressing news. And then Jonas's disappearance made me forget about it."

A blatant lie, but he kept all trace of deceit from his face. Lying without a trace was a useful skill for a lawyer, although he hated using it on his wife.

Livia's brows narrowed. "I don't believe you. You wouldn't forget something that significant. Since you've intentionally kept silent, I wonder if the trial is related to the crimes."

Jupiter Best and Greatest! How had she come to that conclusion? No. Never mind how. What mattered was getting her to stop.

"My decision about the water fraud has nothing to do with Gracchus!"

"Really? Because the more you deny it, the more I'm beginning to suspect Gracchus is the reason you're turning coward and reneging on your promise to Damaris."

How dare she accuse him of breaking a promise! Avitus clenched his fists. "Enough! We are not going to speak of this matter again. I forbid you or your maid from asking anyone about Zeno or anything to do with the water system. Is that clear?"

Livia's eyes blazed. "I thought you were better than other men, but I guess I was wrong." She shifted to face away from him, waves of anger radiating from her furious silence.

Avitus slumped into his seat and closed his eyes. Hades! He'd let his anger get the better of him and treated her just like his father had treated his mother. He wanted to reach over and tell her . . . what? That his seeming disinterest in the water crimes was for her own good?

Pollux. Why were women so difficult?

Or maybe it was just him?

A curse on stubborn, short-sighted, autocratic men! Oops. Livia immediately retracted that thought. Followers of the Way were supposed to love others, not curse them. Even exasperating husbands.

What was wrong with Avitus? Why had he turned from a daring advocate of the people into a cantankerous craven who made lame excuses? She was still mulling over her exasperation the next morning while Roxana helped her dress.

"You seem upset, my lady. I hope your dinner last night wasn't a disappointment?"

"Aunt Livilla was a lovely hostess, and the senator and his wife were charming. It's my husband who's become a problem."

Livia explained her argument with Avitus. "I don't know why he changed his mind, and he won't tell me. I need your help to figure it out."

"Certainly, my lady."

Some maids were vicious gossips, but Roxana was Livia's trusted confidante. She often helped her mistress think through thorny problems.

Roxana pursed her lips. "Perhaps we should start by narrowing down when he changed his mind."

"Good idea. Avitus was still interested in uncovering the water fraud when I brought him the information from Ozias, yet by the time we came home from Auntie's dinner last night he had changed his mind."

"Could it have been something that was said during dinner?" Roxana asked.

Livia played last night's dinner through her memory. Avitus had been subdued the entire evening, and he'd not questioned Laenas like she'd expected. In fact, every time she'd tried to bring the conversation around to water theft, Avitus had changed the subject.

"No, I'm pretty sure he'd already decided to quit before we went to dinner."

"Then his change of heart must have happened earlier that day."

Unfortunately, Livia and Roxana had been gone for most of the day, watching Curio's cook attempt to teach Brisa some basic recipes. (She was not an apt pupil, but that was a problem for another day.)

"I wish I knew what Avitus was doing yesterday. The only thing I know for sure is that he talked with Babak."

"Do you think the silk merchant might be responsible for the master's change of heart?" Roxana said.

"I doubt it, but we shouldn't rule him out completely."

That was a lesson Livia had learned while trying to figure out who had killed her father: Never discount anyone, no matter how unlikely they seem. The true culprit may be the one you least expect. However, her gut told her Babak wasn't the problem.

"Any other ideas?"

"Wasn't Timon supposed to check on someone?" Roxana said.

"That must be it! Timon discovered something about Scaevola that scared Avitus into quitting."

The fact that Avitus hadn't told her about Scaevola until two days ago made it even more likely he was the root of the problem. "We need to learn more about Scaevola."

If only she knew who to ask. Scaevola lived near the Triton, so questioning his neighbors wasn't possible. Who else could give her information about a total stranger? Would they be forced to send Roxana back to her friend in the Subura for information?

"Perhaps you could visit your sister-in-law, my lady? I could ask her slaves if Jonas told them about Scaevola."

"That won't work. If we go to Hortensia's house, Avitus will hear about it. However, we could ask Damaris if Jonas told her about Scaevola. He hasn't forbidden us from talking to her."

It was a slim chance, but it was better than nothing. Livia arrived at the weaver's shop to find Hermas's two daughters busy at their looms, while Hermas strung new warp threads on a third. There was no sign of Judith or Damaris.

Hermas greeted her with his customary, friendly smile. "Welcome, my lady. What can I do for you today?"

"Good morning, Hermas. I'm here to see how my cushions are coming along. Are any of them finished?"

"Yes." Hermas hurried to the rear of the shop and returned with a cushion. The fabric was smooth and the stitches were tiny and tight. The ivy embroidery along the sides added an elegant touch.

"This is lovely. When will the others be ready?"

His face fell. "The embroiderer's son is unwell and she's been tending him. The remaining cushions won't be ready for at least another week."

"That will be fine. I'm not in a hurry."

He sighed in relief. "Thank you for your patience."

Patience? Ha! God must have a sense of humor to commend her for patience on a day when she felt like throwing things. But she took a deep breath and did her best to sound like a paragon of that virtue. "I was hoping to talk to Damaris. Is she here?"

"I'm sorry, but Damaris isn't well today. She's been suffering from nightmares, and this morning she's in bed with a sick head-ache. My wife and Brother Titus are tending her. If you wait a few minutes, they'll return here and I can introduce him to you."

How could someone who was just commended for patience refuse that invitation? Fortunately, Livia wasn't forced to wait long. Judith entered the shop, followed by a man who must be Brother Titus. He was about the same age as Hermas, with a hint of gray in his black hair. He had a serious face softened by friendly eyes that crinkled when he smiled.

Hermas gestured to him. "May I introduce my friend and men-tor, Asyncritus, known to his friends as Brother Titus. And this is the woman who helped us find Damaris. She is a friend of Pansa the baker."

Brother Titus smiled warmly at Livia. "I'm happy to meet you. Hermas says you've recently moved to our section of the city?"

Livia nodded.

"You are welcome to join us any morning."

"I hope to do so soon, but right now things are too unsettled at home."

"I'm sorry to hear that." His gaze filled with compassion. "I sense you are distraught over something, my sister. May I pray for you?"

Her first reaction was to decline. She didn't want to share her concerns with a total stranger. But her soul was in turmoil, and she could see the genuine concern in his face. He was a fellow believer, and both Hermas and Pansa vouched for him. And a niggle of guilt reminded her that she'd been too angry to pray about the situation, especially regarding her frustration with Avitus.

Her story tumbled out, from finding Damaris to last night's argument. "My husband promised to find the men responsible and put a stop to them. We were getting close to unraveling everything, but suddenly he's changed his mind, and he's forbidden me from doing anything about it."

Brother Titus nodded sagely. "I see why you are upset. We all encounter situations when we wish to alter the decisions of others. We may do what we can to influence those with authority over us, but it is not our place to control them. I have found that the more we try to control rather than honor others, the less influence we wield."

That made sense. Livia hated it when others tried to control her. She thought of the difference between her mother's sharp reprimands and the gentle way Placida helped Livia see things in a new light. One tried to change her by exerting control. The other used her influence. And what a difference it made.

Was that the secret to dealing with a husband? Instead of demanding Avitus explain himself, should she try a more subtle approach? But how did one influence a nonemotional, analytically minded male?

Curio might have an idea. Her brother already knew about the crimes, and he was Avitus's friend. Yes, Curio was just the ally she needed to help her convince her husband to give up his lame excuses and get to the bottom of the water fraud.

And if she was heading to Curio's house, she ought to buy some pastries from Eleni along the way. She'd seen how Avitus had gobbled the pistachio cakes she had purchased from Eleni the last time. There was more than one way to exert influence over a man.

CHAPTER 24

Avitus didn't consider himself a Stoic, but he agreed with many of their tenets, including the ideal of temperance. Moderation was the key to a happy life. Losing one's temper was never beneficial. His father had not been a temperate man, and his choleric outbreaks had made everyone in the household miserable. Avitus had vowed not to live that way, but last night he'd lost his temper while arguing with Livia.

After a tiring morning debating a case in the forum, he wasn't looking forward to returning home to an outraged wife who'd had hours to brood over last night's harsh outburst. And he had only himself to blame for it. Why had he allowed himself to lose control of his temper like that? He must embrace another of the Stoic virtues, courage, and face the consequences of his outburst.

Sigh.

He braced himself to be accosted by a furious, broom wielding female spoiling for a fight, but when he entered his atrium, all was quiet. Either Fortuna was smiling on him, or else he was in trouble.

"Where is your mistress?" he asked Momus.

"She went to the weaver's shop, sir. To check on her new cushions."

Excellent news. Livia had chosen the moral high ground and forgiven his fit of spleen. Better yet, she'd turned her attention to household projects.

Delighted at his reprieve from domestic combat, Avitus sat down to record his notes on the case he'd just won. Since the start of his career, he'd kept meticulous notes on every opponent: the techniques he employed, what precedents he brought up, who his main supporters were. As any good lawyer knew, one could never have too much information.

When he'd finished his case notes, he and Timon drafted a list of the information they would require from Babak tomorrow. Only when they'd completed that task did it occur to Avitus that he hadn't heard his wife return home. How long could it take to look at cushions? He sent Timon to check.

The secretary returned with a worried frown. "The mistress hasn't yet returned, sir. She's been gone over three hours."

Far, far too long.

Where was she? Had she disobeyed his direct order out of spite? Had Gracchus's henchmen tracked her down and abducted her?

Stop. He must not imagine the worst. She'd probably bumped into a friend who'd invited her home for cakes and gossip. She was perfectly safe.

No, she's not, a voice whispered in his head. *She's furious at you because she thinks you've dropped the investigation, so she's gone out in the streets, asking questions.*

And he was powerless to do anything about it.

He was beginning to wonder if marrying Livia had been a

mistake. He should have taken his brother's advice and married a placid woman who wouldn't go looking for trouble.

Which was worse, a dull wife he couldn't respect, or a fascinating wife he couldn't control?

The pastry seller was in her usual spot, but her red cart was not. In its place was a ramshackle vehicle patched together from various bits of rough-sawn wood, crudely shaped and unpainted. But what really alarmed Livia were the bruises on Eleni's face.

Roxana muttered a naughty phrase and ran to the cart. "What happened? Were you robbed?"

Eleni's eyes smoldered with anger. "Not exactly. Two men came asking about Zeno."

"Looks like they did more than ask," Grim said in a hard, threatening voice Livia hadn't heard before.

"They started by asking," she said. "One of them demanded I tell him where Zeno hid the stolen tablet. When I pretended I didn't know who he meant, he slapped me and told me to stop lying. He said Zeno's coworkers knew I was Zeno's friend and I needed to give him the tablet, or else. I said I didn't have it, so they hit me some more. Then they had the bright idea the tablet was hidden in the cart so they tipped it over and smashed it to pieces. When they didn't find anything, they finally gave up and left."

"What did they look like?" Grim asked.

"Big men, work-hardened hands and faces. One was bald and walked with a limp. The other was dark and hairy, with scraggly teeth and dark, cruel eyes."

It sounded like the same men who'd killed Zeno and Jonas. Those criminals had to be stopped!

"I'm sorry." Livia said.

"It's lucky you talked to me first, miss," Eleni said fiercely. "If not for you, they would've found Zeno's tablets and probably killed me for having them."

That was thin comfort. If Avitus hadn't quit, this might have been prevented. The incident might be the extra push she needed to convince Avitus to act, so Livia headed directly to Curio's house to get his help.

"Back again?" Curio gave her his lopsided grin. "I hope all that work with Cook yesterday didn't end in disaster."

Livia launched into an explanation of the water fraud discoveries and the attack on Eleni. As she talked, his smile vanished, replaced by a furrowed brow.

"What do you expect me to do about it?" he said when she'd finished. "I've already given Avitus all the information I've uncovered about the suspects."

"And he has chosen to ignore it! Two days ago, he was eager to stop the whole scheme. The next he's mumbling nonsense about government corruption not being his responsibility. He's not acting like himself and I'm worried. You know Avitus better than I do. Help me convince him to change his mind."

Curio sighed and shook his head. "Has it occurred to you that perhaps you're the one who isn't seeing the situation correctly? Avitus never does anything without good reason. If he's pulled away from this investigation, then I'm sure there's a logical explanation. Let's assume he knows more about it than you do."

"Then why won't he tell me?"

"Maybe he doesn't trust you to keep from meddling where you don't belong. It looks to me like you've become obsessed over this crime, just like you were over Father's murder. And look where that got you—in a tavern with a knife at your throat."

He would have to bring that up. Curio still hadn't forgiven her from slipping the protective escort he'd assigned so she could chase down the villain responsible for their father's death.

She gave him a glare. "This situation is completely different. I'm not hunting criminals, I'm trying to get Avitus to hunt them. He promised Damaris he'd bring Jonas's killers to justice. I promised justice to Eleni as well. And now he won't lift a finger."

Curio crossed his arms and raised a cynical eyebrow. "Let this be a lesson to you. Don't promise what you can't deliver. Justice is never a guarantee in this life."

That was a pathetic excuse to quit. "We can't sit back and do nothing. We owe it to them to at least try."

"*You* don't owe them anything. Why do you care so much, anyway?" He paused and looked her in the eye. "Or is the real issue that Avitus isn't doing what you want him to?"

"No!" Livia slammed a fist on her knee. "The issue is Avitus isn't doing what's *right*!"

"You can't decide what's right or wrong without knowing all that Avitus knows." Curio gave her a stern look. "You need to take the plank out of your eye before worrying about the speck in your husband's."

She crinkled her forehead. "What plank?"

"Have you told Avitus that you've become a follower of the Way?

"Don't change the subject on me. I'm not in the mood."

"Don't accuse Avitus of wrong behavior when you're guilty, too. Honor your husband. Tell him the truth and accept his choice, even if you don't like it. Now, unless there's something else you need, I have work to do."

Refused!

Livia left her brother, jaw clenched and thoughts whirling. Was every man in Rome part of a conspiracy to thwart her pursuit of justice?

Triple fish pickle.

She marched from her brother's house without waiting for Roxana and Grim.

"You look ready to throttle someone," Roxana said when she'd caught up to Livia. "Won't your brother help us?"

"No. He's too busy and he doesn't think it's any of my business."

Anger boiled in Livia's gut, making her limbs jangle with energy. She needed to work off her anger before she did something rash. She spun to face her attendants. "We're heading to the Theater of Pompey, and I don't want a word from either of you until we get there. Have I made myself clear?"

They both nodded.

Livia strode off down the street. A bout of brisk exercise would clear her head and burn off the frustration she felt. Except that every few steps she was forced to slow down for trudging slaves, clumps of chatting women, and laden donkeys who stopped suddenly in the middle of the street. It felt like every denizen of Rome was determined to test her patience today.

After the seventh teeth-grinding delay she cut over to a less crowded street. Much better. She picked up her pace and moved along nicely until she came to an ox cart blocking the street while men in dusty tunics manhandled piles of clay roof tiles through the doorway of a multistory building under construction. There was just enough room for a single person to squeeze between the cart and the building opposite.

While she impatiently waited her turn to get past, Livia peered into the house. The open doorway led to the atrium, which was currently being used as a storage yard for building supplies. A man in a spattered tunic passed by carrying a white-rimmed bucket. He reminded her of a different man with a bucket who'd been working in a different house—one with a fountain that hadn't been running. Hmm.

As soon as they were past the cart, Livia turned to Roxana. "Do you remember when I was looking at fresco paintings last week, and I stopped to question some unfriendly workmen in an empty house?"

Roxana nodded.

"Can you find it again?"

Grim shot her a wary look. "We're under strict orders, my lady. The master made it clear we are forbidden—"

Livia stopped his objections with a hand. "I'm aware of my husband's restrictions and I will abide by them. Avitus and Timon believe the best way to uncover the water fraud is to identify the customers, and I was just reminded of a house we passed last week that had a fountain undergoing renovations. It may have nothing to do with the crimes, but what if it does?" She raised an eyebrow at Roxana. "Can you find the house?"

"Possibly. It was near that bakery Momus found for you that had those tasty sausage rolls."

Grim crossed his arms. "I cannot allow it, my lady."

"Don't get difficult. All I plan to do is learn who the house belongs to. The moment we learn the owner's name we'll return home and allow Avitus to handle it. Satisfied?"

The guard's scowl deepened, but he nodded.

"Lead on, Roxana."

CHAPTER 25

They were directed to three incorrect bakeries before they found the one they sought. It was on a busy street, both sides lined with shops. Livia tried to get her bearings. She remembered facing the bakery while Roxana had purchased sausage rolls. And then they'd turned . . . left?

She studied the street again. Definitely left.

"The house we're looking for should be that way, perhaps four blocks. Do you agree, Roxana?"

"Something like that."

Livia led the way, searching for landmarks that looked familiar. They came to a public fountain, but nothing about it triggered a memory.

She beckoned Roxana. "On our previous trip, I remember stopping to rinse my fingers at a fountain after I finished eating. That's when I saw the workman filling his bucket. Does this fountain look familiar?"

Roxana shrugged. "I wasn't paying any attention to fountains, my lady."

And none of the houses in sight showed any signs of construction activity. Fish pickle.

"I guess it must have been farther along."

Grim cleared his throat. "A suggestion, my lady. For safety's sake, you should remain here and send Roxana to search for the house."

"Very well." Livia waved Roxana on.

She trotted away, ogling the shops as she passed. Halfway down the block she paused to admire a necklace.

"What's she doing? I didn't tell her to shop along the way."

"Trying to blend in and look like an innocent shopper. Smart girl."

Oh. Perhaps Livia should act like a shopper as well. She wandered into a basket maker's shop. The wares on sale were primarily one-handled market baskets of various sizes. Livia selected one and tested the heft. A good market basket was sturdy enough to carry a full load but not so heavy that it was burdensome to carry when empty. This one was sturdy, but fairly heavy, and the weaving was lopsided. She returned the basket to its shelf and wandered on. The next shop was a scroll-seller, which she bypassed. Then she came to a shop selling spoons, small ones for dining and larger ones for cooking.

They could use a set of *cochleares*, small spoons with pointy handles designed for prying snails from their shells. Livia had been wanting to teach Brisa how to cook snails, and this would give her a reason to insist on it. Livia selected nine silver cochleares with a swirled pattern on the handles, and then enjoyed a spirited haggle with the shopkeeper before reaching a suitable price.

Grim remained on guard at the shop door, alert and scanning the street.

"Any sign of Roxana?"

"Not yet."

"Hold these while I look at the pottery next door."

She handed the spoons to Grim. He reluctantly took them and tucked them into his belt. The pottery shop featured plain, inexpensive cups and bowls. What Livia wanted was a set of glossy red-ware bowls, but she pretended to look through the display until Roxana finally appeared.

She was grinning. "I found the house, my lady. It's still filled with workmen, only this time there's a big scowling brute standing guard in the doorway. I went a block past and then stopped to ask a nice old woman selling flowers where the oil merchant lived, because I remembered when we were there before, the foreman said something about the owner being an oil merchant. Anyway, the flower seller said a rich fellow from Baetica just bought a house down the street and was having it remodeled. I thanked her and turned back. After I passed the house, I stopped at another shop and asked about a merchant from Baetica. That shopkeeper told me his name was Gaius Ulpius Optatus."

Livia mirrored her maid's exultant smile. "That name matches the top set of initials on Timon's list. Excellent work! I think we've found one of Prochoros's customers."

"We've found more than that, my lady." Roxana's eyes danced with excitement. "As I was talking to a shopkeeper, guess who walked by? The bald, limping goon who hassled us at the Triton."

"Did he see you?" Grim asked.

"Not until I waved to him."

Grim sputtered, nostrils flaring.

Roxana rolled her eyes. "Relax. I kept out of sight and watched where he went." She paused dramatically. "He entered the house belonging to Optatus. What do you think of that, my lady?"

Livia scanned the street, searching for any sign of the thugs. "Good work, but we'd better leave before they spot us. Take us home, Grim."

Roxana's discovery confirmed that Livia' hunch had been right. Optatus was part of the illegal water scheme. But when Avitus heard her news, would he be impressed, or would he go apoplectic that Livia had ignored his orders and endangered herself?

Technically, she hadn't broken his order, but she had ignored his intent.

Grim's voice brought her back to the present. "Turn right at the next cross street, my lady."

"That's not the way home," Roxana said.

"We aren't heading home until I'm sure no one followed you," Grim said.

"I'm not stupid, you know. I made sure they didn't see me."

"Hush, Roxana. Grim's right to be cautious. These men are too dangerous to trifle with. No more arguing."

They turned right. Then left, then right again, pausing for Grim to scan the street behind them at each turn. Livia studied the street from the corners of her eyes while she pretended to admire a display of earrings. With so many people on the street, how could Grim tell if they were being followed?

"Looks safe. You may continue, Mistress."

They advanced another block until they caught up with a group of dawdling ladies. Livia started to overtake them, but Grim said, "Don't draw attention to yourself, my lady. Slow is better."

Livia ground her teeth and took mincing steps to keep pace with the chattering women. Why must her patience be tested yet again, after all the frustration she'd endured this day? Suddenly a young boy raced past her and careened into the middle of the group, sending two of the ladies off balance with shrieks and waving hands. The boy snatched a purse one of the women had foolishly left hanging from her belt then raced away.

"I saw that! Stop, thief!" Livia chased after the boy, quickly overtaking him. She reached out to grab him, but just before her fingers closed on his arm, someone grabbed her.

She was jerked against a large, muscled chest.

"Look what we have here."

She'd heard that raspy voice before. The hairy thug. She tried to break free, but he encircled her waist with one hairy arm and held her tight. The other hand brandished a small dagger. "Don't scream or I'll hurt you."

Fear surged through Livia. She was in the hands of a killer.

Roxana and Grim emerged from the squawking women, heads swiveling as they sought her. Grim saw her first. His eyes locked on Livia's captor. "You there! Back away from the lady."

"Stay where you are," Hairy snarled back. "Or the lady gets a knife in her lungs."

Livia yelped as the point jabbed into her side. Grim stopped, eyes bouncing from Livia to her captor.

"No sudden moves," her captor said. "Tell your guard dog and the little maid to turn around and walk slowly until they reach a carpet shop. Tell them to go inside the shop and stay out of sight. If I see either of their ugly faces looking back at you, the knife goes into your lungs. A punctured lung is a slow, painful way to die."

Livia had to swallow twice before her voice would work. "Do what he says, Grim."

Grim took Roxana by the elbow and turned around. Livia watched helplessly as her servants trudged away.

No, she wasn't helpless. She sent a silent plea to God. *What should I do?*

Keep him talking.

"You're making a grave mistake," Livia said in a voice more confident than she felt. "My husband has powerful friends, including senators."

"So does Nepos."

Her heart skipped a beat at the name. Could Nepos be the marble dealer? "Who's Nepos?"

"Someone you don't want to anger, and right now he's tired of you showing up where you're not wanted. If your husband thinks he can fool us by sending a woman to do his dirty work, he's dumber than most."

Is that what this idiot thought? Did it not cross his chick-pea-sized brain that she might be acting on her own initiative? "What makes you think my husband sent me?"

A nasty laugh sent a wave of foul breath past her cheek. "Why else is a fancy lady like you nosing around houses under construction? A woman should know better than to poke around where she's not wanted. I warned you to stay clear of our business, but you didn't listen, so now you're coming with me."

"Where are you taking me?"

"To the boss. Nepos will want to find out who your husband is and why he's so curious about our projects."

Did that mean Nepos was the man in charge of the fraud? What else could she learn about him? "Does Nepos live nearby?"

"Never said I was taking you to his house. Enough talk, woman. No struggles or I'll use my knife."

Suddenly Grim spun around and something hurtled toward Livia. A spoon. It struck her attacker on the cheek. He roared and raised his hand to protect his head as two more spoons followed the first.

Livia jerked free of his grasp as a fourth spoon struck his temple and sent him to his knees. She sprinted to her slaves as another spoon whizzed past her.

Roxana grabbed her arm. "Come with me, Mistress." They veered into a cross street, ran for two blocks, then turned again and slowed to a walk. Grim caught up with them a block later.

"He's too stunned to follow, but there may be more. Stay right behind me."

They wound their way through back streets, pausing every so often to enter a shop while Grim studied the street for murderous enemies.

It felt like the journey would never end.

CHAPTER 26

Voices at the door! His wife was home at last.

Avitus stopped pacing and stood in the middle of the peristyle, arms crossed, waiting to hear what excuse Livia would give this time.

She entered the garden with Roxana and Grim right behind her. All three were flushed and anxious. Jupiter Best and Greatest, was that blood on his wife's tunic? His anger melted into concern. He hurried to her side. "Are you hurt?"

She shook her head. "I need to sit down."

He guided her to a bench. She sank down without a word. Not a good sign.

Avitus focused on the others. Roxana was wide-eyed and breathing rapidly. Grim was grimmer than ever. Momus hovered at the edge of the peristyle, peering at them anxiously.

He turned back to his wife. "Where have you been?"

She frowned in thought. "I was only looking for the house with the dry fountain. If I'd known they would be there, I wouldn't have gone. We left, but the beggar boy snatched the woman's purse so I ran after him, and the hairy one grabbed me, but Grim bombarded him with spoons and I got away."

Her words made no sense. Avitus settled beside her on the bench. She was trembling, so he took her hand in his. "You're safe now."

With much prompting and backtracking, he pieced together the story. His obsessed wife had gone snooping for more clues. Through a creative interpretation of the facts that defied logic, she'd stumbled onto the house where the thugs were hiding. And the scum had dared to touch her!

He took Livia by the shoulders and forced her to look at him. "I shudder to think what those men might have done to you. How can I protect you if you disregard my warnings and break your promises?"

"I'm sorry." She met his gaze for a moment then looked away. "I shouldn't have gone, but I was angry at you for giving up on the crimes. I wanted to find something that would make you change your mind."

What an idiot I've been. Why had he thought pretending to give up on the investigation would work? All he'd done was incite her to take needless risks, with almost catastrophic consequences. If not for Grim's quick acting, she would have been captured.

"I promise I'll find these men and deal with them, but I can't do it if I'm constantly worried about you. They'll be looking for you. That means you must stay home until they're apprehended. Do you understand?"

She nodded. "I won't fight you anymore." Then she raised her head and looked him in the eyes, her own sparking with anger. "Those men have ruined enough lives. Do whatever you need to find them and stop them!"

"I will." He helped her to her feet. "Roxana, see to your mistress. I think she needs to lie down."

Only after the women were out of sight did he allow his anger to flame to life, filling his chest with heat and tightening his jaw. His wife had been attacked. In broad daylight! What criminal dared attack wealthy ladies with impunity? That might happen in some provincial backwater, but this was Rome, the center of the civilized world. Blatant disregard for the law was not allowed. Not in his city. Not while he lived to do something about it.

And thanks to Livia's almost-disastrous quest, they knew where the killers were hiding. More importantly, they now had a name—Nepos.

Avitus would not squander this opportunity. It was time to go on the offensive. He beckoned Grim and Sorex into his study. "We need to talk."

Grim stood to stiff attention, gaze fixed on the floor at Avitus's feet. "Forgive me for failing you, sir. I should never have allowed the lady to look for the house. I should have been more cautious. I should have suspected there would be more than one. I—"

Avitus silenced him with a look. "Don't waste breath on excuses."

"Yes, sir. I won't fail you again, sir."

"Yes, you will."

Shock and anger flitted across Grim's face, followed by resentment. Avitus recognized the feelings. He'd reacted the same way when Jonas had taught him this lesson. His mentor's voice sounded in his head. *The wise man learns from his failures. The foolish man wallows in them.*

"Much of life is outside our control," he told Grim. "A successful man isn't the one who never fails, but the one who refuses to let failure defeat him. Instead of giving up, you found a way to rescue your mistress. That is exactly the kind of man I need to protect my wife."

The slave remained at attention, but every angle of him softened in relief.

"Now, tell me what happened. I want every detail."

Grim complied.

Even after Grim's report, Livia's reasoning for searching out the house made no sense. The threat, however, was as clear as the sun in a cloudless sky. Gimpy and Hairy had recognized Livia and suspected she was looking into their secrets. If they saw her again, they would kill her.

"Did anyone follow you here?"

"I did my best to avoid it, but the lady was shaken and I dared not delay too long before leading her home."

Then they must prepare for the worst. "Grim, take Sorex and show him where the killers are hiding. You will stay and watch the house. Make sure they don't disappear again. Sorex, you go to my brother and ask for two of his men to serve as additional guards. I want this house as secure as a legionary fort."

"Yes, sir," they said in gruff unison.

When they'd gone, Avitus strode to the atrium. "Keep alert, Momus. The mistress's attackers may have followed her to the house. If you see anyone suspicious, inform me immediately."

"Don't you worry, sir. They won't be laying a hand on the lady while I'm on duty."

But Avitus did worry. He surveyed the street. No threatening faces stared back at him.

Except one.

Roxana's annoying cat walked over and stared up at him with disdainful, unblinking eyes. "Go away, cat. I'm in no mood to put up with you."

The cat didn't move except to twitch the tip of its tail. The little creature was as brash as the criminals. What they needed was a loyal dog to protect them, not a devious, food-stealing cat. As if the cat could read his thoughts, it laid back its ears and hissed at him. Infernal beast!

Momus snapped his fingers. "Come Nemesis. Don't annoy the master. You're needed inside to comfort the lady."

Avitus spun on Momus. "That cat is not allowed in my house."

"Nothing like a purring cat to calm a troubled heart, sir." Momus smiled benevolently as the cat strolled into the atrium.

Hades! Avitus clamped his jaw on a litany of imprecations against felines and stomped off down the street. He completed a circuit of the block without seeing anyone suspicious. Satisfied the killers weren't lurking in the shadows, he returned to the house and considered how to proceed.

A new day offered a new chance to do what was right. How many times had Placida and Pansa counseled Livia to act with patience? Yesterday she'd failed.

In monumental fashion.

Her skin crawled, remembering the hairy man who'd crushed her to his chest, breathing threats and sour breath in her ear. And she had only herself to blame. She'd been so angry that she'd done the very thing Brother Titus had counseled her not to—attempting to control her husband.

What she should have done was comply with Avitus's wishes and trust God to set matters straight. Ultimately her actions proved she didn't trust God or her husband.

It was a sobering realization, and she vowed to atone for it by being a model wife today—a vow she could only keep with the Lord's help.

Dear Jesus, help me be patient and trust my husband to do what is right. And thank you that, despite my failure, you have changed his mind.

Before he left, Avitus called her to the atrium. "I've ordered Grim to keep watch on the house belonging to Optatus, to make sure the killers don't disappear again. We don't know if the criminals followed you home yesterday, so I've added additional guards, just in case." He pointed to two sturdy men who stiffened to attention under his scrutiny.

"They will keep you safe, so long as you stay home like we agreed." He stabbed her with his intense lawyer's stare.

Expecting her to argue? Could she blame him, based on how she'd behaved lately? She bowed her head demurely. "I give you my word. Roxana and I will remain in the house all day."

He narrowed his eyes. "Forgive me if I find your sudden meekness a trifle suspicious."

Livia crossed her arms. "Perhaps you are confusing meekness with cooperation. I promise to stay home so that you can devote your full attention to finding Nepos. May God grant you success."

After searching her eyes for an uncomfortably long moment, he appeared to accept her promise. "Babak's painters should arrive later. I've instructed Momus to admit them." He shook a warning finger at her. "But remember, I've only agreed to repaint the dining room, so don't get carried away."

"I promise."

Now that they had a name, finding the marble dealer should be possible, and the most logical place to search for him was the busy warehouse district along the Tiber River. Avitus, Sorex and Timon hiked across the city and out the Triple Gate to the banks of the Tiber River. The streets near the river were crowded with stevedores, mule drivers, shouting men, and containers of all sizes being transported from barges to the multitude of large buildings that housed the goods arriving daily from the port of Ostia downriver.

Before he could search for Nepos, Avitus must keep his appointment with Babak. He passed through the entrance of the silk merchant's warehouse into a courtyard paved with a black and white mosaic featuring Mercury. An appropriate choice for a man of commerce. On either side of the entrance were three storage bays protected by heavy wooden doors. Could Babak possibly own that much silk?

They were ushered across the courtyard to an office. The room was filled with rows of scrolls peeking from pigeonholes and shelves piled with stacks of wax tablets.

Hmm. Somewhere in that mass of records there ought to be useful information on marble dealers. Perhaps he could coax the merchant to assist him?

"Greetings, Advocate," Babak said. "My clerks will supply you with any documents you wish to view." He gestured at two clerks. One was wizened and thin as a post, the other barely more than a boy. The older clerk's grandson, perhaps?

Avitus asked for all the records related to the disputed shipment. Manifests, sales contracts, barge invoices, etc. Despite the volume of records, the clerks located every document he requested with commendable alacrity. While Timon copied the pertinent details, Avitus asked Babak for a list of men whom they could call on to testify. "We need men who can vouch for your integrity, as well as men who will testify regarding your opponent's dishonesty."

When Avitus had compiled a suitable list, he said, "I wish all my clients were as organized as you are. You keep excellent records."

"Thank you, Excellency. "

"It occurs to me that a merchant who keeps such stellar records might be able to assist me on an unrelated matter."

Babak broke into a beatific smile. "Nothing would delight me more than to be of service. What is it you seek?"

"I occasionally assist government authorities in inquiries regarding corruption. It has come to our attention that certain men of this city are operating a large-scale scam. At present we are not sure how wide this web of corruption has spread, but we suspect it leads even into the senate. From what we can ascertain, a key player in this reprehensible activity has a connection to the shipment of marble. Might you be able to help us find this individual?"

Babak's face had grown wary at the mention of government authorities, but now he relaxed. "The advocate wishes information on shippers who deal in marble?"

"Just so."

"As you are surely aware, I do not myself deal in marble," Babak said, "but a wise merchant keeps his eyes and ears open at all times."

Exactly what Avitus had been hoping. He outlined the information they sought on marble dealers. When he'd finished, Babak snapped his fingers and the older of his clerks stepped forward.

"Sir?"

"You heard the advocate. Find him what we know about anyone named Nepos who deals in marble."

The clerk rubbed an ink-stained finger along his chin then plucked a tattered scroll from the shelf. The clerk consulted four additional scrolls before he was satisfied with his efforts. When all the information had been copied, the clerk handed a list to Avitus with a deep bow.

"Thank you," Avitus said to Babak. "This will help immensely."

The list Babak's clerk provided included five men named Nepos. Two were ship captains that sometimes transported marble from far provinces like *Aegyptus* and *Numidia*. Avitus sent Timon to check on them. Avitus and Sorex would locate the remaining three, who owned warehouses in Rome. The hunt for Nepos had begun.

CHAPTER 27

A few hours later, Livia stood in her dining room with the head painter.

"Good lines in this room, miss. What do you have in mind?"

She explained her vision for creating a smaller version of the scenes in Babak and Nahla's peristyle.

He scratched his chin with a pigment-stained finger. "Sounds possible. May I show you what I propose?" He took a stub of charcoal and drew a tree and half a bush with a few deft strokes. Next, he sketched a Corinthian column with a few parallel lines topped by a squiggle of acanthus leaves. On the other side of the column, he continued the bush and added a clump of flowers and a fountain.

"You see? The entire wall is one scene divided into sections as if you were looking through a colonnade."

Livia stood back to study his handiwork. It was exactly the kind of look she wanted. "I like it."

The painter bobbed his head. "Thank you. I'll purchase the necessary materials and return tomorrow with the crew to begin work." He took careful measurements of the room with a length of knotted twine then excused himself.

When he was gone, Livia reclined in each dining couch and squinted at the walls, imagining how the new frescoes would look from the vantage point of guests. Since one side of the room was open to the peristyle, the other three walls should complement it rather than compete with it.

"I was wondering, my lady?"

"Yes, Roxana."

"Would it be possible to include a cat in one of the scenes? Maybe only her face, hiding behind a clump of flowers?"

Livia chuckled. "Can you imagine what Avitus would say if he noticed a cat in his dining room? But I like the idea of including animals. Perhaps a few birds, too."

"The birds of the air above the lilies of the fields? Like Pansa always talks about?"

Livia caught her breath. "That's a grand idea. We can ask the painter to include details that remind us of the stories the Lord Jesus told."

"Brilliant, my lady. Our secrets, right on the walls in front of everyone's noses."

Secrets.

The word made her squirm. She'd promised both Curio and Placida that she would tell Avitus about her faith. As soon as this business with the water fraud was over, she must sit down and have a long talk with her husband.

Nissa stuck her head into the room. "Roxana, there you are. I was outside and I saw some boys tormenting a cat. It looked like Nemesis."

"Where? Show me!" Roxana dashed from the room.

"Roxana! Come back here!"

Too late. Livia clambered from the dining couch and trotted to the atrium, but Roxana and Nissa were out the door.

Fish pickle! Livia had promised Avitus they would stay inside. What would happen if the thugs were watching the house and saw Roxana? What would they do to her?

She turned to Momus, who was squatting with Publius's extra guards, playing knucklebones. "Why didn't you stop her?"

"Who?"

"Roxana."

Momus shrugged. "No one gave us orders about Roxana."

Well, rancid fish pickle.

"You'd better go find her. If those thugs are watching our house, they'll recognize her."

Momus ambled to the doorway and squinted into the street. "We've been searching the block since last night, my lady. We haven't found anyone suspicious, so I wouldn't worry."

"Let's hope you're right."

She peered over the doorkeeper's arm, frustrated and anxious. This must be how Avitus felt when he discovered Livia had been investigating the Triton or searching the streets for blind beggars. No wonder he got cross with her.

Roxana trotted home a few minutes later, carrying a hissing Nemesis in her arms. Both maid and cat looked ready to bite someone.

Livia was mad enough to bite back. "You're lucky those thugs weren't out there waiting for you. Don't you dare leave this house again without my permission."

"Sorry, my lady."

"You'd better be. Put the cat down and get busy clearing the dining room so the painters can begin work tomorrow."

The first Nepos whom Avitus and Sorex visited was at least sixty and could barely walk. He kept his business going by sitting on a padded bench and shouting orders at a long-suffering nephew who appeared to have as much enthusiasm for life as a slug. Avitus could not imagine this pair running a complicated fraud.

The second Nepos was an eager young merchant from Cyrene. He had the drive and the intelligence, but his warehouse space was located inside a large building with more than twenty separate storage areas around a central courtyard. This Nepos would have a difficult time keeping illegal goings-on from curious neighboring merchants.

The final warehouse was more promising, one of several units in a long dreary row, each with a stout door opening directly onto the street. Avitus kicked at weeds growing in one of the doorways. "Looks like half the warehouses in this block are empty. A convenient location for a businessman who wanted his activities to go unnoticed."

Sorex nodded. "Very suspicious."

Inside, the warehouse was one large room. No loft overhead. No storage chests or other hiding places to store illegal plumbing supplies. A brawny man who looked strong enough to lift the large stone slabs stacked around the building strode to meet them. "Can I help you?" he said in voice that was anything but welcoming.

"I'm looking for Nepos the marble importer," Avitus said.

"I'm his clerk," the man replied.

Avitus harrumphed, indicating he was not pleased to be dealing with a mere clerk. "I'm renovating a house and I need marble for a new fountain and other improvements." He rattled off half a dozen colors of marble, along with the quantity he wanted. The clerk's eyes glinted with avarice as the list continued, each marble more expensive than the last.

"We don't have porphyry in stock," the brawny clerk said, "but I can show you some Numidian yellow and Theban green."

He muscled aside a few slabs before dragging samples into the light. Avitus made murmurs of approval.

"You buying these now?"

"I would prefer to discuss my purchases with Nepos himself. Will he be back later today?"

"He rarely comes here. Nepos has a showroom on the Caelian Hill near the shrine to Minerva. That way his fancy customers don't have to come all the way out here."

Implying that Nepos only dealt with men who were too wealthy to dirty their sandals visiting a warehouse.

Extremely promising.

"What do you think?" Avitus asked Sorex once they'd left the warehouse. "The clerk acted like a thug but I didn't see any place to hide plumbing supplies."

Sorex gestured to the seemingly vacant warehouses. "Could be using more than one warehouse."

"Good point. Let's hope Nepos and his fancy showroom give us something more to go on."

They cut around the south side of the city wall and entered through the Gate of the Oak Nymphs, where the street called Via Tusculana exited the city. It was past midday, so they stopped at a hot food shop for a quick bowl of stew washed down with watery sour wine.

The host was friendly. When Sorex asked him where to find Nepos he made a face. "What do you want with him?"

"My master wants some fancy marble this Nepos is supposed to sell."

"You've not met him, then?"

They shook their heads.

"He's a nasty piece of work. Vile temper, rude, and dishonest as the day is long. If you want my advice, get your marble from someone else. I've never seen him have a return customer, and that tells you something, doesn't it?"

Avitus paid for their meal and thanked the man for his advice.

They approached Nepos's shop with care, pausing a block away to study it. While they watched, two men emerged. The first man was bulky, with the scarred face and swaggering gait of a gladiator. The second man must be Nepos. He was—

Avitus turned away, stomach churning. A memory exploded in his head: a younger version of the face he'd just glimpsed, leering cruelly. He stumbled into the nearest shop, heart pounding.

"Looks like you've just seen a shade," the shopkeeper said, concern wrinkling his forehead. "Is everything all right?"

"I'm fine." Avitus straightened and brushed imaginary dust from his tunic. "Just someone I want to avoid."

The shopkeeper glanced out the doorway and nodded. "Don't blame you. We all avoid that one when we can." He sidled to the doorway, pretending to straighten his display baskets. "He'll be out of sight in a moment or two . . . and now he's gone."

"Thank you." Avitus passed the kindly shopkeeper a sestertius. "May Fortuna smile kindly on you and your household."

He left the shop, heading in the opposite direction from Nepos. Sorex followed silently, but Avitus could feel the unasked questions burning in his faithful slave's mind.

"I recognized Nepos."

"So I gathered, sir. You turned pale as a shroud when you laid eyes on him. Who is he?"

Nepos! After all these years. Avitus found himself rubbing the burn scar on his arm and forced his hands to his sides.

"He's a relative of Gracchus."

Sorex gave a low rumbling growl. "Then we've found our man?"

"I think so."

Nepos's family owned vineyards near the coast, yet here he was, pretending to be a marble dealer. It couldn't be a coincidence.

"Want me to go back and see what I can learn about him, sir?"

"No. If Nepos has been in Rome running the piping fraud all this time, he's sure to have seen Publius and me in the forum. Which means he would recognize you and Timon as well."

Sorex grunted his understanding. "We need someone else to reconnoiter who Nepos won't recognize. Like maybe Curio?"

"That's what I'm thinking."

After Avitus explained things, Curio agreed to do some quiet snooping. Avitus thanked his brother-in-law and turned his steps toward home.

If Nepos was leading the fraud, then Gracchus was behind everything for sure. And opposing Gracchus was a dangerous endeavor. Avitus couldn't make that choice without explaining the risks to Livia and getting her unequivocal promise of cooperation.

Avitus found Livia and her maid discussing sketches that had been drawn on the dining room walls. She looked up, surprised. "I wasn't expecting you back for hours. Did you find Nepos?"

"I did. Come into my study and I'll explain."

Avitus indicated Livia take a chair then sat facing her. He took a deep breath, squared his shoulders, and began. "I think we've identified the Nepos who's behind the fraud, but there's a problem. He's a relative of Gracchus."

"The one who cheated you at the trial? I thought you said he wasn't involved."

"I was mistaken. Before I explain how Gracchus is involved, I need you to understand how our feud began. It starts with this." He touched his scarred cheek.

Her eyes widened.

"My father and Gracchus's father were friends. We often spent time at each other's villas, especially during the summer when we escaped the heat of Rome. Publius and I dreaded the visits. Even as a child Gracchus was cruel, vindictive, and self-centered. The year I was twelve, we stayed at their villa for an extended visit. Jonas had been teaching us sword skills, and Father insisted we continue our lessons. We were joined by Gracchus and his cousin Nepos.

"Every day Gracchus taunted the rest of us. He was older and stronger and took pleasure in humiliating us with his superior skills. Publius and I got the brunt of it, but he taunted Nepos, too."

Livia's eyes narrowed. "I hate bullies."

"So did we. We complained to Jonas, but he told us not to let Gracchus rile us. He said a man's honor was proven by character in the face of adversity. Eventually Jonas grew tired of Gracchus and his insults. He secretly taught Publius moves to disarm Gracchus. It worked. Gracchus was so shocked at losing he quit attending the lessons. After that, Nepos began to act friendly. He said he'd never seen anyone best Gracchus before.

"One day Nepos told us Gracchus and his friends were planning to celebrate Bacchanalian rites that night at a neighboring villa. He proposed we sneak out of the house after dark to spy on them. To youths on the cusp of manhood, a glimpse of wild and forbidden rites seemed like a daring plan. To make it sweeter, Nepos claimed we might witness something that could be used to blackmail Gracchus into leaving us alone for good.

"We followed Nepos through a grove of trees to a little dell lit by a bonfire. Gracchus and his cronies were sitting around the fire, drinking wine. We were suspicious when we didn't see any women, but Nepos told us to be patient. The entertainment would arrive soon."

Livia listened in rapt silence, eyes round in anticipation like a theatergoer waiting for a fatal twist in the plot, which was exactly what he must deliver.

"Then Nepos shouted, 'Now!' In moments Gracchus and his leering friends had surrounded us. Gracchus drew a sword and pointed it at Publius. 'No one makes me look bad and gets away with it,' he said. They dragged us into the clearing. While Nepos held me down and laughed, the others forced Publius to strip naked. Then Gracchus prodded him to the center of the clearing, tossed him an old sword, and told him to defend himself. Publius did his best, but he was soon bleeding from half a dozen cuts while Gracchus remained unmarked. I began to fear it wouldn't stop until Publius was seriously hurt.

"Then Gracchus took a swipe that would have split Publius's head if he hadn't thrown himself to his knees. Gracchus laughed and gave him a vicious kick. Then he raised his sword. I was sure he was about to kill my brother."

Avitus took a shaky breath, reliving the desperation of that moment. "I broke free of Nepos and drove my shoulder into Gracchus's groin with as much force as I could muster. He screamed, dropped his sword and bent double. Everyone else froze, staring in horrified fascination as Gracchus writhed and cursed. I grabbed the sword and stood over Publius to protect him. Gracchus staggered to his feet. He grabbed me, shook me like a rat then tossed me aside—right into the fire."

Livia cried out in alarm.

"After that everything is a blur. Publius dragged me from the fire and we stumbled home, where Jonas tended my wounds. The next morning, we told my parents what had happened. Gracchus and Nepos denied it, claiming they'd been at a friend's house all evening. Their friends corroborated their testimony, making us look like liars. Father was furious."

Livia's eyes narrowed. "Your father believed Gracchus instead of you?"

"We were guests in Gracchus's house and we had no way to prove our version of the story. Honor demanded Father accept Gracchus's version. To his way of thinking, it was our fault that we'd allowed ourselves to be humiliated."

Livia jumped to her feet and uttered an unladylike phrase. She grabbed his hands, eyes blazing. "No wonder you hate Gracchus so fiercely! It would have eaten me alive to be called a liar after all you'd suffered."

It had been eating Avitus's soul since the day it happened. His face and his dignitas had been forever damaged, and his father had never forgiven him. All while Gracchus continued to thrive.

"Now that I've given you the history of our feud with Gracchus, I hope you understand the risks we face. Gracchus is as vindictive today as he was back then. If we go after him, I can't promise we'll succeed unscathed. He won't hesitate to hurt you if he discovers who you are. When I realized I had been allowing you to pry into one of his schemes, I was alarmed. I foolishly thought I could convince you to drop the matter without explaining the real issue."

She crinkled her brow. "You weren't actually giving up?"

He shook his head. "Publius and I will never stop fighting him, but I'd hoped to avoid telling you the shameful truth about our history. I see now that was a mistake."

"Thank you for explaining," Livia said gravely. She reached up and ran a finger along his scarred cheek. "I'll never look at these scars again without remembering the injustice you've suffered. I knew you were a man of courage and honor, but until this moment I didn't guess the depths of your character. You're ten times the man Gracchus is, no matter how much dignitas he thinks he wields."

Warmth spread from his cheek to his face and chest, melting the shame that had frozen him for so long. For a moment he had a strange impulse to laugh. Never in his wildest dreams would he have imagined Livia's tender response. Or her fierce devotion.

It was a completely novel feeling. Who would have guessed that sharing his darkest secret with his wife would lead to joy rather than shame? He pulled his wife to him and kissed her.

She kissed him back. With passion.

CHAPTER 28

Until last night Livia had believed Avitus would always be impossibly distant and withdrawn, someone she could co-exist with but would never come to know, let alone love.

This morning everything was different.

Today, instead of pretending to be asleep, she sat up and greeted him. He returned her greeting with a kiss.

When he slipped from the covers, Livia looked at his scarred body in the light of day. She was captured by the way his muscles rippled as he bent at the washbasin to rinse the sleep from his face. His wiry form moved with the lithe grace of a man who exercised regularly. Why had she never noticed this before?

Because she'd never looked for it. She'd been so convinced he would always be distant and unfeeling that she'd not bothered to notice his other qualities. *You see what you look for.* One of Placida's mottoes, and so often true.

In the future, Livia would look for things to love about Avitus, instead of focusing on the things she wished to change. Starting now.

Her husband dried his face and hands. After shrugging into a fresh tunic, he called for Sorex to help him don his toga. That meant he had official business.

"Do you have another court case today?"

"Only a preliminary hearing with the praetor. After that I must tell Publius about Nepos so we can decide how to proceed."

Avitus stood with arms outstretched while Sorex wound the bulky garment around him and painstakingly adjusted the folds. Avitus caught her watching and rolled his eyes. She giggled. Sorex froze, flicked a glance at both of them then returned to his work, a faint smile creasing his gruff face.

When the toga was arranged to his satisfaction, Sorex withdrew. Husband and wife regarded each other shyly. "I wish you a good day," Livia said. "I will abide by my promise and stay home. May God's blessing go with you."

"Thank you." He smiled, brushed his fingers along her cheek and was gone.

A perfectly mundane exchange, but so different from anything that had come previously that it left Livia feeling giddy. Could Placida have been right all along? Could she and Avitus develop actual feelings for one another? Could she find it in her heart to love this frustrating and enigmatic man?

Avitus had known adapting to marriage would be a challenge. He'd expected a wife to disrupt his routines and embark on a whirlwind of home improvements. Publius had prepared him for that, but he'd said nothing about how to handle love.

Emotions complicated everything. Emotions clouded his thinking. But this morning Avitus wasn't complaining. The simple exchange he'd shared with Livia buoyed his spirits all the way to the forum.

When his business there was finished, he headed to his brother's house and found Publius reading a scroll in his peristyle. "Good morning. We need to talk."

"Indeed?" Publius set his scroll aside. "Did you find the man behind the water scheme?"

"Yes, and you're not going to believe who I discovered: Gracchus's cousin Nepos."

Publius froze for five heartbeats, mouth slightly ajar. Then he blinked. "You're certain it's Nepos, not someone who looks like him?"

Avitus didn't dignify that question with an answer. He explained how they'd found Nepos as a result of Livia's almost-kidnapping.

"Jupiter, Best and Greatest. They actually grabbed her in a public street? Gracchus has overstepped himself this time. First the trial and now this." Publius slammed a fist on his knee. "We cannot allow him to continue flaunting our laws with such impunity."

No, they couldn't, especially when Livia was the victim.

"Now that we've identified Nepos," Avitus said, "I'm convinced your theory about Gracchus and the water lines is correct. If we can prove it, we can make Gracchus and Nepos pay."

"I'm all ears. How do we prove it?"

"We start by keeping track of the criminals. Can you spare men to watch the house where Livia discovered the killers? She says it belongs to Optatus, by the way. Is he one of Gracchus's new clientes?"

"Indeed, he is. Meanwhile, I've spoken with a few of the other clientes to verify they have running water in their city homes. We can check to see if they have the proper licenses. If they don't, we have our proof."

"That won't be enough," Avitus said. "Proving those men have illegal pipes would implicate Nepos, but not Gracchus. What we need is a customer who can testify that Gracchus offered him a water connection, and that Nepos accepted money to have the plumbing installed."

"That may be possible," Publius said. "I'll have to consider which of Gracchus's new clientes I can convince to cooperate with us."

That was as likely as snow in August.

"None of his clientes are going to testify against him in court. Not when they face hefty fines for admitting they have illegal water. And I don't trust anyone who has become a cliens of Gracchus, anyway."

Publius made a frustrated noise in the back of his throat. "How do you expect us to get a customer testimony if you don't trust any of the customers?"

Avitus grinned at his brother, the solution suddenly clear in his head. "We create our own. We send someone posing as a customer, who can pretend to purchase a water connection and then report it for us."

"Brilliant!" Publius pounded his knee again, this time in glee. "A false customer to gather the proof we need. I like it. And I have a cliens who could play the part convincingly."

"I don't think that's a good idea. If Nepos has been in Rome for the last year or more, he's certain to have learned all he can about us, including our households, and our clientes. We'll need someone he won't link back to either of us."

Avitus tapped his fingers as he thought through his list of contacts that could be trusted. Perhaps he could ask Turpio, his actor friend?

"How about your brother-in-law?" Publius said.

"He's a possibility. I'll ask him. Meanwhile, I'd still like to post a watchman at Optatus's house. And Scaevola's, too."

"Very well, I'll send men to keep the houses under surveillance.

What else do we need?"

"One last thing. We need to figure out who in the water commission we can trust to listen to our evidence. How well do you know the ex-commissioner, Laenas? Can he be persuaded to help us?"

"Very likely. He's a man of duty and honor, and he's an outspoken opponent of Gracchus."

"Will you talk to him?"

"It would help if I had something to show him. Can I have those tablets you discovered?"

Timon pulled Zeno's tablets from his satchel and handed them to Publius.

"Excellent. These ought to pique Laenas's interest. I'll go at once and see if he's available."

The brothers exchanged a look. After all these years and so many frustrating losses, would they finally be able to watch Gracchus suffer for his crimes?

CHAPTER 29

On the short walk to Curio's, Avitus considered the risks of asking his brother-in-law to play the customer. Curio and Avitus had always kept their relationship secret, and the marriage to Livia had been a small, quiet ceremony, thus it was not common knowledge that the two men were related. Therefore, the risk of Nepos recognizing Curio was low enough, assuming he hadn't attracted undue attention during yesterday's surveillance.

But first, Avitus would listen to what Curio had learned about their enemy. He took a seat in Curio's study and raised an eyebrow. "What did you discover?"

"This Nepos you sent me to ask about is a thoroughly odious man." Curio grimaced and took a sip of wine, as if to wash the bad taste from his mouth.

Avitus didn't blame him. Nepos left a bad taste in his mouth, too. "Sounds like he's the same belligerent oaf I remember. Thanks for checking into him for me. What did you learn?"

"Nepos keeps to himself. Obviously wealthy, yet he rarely entertains. Comes and goes at odd hours. Always keeps two men on guard at his door. All of which suggests a man who has things to hide."

Yes, it did. Nepos was looking more guilty by the moment, but they needed proof to link him to the water fraud. "Has anyone seen him talking with Hairy or Gimpy?"

"Not that I discovered, but I did verify he's a cliens of Gracchus."

That was no surprise. "Did you find anything that could point to illegal dealings?"

"Possibly." Curio gave Avitus his lopsided grin.

"I'm all ears."

"The shop next door to Nepos's premises is empty. I didn't see any other vacant shops nearby, so this one seemed odd. I started asking about it. Turns out Nepos's shop and the one next door were previously owned by brothers who left Rome at the same time. Rather abruptly, I'm told. Nepos moved into the larger shop, and the other has been vacant ever since. When I asked the landlord, I was informed the space is not available for rent. Isn't that curious?"

"Are you suggesting the vacant shop isn't really vacant?"

"I am. Someone has been through that door recently. There were fresh skid marks across the lintel. So I made the acquaintance of the tenants who live above the empty shop, and they told me they sometimes hear voices and other noises, but they're too afraid of Nepos to ask questions."

Aha! It wasn't firm proof, but they were getting closer. Avitus raised his wine cup in salute. "Well done."

"Thank you." Curio matched the salute and took a sip. "If you want, I can arrange for certain people I know to break in and take a look inside that shop."

"That won't be necessary. Publius and I have come up with a less risky way to learn what we need." Avitus explained their theory about Gracchus being the mastermind, and their idea for getting an eyewitness testimony about Nepos's part in the fraud. "Would it be possible for you to pose as a customer, or did Nepos's guards notice you asking questions?"

"I went disguised as a poor craftsman and I stayed clear of Nepos and his guards. I doubt they paid me a second glance."

"Then you're willing to return? Livia isn't safe until Nepos and his underlings are arrested."

Curio nodded. "You know I'll do whatever I can to help you. Any suggestions on how I approach the subject? What if there's a code phrase or a token of some kind?"

An apt concern that Avitus had been pondering. "I don't think we need to worry. Nepos isn't particularly bright. He's likely to bungle code phrases or other complicated procedures. If I were Gracchus, I'd keep things as simple as possible. I doubt random strangers show up at Nepos's marble shop asking about plumbing unless Gracchus has sent them."

"That's good to know. What kind of man do I need to impersonate?"

Avitus explained Publius's theory about newly arrived wealthy provincials wanting access to water rights.

"I can make that work," Curio said in a heavy accent. "We have relatives in *Ariminum* who fit that profile. I'll pretend to be one of them."

Avitus laughed. "You have the accent down perfectly. Thanks for doing this."

"You're welcome. If I leave now, I'll be finished by midafternoon. Do you want to come back this evening to hear what I learn?"

"Livia will want to hear as well, so could you come to my house instead?"

"No problem. See you around the ninth hour."

"Done."

Avitus left Curio's house feeling more hopeful than he had in days. For the first time since Jonas went missing, they were on the offensive instead of chasing three steps behind.

Maybe the gods were finally smiling on him.

Avitus arrived home to find his dining couches piled in a corner of the peristyle and men's voices coming from the dining room. Ah yes, the painters. He'd have to get rid of them before Curio arrived.

Livia and her maid stood in the middle of the dining room talking with one painter while two others assembled a scaffold. The room was filled with tarps, sacks of plaster, buckets, trowels, paint brushes, and baskets of colored lumps that would be ground to create the pigments from which the painters mixed their paints.

Livia waved him over. "You're back just in time to help me with the final decisions."

She explained her vision for each panel. Avitus nodded and smiled, pleased to see his wife happy. "Very nice," he said when she was finished. "I trust your judgment."

After a discussion about payments, the painters took their leave, promising to return in the morning and begin work.

When they were gone, Livia quirked an eyebrow. "You seemed in a hurry to be rid of them. What's going on? Do you have news?"

"I do." He told Livia about sending Curio to impersonate a customer. "He's on his way to Nepos's shop now. I've asked him to come here when he's finished so you can hear what he discovers."

"You did?" She gave him a dazzling smile.

And then she kissed him.

Perhaps the novelty of a kiss would fade with time and familiarity, but for now he savored the warm flutter it caused in his heart. He would do whatever it took to keep her safe.

Right now, that meant putting a stop to Nepos and his henchman. Avitus and his allies gathered two hours later to discuss their latest findings.

"Let's make this quick," Publius said when he arrived. "I haven't had a chance to bathe yet, and we have guests coming for dinner."

He dropped onto a stool and noticed Livia. His eyebrows rose, and then lowered into a bristling line. "This is serious business, brother. No place for a woman."

"Livia has done as much as anyone to uncover these crimes," Avitus replied. "She's earned a right to stay."

Publius harrumphed and gave her a dark look. Livia gave Avitus's hand a quick squeeze of thanks. He gave her a tiny wink in return. (Who would have imagined he would ever wink at a woman? Amazing.) But, to business.

Avitus looked into each serious face, one at a time. "We all know what's at stake here."

They nodded.

"Let's start by hearing from Publius. What did Senator Laenas say about our suspicions?"

"Ex-commissioner Laenas is eager to help us. He was impressed by the detailed pipe information in the tablet, and he's sent a man to locate a few of the pipes. Once he verifies that the tablet does in fact list illegally connected pipes, Laenas is happy to report the whole scheme to the proper authorities. He approves of our plan to send a false customer to learn exactly who is involved and what parts they play. Once we have that information, he asks that we bring everything to him and he'll take over."

"Not sure I like that." Curio frowned and shook his head. "What if he's part of the scam? How do we know we can trust him?"

A reasonable question, but Publius drew himself up and gave Curio a withering glare. "Because he gave me his word."

"A gentleman's agreement, eh? That works for me."

"I'm so glad you approve," Publius said acidly.

"Thank you for arranging things with Laenas," Avitus said, steering the conversation back on track. "Tell us what you learned, Curio."

Curio began by describing Nepos's shop and his suspicions of the vacant one next door.

Livia's eyes lit up. "I assume you're going to take a look inside?"

Publius scowled at her for interrupting. Avitus shot her a warning look. "We have a less risky plan to get the information. Please continue."

Curio did so. "I told Nepos I was adding a fountain to my garden and wanted marble for the facade. I waited to see if he would bring up water connections on his own, but he didn't. After discussing various marbles he had on offer, I mentioned that I'd been talking to Senator Gracchus, who told me that Nepos could arrange to have my new fountain linked to the water lines. I can't describe his reaction. He managed to go on full alert like a guard dog sensing danger while at the same time becoming all sly and conspiratorial. The shifty look lasted about three heartbeats then he gave me a smile as false as a crocodile's. 'I wasn't aware the senator was still sending me customers,' he said."

Avitus exhaled sharply. Would fate snatch victory from their hands after letting them get so close? "Don't tell me he refused you?"

"No. I told him I'd just made Senator Gracchus's acquaintance, and I was sure my esteemed new friend wouldn't have mentioned the plumbing opportunity unless the offer were still valid."

"He believed you?"

"Seemed to. He got down to business without any more questions. First off, he demanded a five hundred sestertii deposit before he would introduce me to the plumbers. Are we willing to pay that much to go through with the ruse?"

"I am." Publius said. "I'll consider it a good investment, if we can prove Nepos and Gracchus are behind the fraud."

"I was hoping you'd say that, because I've agreed to meet them tonight. Can you get the money together that quickly?"

"Why such a rush?" Publius frowned at Curio. "Seems suspicious."

Curio laughed. "Of course it's suspicious. He's running an illegal plumbing scam. That's why the meeting is two hours after dark, when honest men are home in their beds."

Publius's frown deepened. "This is no time for levity. What if he suspects you? If he connects you to Avitus, our plans are ruined."

"Sorry, just trying to lighten the mood." Curio adopted a serious tone. "Don't worry, I know how to deal with dishonest men. I made sure I lost the man he sent to follow me before coming here, and I agreed to meet tonight because I thought it best to make the arrangements before Nepos had a chance to talk to Gracchus."

"I see." Publius nodded, mollified. "In that case, carry on. I can provide the coin you require. What's our plan?"

"Here's what I propose," Avitus said. "As soon as our meeting is over, we'll position men near Nepos's shop to keep watch and act as backup in case things go wrong. Curio will arrive tonight at the appointed time, bringing the money provided by Publius. After his meeting, Curio will go directly to Laenas's home and report everything he observed. Meanwhile, our backup men can follow Nepos's conspirators to wherever they are currently residing. Any questions?"

Curio and Publius shook their heads, but Livia pursed her lips.

"Aren't you missing an opportunity?" she said. "Tonight's meeting is the perfect chance to get a look inside the vacant shop. Curio can distract Nepos's guards while someone slips through the door."

Avitus swallowed his frustration. "I realize it's tempting to see what's inside, but we don't want to jeopardize our main plan. We can't risk the guards getting suspicious before Curio has a chance to meet with Nepos."

"You're forgetting that Nepos's shop is on a corner," Curio said. "His door opens onto one street and the vacant shop opens onto the other, so Nepos's guards can't see someone at the door to the vacant shop. Livia's right; it's the perfect time to sneak in for a look."

"I agree as well," Publius said. "It may give us more evidence to take to Laenas."

Avitus groaned inwardly. They were now talking about coordinating three different groups, all with different missions.

"Breaking into the shop complicates our plan and adds additional men. I don't think the risk is worth it."

"It's only two more," Curio said. "I know someone we can trust to get the door open, and Timon is perfect to take a quick inventory of what he finds inside."

"Yes, but—"

"I like it." Publius smiled for the first time since his arrival. "Curio will get the testimony we need about Nepos, Timon can find out what's in the shop next door, and Avitus can act as coordinator and lookout. Then you can accompany Curio and present all our evidence to Laenas."

Avitus swallowed the rebuttal he'd been about to make. Joining Curio wasn't a bad idea. Avitus understood the legal actions they hoped to take against Nepos. It would be in their best interest if he spoke to Laenas directly.

"Very well, you've convinced me."

They finalized timelines, signals, and other details. When everyone was satisfied, Avitus looked from one face to the next, ending with his wife. He held her gaze. "My thanks to each of you for your invaluable help. Together we can bring the men responsible for murdering Jonas to justice."

CHAPTER 30

Avitus and Curio rushed off after the meeting without a thought about dinner. Typical men, never paying attention to practical things. They would have to fend for themselves, but at least Livia could see the rest of them were fed.

She went to the kitchen and ordered Brisa to pack a cold supper for Sorex and the two guards belonging to Publius. They thanked her and left to take up their position as backup.

After the men were gone, she and Roxana lifted up their hands in prayer, asking God to protect everyone and grant Curio a successful mission. May Nepos and the rest of the evildoers soon face justice!

When they finished praying, Livia tried to keep herself busy during the long wait until Avitus returned. After discussing menus with Brisa and inspecting her flowerbeds, Livia looked around for something else to do. Grim and Momus were playing a quiet game of knucklebones in the atrium. Brisa and Nissa weren't shouting at each other. Nemesis wasn't slinking around the house trying to filch a snack.

Everything was in perfect order. Fish pickle! Livia would

have to emulate her mother, who passed many serene hours listening to poetry or dictating letters to friends. Except that Roxana's reading ability wasn't yet sufficient to recite poetry, and Livia had no need to send anyone a letter.

Pretending to write a letter would be good practice for Roxana, however. Livia settled on her favorite bench in the peristyle and began to dictate. "Livia Aemilia, to my dear friend Fabia. Greetings…"

She managed two sentences before her mind went completely blank. Sigh.

"It's no use. I can't compose a lighthearted epistle when my thoughts are churning."

"I don't blame you." Roxana set the tablet aside and gave Livia an impish smile. "You know what would suit my mood, my lady? I wish you and I could have a duel like the master and Sorex do."

Livia rolled her eyes. "Can you imagine what Avitus would say if he saw us handling swords?"

Women who trained to fight as gladiators were considered even more infamous than their male counterparts. Livia had no qualms about ignoring stuffy conventions, but there were some lines she could not cross.

Roxana set her hands on her hips and looked around the peristyle. "We need something to distract us. Maybe a game? Or I could try a new hairstyle? I saw a plait the other day that might suit you."

Why not? Livia sent Roxana for her comb and hairpins. Just as the maid returned, a voice sounded in the atrium. A moment later Momus appeared, followed by Dap.

Praise God, a distraction!

Momus dipped his head. "The lad has something he insists he must tell you, my lady."

Livia waved the boy to speak. He bowed to her then turned to Roxana. "I saw some boys tormenting a cat in an apartment building down the street. I think it's Nemesis."

Roxana uttered a naughty phrase then slapped a hand over her mouth. "Sorry, my lady. May I go?"

It had been two days since her incident with the thugs, and none of Avitus's extra-alert guards had seen any sign of killers lurking in the shadows. "Go rescue your cat, but come right back."

Roxana and Dap hurried off, leaving Livia alone with her thoughts. Would Curio succeed tonight, or would Nepos refuse to cooperate? Would the information be enough to convince Laenas? What if Nepos wasn't involved in the water fraud after all?

Enough!

Livia went to the kitchen to check on Brisa and Nissa. She found the housekeeper polishing a copper casserole pan. Brisa set her rag aside and leaped to her feet. "May I help you, my lady? Did you want something to eat?"

"No thank you. Isn't Nissa supposed to be doing that?"

Brisa made a rude noise in the back of her throat. "She spent all afternoon at it, and you can see what a shoddy job she made of it." Brisa held out the pan, pointing to a section that wasn't polished to mirror brightness.

Not this again. Livia was tempted to walk away and deal with her squabbling servants later, but that would mean sitting in the peristyle watching her toenails grow until Avitus returned.

She took a deep breath and spoke as patiently as she could. "Your master bought Nissa to do jobs like polishing the pots so you could pay attention to more important things. Where is she?"

"I sent her to scrub the floor in the guest room."

Which was probably already spotless.

"You mustn't do Nissa's work for her. Leave that for to-morrow."

Brisa wrinkled her face. "That stupid girl will never learn to do it properly! She's hopeless and I'm sick of her. The master deserves better than this." Brisa tapped the pan.

Argh! How was Livia going to get it through Brisa's stubborn gray head that Avitus didn't care how shiny his casserole pans were? No one could live up to the fussy woman's standards.

A man's voice boomed from the direction of the atrium. Could Avitus be home already? No, it was Grim's voice. Angry. Probably arguing with Roxana about allowing Nemesis into the house.

Livia started for the atrium to scold them both.

"Stop, my lady." Brisa grabbed a heavy ladle. "You wait here while I see what's the problem."

"It's only Grim and Roxana arguing."

More shouts rang out. A different voice. Uh oh. Maybe it wasn't Roxana. But who else would Grim have allowed in?

A man appeared in the passage and shouted over his shoulder. "Found 'em. Over here."

Lord have mercy! How had a stranger gotten into the house? Livia looked around for a suitable weapon, and grabbed a broom.

Brisa planted herself in the kitchen doorway and brandished her ladle. "If you've come to rob us, you've chosen the wrong house. There's no silver kept in the kitchen and the master's got the key to the strongbox with him."

"We've come for something more valuable than silver. Out of my way, you old biddy." The stranger reached for Brisa. She swung the ladle and struck his arm with a sharp thwack. He roared and stepped back, cursing.

Brisa cocked her ladle for another blow. "Go away, you filthy thief or I'll smash your skull."

She swung again. This time her attacker sidestepped the ladle, jerked it from her grasp, and smashed his fist into the old woman's temple. She crumpled to the floor.

Livia gripped the broom with both hands, ready to strike. "Keep your distance."

He laughed and stepped over Brisa's prone form. "You're the one we want, my beauty."

A second man appeared. The hairy thug! Livia felt the blood drain from her face. How had they found her?

"There you are, you nosy little wench," Hairy said. "This time your slaves won't be coming to your rescue. Put down that broom like a good girl."

She gripped the broom so tightly her knuckles turned white. "No."

"You're coming with me one way or another. Cooperate and you'll have fewer bruises to show for it. What'll it be?" He took a step toward her.

Livia's pulse throbbed in her temple but she kept the fear from her voice. "Touch me and my husband will see you punished."

"Your interfering husband left the house hours ago. Nepos is expecting him. That's why he sent me to fetch you."

They knew Avitus was coming! He was walking into a trap! Livia's heart pounded even faster.

Hairy lunged and grabbed the broom. The other man came behind her and seized her arms. They were too strong for her to pull free, so she went limp.

"Smart girl," Hairy said. "Tie her up."

The man who'd smashed Brisa tied a gag around Livia's mouth and trussed her hands and feet. Then he heaved her over his shoulder like a sack of grain.

"Hold it." Hairy said. "The boss wants me to get a token." He grabbed her by the hair and tilted her face so she was looking up at him. "Hold still if you don't want me to shred your ear."

Her skin crawled as he fumbled with her earring. He stood back and dangled it in front of her. "Nepos is looking forward to showing this pretty little thing to your husband and making him pay dearly to get you back."

He laughed. Then he let go of her hair, so her nose smashed into her captor's back.

The filthy swine!

Livia was carried to the atrium, where a curtained litter waited. As she was stuffed inside, she caught a glimpse of Grim and Momus sprawled on the floor. The blood pooling under Momus's head almost undid her completely. She closed her eyes and fought the sobs threatening to rack her body.

Lord God, please protect us, or all is lost.

Roxana followed Dap into the street. It wasn't full dark, but the brightest stars were visible and the street was blanketed in shadows. This neighborhood wasn't as dangerous after dark as the rough streets she'd grown up in, but Roxana was still wary. The sooner she rescued her cat and returned to the house, the better.

Dap led her to an apartment building three blocks away. "In there." He pointed through the tunnel-like entryway that led to the central courtyard.

Roxana thanked him and hurried into the building. Unlike

the mistress's flower-filled peristyle, this space was crowded with drying laundry and the detritus of several dozen families. In one corner of the twilit courtyard, a clump of children clustered around an overturned basket that lurched as something inside tried to get away. A boy jabbed a stick through a hole in the basket, prompting an enraged feline yowl.

Roxana strode over to them, grabbed the boy by the tunic and jerked him backward. "Stop it!"

She yanked the stick from his grasp and waved it in the faces of the young hoodlums. "Shame on you, teasing a helpless animal. How would you like to be stuck in a cage while people poked at you? Huh?" She shoved the stick in one surprised face after another. The children turned and fled.

"Nasty little beasts."

As if in agreement, a low hiss came from the basket. "Easy, now. I'm going to let you out." Roxana slowly tipped the basket. Nemesis darted out, ears back and tail lashing.

"Aha! It *was* you. How did you let yourself get caught by a pack of scruffy, no-good, barefoot urchins?"

Nemesis didn't answer, but the bit of dried fish lying under the basket suggested greed had been her downfall.

"You'd better come home with me. Lucky for you the master's away tonight."

Roxana headed back to the street. The cat followed. Halfway home they were forced to step into a recessed entryway to allow a litter to pass. Despite the evening's oppressive heat, the litter's occupant rode with the curtains closed. Who cared so much about privacy that they would roast inside a stuffy litter after dark? Then she caught sight of a man walking behind the litter.

The hairy thug!

Hot needles of alarm shot through Roxana. She pulled into the shadows until he passed by, then darted to the house. Grim and Momus lay sprawled on the atrium floor. Unmoving.

Lord help her! Were they dead? Should she help them? But what about the mistress?

She ran back to the street and spied the litter, just visible in the twilight. It was already two blocks away. The mistress was in serious trouble, and what was a lone slave girl going to do? The only thing she could. She started after the litter.

CHAPTER 31

"Roxana! Wait." Dap ran up to her. "Is Nemesis all right?"

"Dap, thank God I found you. Nemesis is fine, but I think those men have kidnapped the mistress. Can you follow that litter and see where they go? Then come tell me. And stay out of sight, you hear me? They're dangerous."

"Don't worry, I know how to be invisible when I need to be." He raced off, weaving through the crowd.

"Thank you, Lord Jesus," Roxana whispered. "Please keep the mistress safe and show me what to do." She returned to the atrium and found Nemesis sitting beside Grim. A trickle of blood oozed from his temple where a large knot had formed. Nemesis looked up at Roxana.

"Do you think he's alive?" she asked the cat.

Nemesis placed a paw on Grim's shoulder and sniffed at the wound. Then she licked him on the nose. His eyes shot open. He groaned and flailed an arm at the cat, who hissed and darted out of reach.

Sagging with relief, Roxana squatted beside him. "You're alive. How do you feel?"

Grim groaned, raised himself on an elbow, took in the room. "Where'd they go? Where's the mistress?"

"I think they kidnapped her."

Cursing, Grim pushed to his feet, staggered, and dropped to his knees with a grunt of pain.

"Careful. You've got a nasty bump on your head. Better take it slow."

"No time. We must find the mistress."

He started to rise, but Roxana grabbed his shoulders.

"Stay where you are. I've sent Dap to follow the mistress. The litter's out of sight by now, anyway, so there's nothing we can do."

"I'm supposed to rest easy and trust the lady's safety to a dirty street urchin?"

"Dap's not dirty, and what other choice did I have? Someone had to stay here and tend the wounded. Stop complaining and let me see that knot."

He pushed her hands away. "Leave me alone. Go tend Momus."

The doorkeeper lay on the other side of the atrium. His face was covered in blood from a gash on his forehead and another on his forearm. *Please, may he not be dead.* Roxana knelt beside him and felt his neck for signs of life. There was a faint pulse.

Brisa staggered into view. One hand held a damp rag to her temple, the other gripped a ladle. Wild-eyed, she glanced from Roxana to Grim. "Where's the mistress?" Then she saw Momus. "Juno and Minerva, have they killed him?"

She tottered over and dropped to his side. "Momus!"

"It's all right. He's alive."

Brisa let out a sob and dabbed at the gash on Momus's forehead.

Roxana placed her hands over Brisa's. "That's right. Good thinking. You hold your rag right there to stop the bleeding while I run to the kitchen and get more."

By the time Roxana returned with clean rags, Grim was standing in the doorway. "I can't see the litter. Which way did they go?"

"Don't be stupid, Grim. You've a knot on your head the size of a pomegranate and your face is pale as a lamb. You'll never catch them."

Grim raised a hand to his head and winced as his fingers explored the knot. He huffed an exasperated breath then crossed his arms. "I'll see to Momus. You go find Nissa and fetch a basin of water."

Normally Roxana would have bristled at his bossy tone, but right now she was too sick with worry to argue.

When full night settled over the city, Avitus, Curio and three attendants set out for Nepos's shop. The daytime ban on carts ended at dusk, so the streets were filled with shouts, braying donkeys, and the creak of axles. The racket would help disguise their furtive actions when they reached Nepos's shop, but the flood of delivery carts was a nuisance on the way there. They skirted slow-moving vehicles as they worked their way south along the busy Via Tusculana.

When they reached the Shrine of Minerva, Avitus and his conspirators paused to go over their plan. He insisted they each practice the signals for warning, rescue needed, and all clear. "Nepos and his henchmen aren't afraid to kill to protect their interests, so watch out. If you sense danger, get out of there."

Curio slapped him on the shoulder. "We'll be on our guard. Don't worry."

"Thanks again for doing this. Publius and I have waited a long time to pay Nepos back for the pain he caused us."

"You're welcome."

From this point on, Curio and his attendants went ahead while Avitus stayed thirty paces behind and out of sight. When he was one block from Nepos's shop, Avitus whistled the first line of a popular legionary ditty. It was returned with a four-note signal. The tension in Avitus's stomach relaxed slightly. Sorex and Publius's two men were in place and ready to help if needed.

That detail settled, Avitus found an alcove to hide in while Curio approached the marble shop. An ox cart rumbled through the intersection, momentarily blocking Avitus's view. When he could see again, the last of Curio's attendants was passing into Nepos's shop. The guard followed, closing the door behind him. Excellent! So far, everything was going according to plan. Time to make their next move.

Only, the oxcart halted in the middle of the street while the carter delivered three large bundles to a shop owner. Avitus ground his teeth while the men chatted. Every few seconds he glanced at Nepos's door, the knot in his stomach growing tighter by the moment.

Finally, the deliveryman climbed onto his cart and it creaked away. Avitus slipped from his hiding spot. His limbs were surging with tension, and he had to force himself to walk at a normal pace. He strolled past the vacant shop and whistled the legionary ditty again.

No answering signal. Avitus continued along the street. After counting to twenty he whistled the tune again. Still no answer. Where was Timon? He and Curio's thieving friend should have been in place hours ago. He resisted the urge to peer into the shadows. *Stick to the plan.* He counted to twenty again. Whistled.

Nothing.

Two men turned onto the street. They strode along at a no-nonsense clip, looking from side to side. Pollux! A pair of zealous vigiles on the lookout for trouble. The men spotted Avitus and approached. "Evening, sir. Looking for something?"

Uh oh. He was a stranger walking the nighttime streets without attendants. How could he explain his presence? He gave them his best impersonation of an anxious but embarrassed father.

"I'm looking for my daughter's cat. She slipped out the door." Avitus whistled the signal for *Watch Out* and then called, "Here, Smoky."

The men came closer, peering at him suspiciously.

"Have you seen him?" Avitus gave them an earnest smile. "A black cat with two white feet?"

The men exchanged glances. "What do you think?"

"Burn scars on half the face. It's him." They grabbed Avitus by the arms. "Nepos has been expecting you."

Panic jangled every nerve. *No! It can't be.* Avitus went rigid. "Let me go. You're mistaking me for someone else."

"Don't think so. You're Aulus Memmius Avitus. Come with us and don't make us hurt you."

Thoughts swirled in his head so fast Avitus felt dizzy. These vigiles had been waiting for him. It was a trap! How had Nepos known? What would they do to him? He'd better signal Sorex to rescue him before his captors dragged him away. He filled his lungs.

Stop. Slow down. Think first, then act.

He released the breath. If this was a trap then Curio was in danger, too. If Avitus gave the rescue signal now then Nepos's men would be alerted. Better to let his captors take him into the shop and hope Sorex and Timon would find a way to rescue Avitus and Curio together.

Avitus relaxed and allowed the vigiles to march him into Nepos's shop. The interior was brightly lit with torches set in wall brackets. The pair prodded him past a display of marble statuary to the rear of the shop, where Curio and his attendants stood surrounded by armed men. Avitus was shoved to stand beside Curio.

Their eyes met. Curio gave a tiny tilt of the head followed by a raised eyebrow, asking if they should fight. Avitus gave a tiny shake. Nepos's thugs wouldn't hesitate to kill Curio's attendants. Better to wait for Sorex.

"And here's our final guest," Nepos said. "Thank you for bringing him, boys." Nepos tossed one of the vigiles a bag that clinked when he caught it. "Always a pleasure doing business with you."

The vigiles left. Two men took their places guarding Avitus and Curio. One was bald. The other had shaggy black hair and a week's worth of beard.

Nepos sat down on a marble bench facing Avitus. He took a sip of wine from a silver cup then flicked his fingers. "Tie up the slaves while I talk with my old friend and his spy."

Curio's attendants were prodded to the side of the room and bound. Meanwhile, Nepos dipped his hand into a bulging leather sack that sat on the floor at his feet. He pulled out a handful of coins that glinted silver and gold in the flickering light. He let the coins slip through his fingers back into the sack and grinned at them. The greedy scum was enjoying this.

"As you can see, your clever little plan failed," Nepos said. "Did you think I wouldn't check your story? Gracchus hasn't spoken to anyone about our scheme since Publius's meddling freedman started poking around. When your spy asked about a water hookup, I was suspicious, so I sent a young scamp to follow him."

Curio drew a breath and Nepos laughed, an ugly sound that set Avitus's teeth on edge.

"Your spy was so busy trying to lose my door guard that he didn't notice the lad. Led the boy right to your door." Nepos laughed again. "And that means all your clever plans have come to nothing."

But Avitus had allies Nepos didn't know about. The cocky dolt hadn't even ordered his men to bind Avitus or Curio. If they pretended to be helpless and kept Nepos talking, Sorex and the others would have time to come up with a rescue plan.

Avitus adopted a flustered-but-imperious tone. "What are you going to do with me? Even Gracchus can't murder a senator's son with impunity."

"Gracchus had no intentions of killing anyone. Too messy, dealing with dead bodies. He much prefers other methods. And since you asked, let's get down to business."

Nepos stood, drew a gladius and strutted in front of them. "Gracchus and I don't appreciate your meddling, so here's how things are going to work. First of all, you and your spy will each pay Gracchus an additional five hundred sestertii for the trouble you've caused us. Secondly, you will both swear a binding oath that you will not reveal our water arrangements to anyone."

He paused to place the tip of the sword on Avitus's chest. "Break your promise and Gracchus will destroy you."

How Avitus wanted to grab this swaggering oaf by the throat and squeeze the life out of him. Instead, he frowned and kept the fool talking.

"What will you do if we refuse to swear the oath?"

"I thought you might ask." Nepos raised the gladius until the point hovered in front of Avitus's face. "To ensure your co-operation, I ordered my men to capture your wife."

CHAPTER 32

Livia lay in the dark, cords cutting painfully into her wrists and ankles with each jolt of the litter. The pain gave her focus. These men caused pain. To Eleni, Jonas, Damaris, Zeno. And now they threatened Avitus too.

They must be stopped.

She had to figure out a way to fight back. Perhaps she could roll from the litter and escape? No, that wouldn't work. She couldn't run with her ankles bound. Better to conserve her strength and wait for a better opportunity. Maybe they would untie her once they reached their destination? She'd have to be ready to move if they did.

After crossing what felt like half the city, the litter finally came to a halt. The man who had crumpled Brisa with a blow of his meaty fist dragged Livia from the litter, tossed her over his shoulder and lugged her up two flights of stairs. Another of her captors led the way with a torch. They entered a room and her captor dumped her on the floor. The other man lit a lamp and set it in a wall niche.

Then he came close, bent down, and gave her a long, lascivious once-over. "Hairy said you were a tasty little strumpet. Too bad we can't have a bit of fun with you, but the boss wants you untouched. Pity." He licked his lips and gave her a leer that sent outrage racing through her body, melting her fear. May this vile, black-hearted, degenerate lout be eaten alive by worms! And the rest of them, too.

The lout straightened. "Behave while I'm gone, little lady. I'll be back in a few hours, once Nepos makes your husband beg for your life." He shifted his gaze to Livia's captor. "Keep watch, but no handling the merchandise."

"You told me already."

"Then don't forget. And no sleeping on the job."

Her captor made a rude gesture at his partner's departing back. Then he sat down on a bed, the apartment's lone piece of furniture. He leaned against the wall and stared at a spider making a web above the door.

Livia huddled on the floor, knees to her chest. The gag pressed painfully into the corners of her mouth and her wrists burned from the ropes rubbing whenever she moved. At least the men hadn't done anything worse, but how long would that last? She needed to get away before her captors turned nasty. And she had to warn Avitus.

They were on the third story of an apartment building, so the room's small window wouldn't be any use. That left the door, which was locked on the inside by a simple wooden bar. If she could get to the door without her guard noticing, she'd be able to open it. Making it to the door wouldn't be easy with bound ankles, but at least there was hope.

After a few minutes, she shifted position, easing the tension in her bound ankles. Her guard barely glanced at her. Good. Despite the tension throbbing in her veins, she forced her muscles to relax. She must remain still until her captor dozed off. *Dear Lord, please help me have patience. You know how difficult it is for me to wait when everything inside me longs to act. Protect me and guide me. Help me get free so I can warn Avitus and Curio before it's too late.*

To keep her impatience at bay, she mentally recited every psalm and passage of the Lord's teaching she could remember. Gradually her captor's head drooped. Lifted. Drooped again. Finally, he started to snore.

Time to act.

With her wrists bound behind her, she couldn't crawl, so she slid herself backward with her feet. One hands-breadth. Two. Three. She paused. Counted to ten.

Her captor didn't twitch.

She continued on, slow and silent. Push. Slide. Pause. As she inched her way across the room, her fingers bumped into something small, hard, and curved. A palm-sized clay oil lamp with a cracked rim. If she smashed it, she might create a jagged shard that would be sharp enough to slice through the rope binding her wrists and ankles.

She couldn't risk the noise, however, so she gripped the lamp in her hands and continued on. Push. Slide. Pause. Push. Slide. Pause.

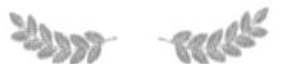

Avitus went taut. *These vile scum had Livia!*

He would not give them the satisfaction of a reaction. Shoulders back, face composed and eyes radiating cold disdain, he stared at Nepos. "Why should I believe a liar like you?"

The wretch smirked. "I have proof. Your little wench was wearing a pale yellow tunic and matching earrings. I have one of them, in case you doubt me." Nepos pulled something from his belt pouch and dangled it in front of Avitus. He gave it a shake, sending the amber beads swinging.

Avitus's stomach clenched. He remembered the earring flashing beneath his wife's hair when he'd bid her goodbye. It took every ounce of will to keep from leaping for Nepos's throat.

Stay calm, he told himself. As long as Nepos needed Livia as a hostage, she would be kept safe. And that meant they had time.

"Now that you see how helpless you are, let's try again. Only..." Nepos stopped his strutting. "This time you'll kneel."

He snapped his fingers. Strong hands pressed on Avitus's shoulders. He and Curio both dropped to their knees.

"That's better."

While Nepos repeated his demands, Avitus assessed the situation. Curio's attendants were in the back corner of the shop, bound hand and foot. Curio knelt beside Avitus, while Gimpy and Hairy stood just behind them, daggers at the ready. Four more men waited near the front entrance.

Would Sorex be able to break his way through the door? Was there another way into the shop? Avitus could see two curtained doorways. The one behind Nepos probably led to living quarters. And the one to his right? He cast quick glances at it, trying to guess what kind of room was behind the curtain without Nepos noticing his interest.

At his third glance he thought he saw a flicker of light. The next glance confirmed it. A faint glow was now coming from the gap below the curtain. Was it a rescue? He must be ready.

"Once you swear your oath," Nepos was saying, "we'll talk about how much it will cost you to get your wife back in one piece."

"You won't get away with this" Avitus said.

"Who's going to stop me?" Nepos waved his sword in Avitus's face. "You, little Avi?"

Avitus locked eyes with his enemy, staring him down, forcing Nepos to be the first to look away. The tiny victory felt good.

And then someone pounded on the door.

Avitus threw himself sideways, rolled onto his back and thrust his heel into Hairy's groin with a much force as possible. Hairy howled in pain and bent double, his dagger clattering to the ground. An instant later Sorex rushed from behind the curtain and sent the thug sprawling with a thwack from a shovel.

Others rushed past, heading for the front.

"Here." Sorex stuffed the shovel into Avitus's hands and bounded past to assist Curio with Gimpy. Avitus got to his feet. Timon and Publius's slaves were engaged with the men near the front entrance. That left Nepos, who stood with his back to a marble statue of Venus, his eyes and the point of his sword darting back and forth.

Avitus approached his old enemy. Nepos brought his sword up. "Stay back or I'll hurt you."

Nepos had the advantage in height, strength, and weapon. But Jonas had taught Avitus how to defend himself with every imaginable weapon, including everyday items like shovels.

He gripped the shovel halfway up the handle, finding its balance. Then he rotated it so the spade end was up. He advanced on Nepos. Feinted high. Nepos's sword swung up to block the blow. Avitus ducked inside the blade, slammed the other end of the handle into Nepos's stomach, twisted his wrists and struck with the shovel end, forcing his opponent off balance. Another tap to the head sent Nepos to his knees. One final chop and Nepos slumped to the ground.

Avitus looked around. All their enemies lay on the floor, unmoving or under guard.

"Good work. Bind the prisoners before they give us any more trouble."

While the others moved to obey, Avitus grabbed a fallen dagger, sliced a strip of cloth from the hem of the nearest unconscious guard and cinched it around Nepos's wrists. When they were securely bound, he rolled Nepos onto his back and slapped his cheek.

The eyes fluttered open. Focused. Nepos let loose a long stream of crude invective. Then his lip curled into a sneer. "You think you've won, but you're wrong. You're going to untie me and my men immediately. Because if your wife's captors don't hear from me before daybreak, they have orders to kill her."

Roxana paced the atrium, every nerve jangling. Dap should have been back by now. Where was he? Had he lost the litter? Had he been captured?

Grim, who was stretched out on the floor, opened one eye. "Pacing wastes energy. You should rest while you can. It's going to be a long night."

"I can't rest when my mistress is out there somewhere, in danger."

"Suit yourself." Grim shut his eye and exhaled a long, slow breath.

"Insufferable man." Roxana stalked to the peristyle where she wouldn't have to look at him. Nemesis, curled on a bench, raised her head, one ear cocked in question. "You're napping too, I see. Don't let me stop you."

Nissa had been sleeping too, or at least that's the excuse she'd given Roxana to explain why she hadn't been attacked like the rest of the household. The girl claimed she'd fallen sound asleep in the guest room and hadn't heard a thing—which sounded like a pile of donkey dung to Roxana. More likely Nissa had been hiding under the bed to save her own skin instead of coming to the assistance of her mistress.

So Roxana had ordered Nissa to fetch water and scrub Momus's blood from the atrium floor. Meanwhile, Roxana and Grim had bandaged Brisa and Momus and sent them to bed. Next, they'd gathered water skins, spare torches, and a small dagger.

Now they waited. And paced. And waited.

CHAPTER 33

Avitus stared down at his sneering enemy. Inside he was screaming, but he didn't allow a single muscle to twitch. Nepos might think he'd defeated them, but all was not lost and Avitus would not despair. They had until daybreak to find Livia and rescue her.

"You're in no position to make threats, Nepos. I have powerful friends who are eager to bring you and your henchmen to the authorities to answer for your crimes. You may as well get comfortable, because it's going to be a long night."

"You were always a naive fool. You'll never find her. Every hour you delay will cost you."

"Someone gag this piece of vermin."

Sorex grabbed Nepos by the tunic and dragged him to where the others were laid in a tidy row. Curio's attendants had been freed, and now guarded their erstwhile captors with grim determination.

Avitus beckoned Timon. "Tell me what happened. Why didn't you return my signal?"

Timon blew out his cheeks. "I heard you, but I didn't respond because I'd seen those two vigiles pacing the street and I didn't want to give away my position. As soon as they took you away, I sent Curio's friend to pick the lock on the empty shop while I ran to tell Sorex what had happened. By the time I returned, the vacant shop was standing open. Let me show you what I found."

Timon pulled a torch from a bracket and led Avitus to the curtained doorway. He pulled the curtain aside, revealing a small storeroom with an unusual detail—a wooden door in the opposite wall. Avitus pushed it open and went through into a much larger space. Timon entered behind him and held the torch so Avitus could see. The room was cluttered with wooden chests, a pile of tools, and a bundle of long objects that looked like lead pipe.

"I take it this is the vacant shop?"

"Yes, sir. I haven't had a chance to inspect the merchandise yet, but that sure looks like a bundle of lead piping."

"We can worry about the inventory later. Right now, we have eight hours to find and rescue Livia."

Avitus summoned Sorex and Curio to discuss the situation and come up with a plan. After considering the options, Curio agreed to stay behind with his men to guard their prisoners. The rest of them would search for Livia. Avitus sent one of Publius's slaves to check with the man watching Optatus's house and the other to check with the man watching Scaevola's. He sent Timon to check on Prochoros. The dishonest foreman hadn't been among the men they'd captured tonight, which meant Prochoros might have played a part in kidnapping Livia.

While his allies sought for Livia in all the most likely locations, Avitus and Sorex would go home and hope someone had news about what had happened. Before they left, Curio gripped Avitus's arm. "Good hunting, my friend. I'll be praying for you."

Avitus hoped Curio's God was listening, because right now they needed all the divine help they could get.

As the hours dragged on, Roxana questioned her decisions. She shouldn't have abandoned her mistress. She should have followed the litter herself instead of trusting Dap. She was a fool and a failure. Why had she thought she could trust a boy she hardly knew to handle so dangerous a job? What would they do if he didn't return?

Finally, Dap did return, chest heaving. Roxana ran to the atrium. "Did you find her? Is the mistress in danger? Where are they? Let's go."

"Hush, woman," Grim said. "Give the boy a chance to catch his breath." He handed Dap a water skin. "Take a drink, boy."

Dap took a long, greedy swig then wiped his mouth. "The men took the lady to an apartment building off the Via Tusculana. I saw her when they pulled her from the litter. She didn't look hurt, but they have her tied up and gagged."

"Clever, boy. Have another drink, and then you can take me to her."

Oh no he didn't! Grim was not leaving her behind. Roxana crossed her arms and scowled at him. "I'm coming, too."

"No, you're not. This is men's work."

Roxana slung the sack of supplies over her shoulder. "Listen, sourpuss, I've seen what a nasty clout to the head can do to a man. I'm coming with you whether you like it or not."

He muttered a curse. "Has anyone ever told you how annoying you are?"

"Frequently, but I don't bother to listen."

"You'll listen this time. You. Are. Not. Coming."

"Oh. Yes. I. Am." Roxana grabbed a torch, lit it in the flame of an oil lamp, and marched into the street. "Hurry up, you two. We don't have time to waste." She turned to Nissa. "Once we're gone, bar the door. You'll have to act as doorkeeper until we get back."

Nissa nodded. Grim spluttered a protest.

Dap tugged his arm. "She'll follow us if you try to leave her behind, so you might as well let her come."

"I give up." Grim stomped out the door and jabbed a finger in her chest. "Fine, but keep your mouth shut. I don't need excitable women filling the air with endless chatter."

Victory! Roxana hid her elation behind a solemn nod. "I'll do whatever you say."

"You'd better, or I'll tie you up and leave you behind." Grim lit his torch, muttering curses about impossible women.

Dap led them on a long journey through the nighttime streets. Roxana wanted to jog the whole way, but Grim insisted they walk at a slow pace. "We don't want to attract attention, and we need to conserve energy so we're ready when we get there."

Roxana had promised to keep quiet, so she couldn't argue as they trudged along, avoiding noisy ox carts and juicy piles of fresh dung.

After crossing half the city, Dap stopped in front of a nondescript building that looked much like the ones on either side. "They took the lady in there." He acted sure of himself, but how could they be certain?

Grim must have been thinking the same thing. "You're sure this is the right building, boy?"

"Yes." Dap pointed with his torch. "I recognize the pot of

pink flowers in that window and the drawing of Neptune beside that door."

Roxana breathed a sigh of relief. They'd found the right building. But they still had to find the mistress, locked somewhere among the dozens of apartments inside.

"Any idea which room they took her to?" she asked.

Dap shook his head. "I didn't follow them inside, but it sounded like they climbed the stairs."

"You two wait over there while I take a look." Grim waved them to a portico then disappeared into the building. He was gone a long time, and when he returned his face was more morose than ever.

"Five floors and nothing to tell which room the lady might be in. I hate to admit it, but I'm glad I brought you along." He scowled at Roxana. "While Dap stays here and keeps a lookout in case the thugs return, you and I are going inside to find the mistress. For once I'm asking you to do what you do best: make a nuisance of yourself."

Roxana glared at him. "This is no time for jokes."

"I'm not joking. I want you to act drunk. Sing an obnoxious song loud as you can."

The knock to Grim's head had clearly scrambled his brains. "Whatever for?"

"To annoy the tenants, so they open their doors and complain. I'll be watching for which doors stay closed."

"That's a stupid plan," Roxana said.

"Have a better one?"

"Yes. Call out the mistress's name."

Grim rolled his eyes. "That will warn her captors we're coming. And did you not hear Dap say the mistress was gagged?"

Olympus, the man was annoying. Especially when he was right. "Fine, you win. But there's one problem. I can't sing."

"Good."

"Huh?"

"The worse you sound, the better. Just make some noise, woman." He shooed her toward the entryway.

It was a crazy plan, but Roxana opened her mouth and belted out a song.

CHAPTER 34

Avitus arrived at his house to find his door closed and barred, which meant someone must be alive inside. Sorex pounded on it, and a moment later they heard the shrill voice of Nissa. "Who's there?"

"The master. Let us in."

She unbarred the door and stood blinking at them in sleepy confusion. While Sorex inspected the house for threats, Avitus questioned Nissa. The attackers had come at dusk, overpowered his slaves, and whisked Livia away in a litter.

If only he'd left Publius's guards here instead of taking them along. Then perhaps Livia would be safe. He should have anticipated an attack on his house. But he hadn't, and now he must find her and get her back. He waved Nissa to continue her tale.

"Luckily, Roxana was out rescuing her cat. She saw the litter leaving and sent Dap to follow it."

"Who's Dap?"

Nissa shrugged. "Just a street urchin who does odd jobs and teaches Roxana's cat to do tricks."

"Why in Hades did Roxana trust a street urchin to follow her mistress instead of going herself?"

Nissa shrugged again. "Maybe because Grim and Momus were bleeding all over the floor?"

Hardly a cogent explanation, but what did he expect from a frightened slave girl? He reined in his impatience and got the rest of the story from Nissa. The street urchin had returned to lead Grim to Livia. If only Avitus had more confidence in their success.

He questioned Brisa and Momus, hoping for more useful details. All they could do was confirm Nissa's story.

"Dap's a clever lad," Momus added. "If he says he knows where the mistress is, I'd believe him."

But it had been hours since Grim and Roxana left to rescue her. After so long, Avitus didn't hold out much hope.

"Do any of you know where they went?"

The girl shook her head. "Not really, sir. Dap said they'd taken her somewhere off the Via Tusculana."

Hades! None of the places Avitus had thought to check were anywhere close to that street. If Nissa was right, his men were looking for Livia in the wrong area of the city.

Avitus sent his injured slaves back to bed and ordered Nissa to remain guarding the door. "I'm going to my brother's house. The moment Grim or Roxana returns, send them to me."

"Yes, sir."

Avitus set out for Publius's. It was past midnight, his house was being guarded by a fourteen-year-old girl, and their best hope of finding his abducted wife was a young street urchin who played with cats.

How the gods must be laughing. He hoped the others would have better news.

They didn't.

Livia hadn't been taken to Optatus's or Scaevola's houses. Nor had she been seen with Prochoros. "The man was hopelessly drunk," Timon reported. "And the tavern keeper said he'd been there all the night. I hired someone to help me get Prochoros back to his apartment. I found two iron-bound chests hidden in his back room, but no sign of the mistress. Sorry, sir."

By this time Publius had been roused and he joined them to discuss what to do next. Avitus explained all he had learned from Nissa.

"Sounds like a fool's hope," Publius said in a voice still raspy from sleep. "If they haven't returned by now, they must be lost somewhere. We should inform Laenas. Let him have Nepos and his men questioned to find out where they've hidden Livia."

"Absolutely not." Avitus said. "They'll kill her if they don't hear from Nepos by daybreak."

"I doubt that threat is true," Publius said. "Nepos only told you that after you'd defeated him."

"I can't take that chance. Until she's safe, we leave Laenas out of it."

Publius harrumphed. "That doesn't leave you many options."

"I'm aware of that," Avitus snapped. Part of him wanted to send every slave in Publius's house out to search for Livia, but the saner part of his mind told him it was pointless.

"Much as I hate the idea, I may have to return to Nepos and negotiate her release. But I'll put it off as long as possible. There's still a chance Grim will succeed in locating her. If so, I'll need runners."

Avitus turned to Publius. "Will you loan me your three fastest slaves? We'll send one to my house to wait for Grim. We'll station the other two along the route, with Timon waiting at the Shrine of Minerva to bring the news to Nepos's shop. That way, if Grim returns in time, I can hear about it as quickly as possible."

But would Grim find her before it was too late?

Push. Slide. Pause. Livia's progress had been excruciatingly slow, scooting a few inches at a time, freezing whenever her captor moved, waiting for his even breathing to resume. But she was almost there. One last push and Livia could touch the door.

Push. Slide. Wood!

Now for the next stage of her escape. She set the clay lamp on the floor and rose to her feet, leaning a shoulder against the door for balance. When she was upright, she twisted so her back was to the door and her bound hands could reach the heavy bar that kept it closed. She gripped the bar as best she could and worked it out of the bracket. Slowly. Slowly. The bar slid a finger's width. And another.

At last, the bar was clear. Livia took a deep breath, grabbed the door, and pulled…

Fish pickle.

She was standing in the way of the door's swing.

Maybe she ought to think through her plan before going any farther? Once she got the door open, she'd need to free her legs so she could walk. That meant shattering the lamp, which was likely to rouse the guard. Hmm, perhaps she could slide herself down the hallway first, so the guard wouldn't hear the lamp shatter? That seemed the best idea.

She lowered herself to the floor, grabbed the lamp, and scooted until she was clear of the door's swing. Then she stood, but she couldn't grip the door and hold the lamp at the same time. She'd have to get the door open first and then pick up the lamp.

She lowered herself once again. Voices echoed from the stairwell. Singing. Growing louder. Livia froze and prayed the noisy tenants would go to a different hallway.

They didn't. The singers came closer. Her guard opened his eyes, saw her, and sat upright. "Hey you. Get away from the door."

Livia shot to her feet and tugged the door with as much force as she could muster. If she could dive through before—

Too late. Her guard leaped across the room, kicked the door shut and yanked her backward. She toppled to the floor, landing hard and shattering the lamp. Her captor pounced on her, holding her down so that sharp bits of the smashed lamp poked into her back.

"I think I saw her," someone shouted from the hallway.

Was that Grim's voice? Livia thrashed, trying to get free. Her guard twisted, pressing her down with his arms while holding the door shut with his feet. Livia's fingers found a chunk of the shattered lamp. She worked it into her fist.

Someone pounded on the door. "Hello?"

Definitely Grim's voice. Livia arched upward with all her might. Then she twisted, stabbing blindly with the clay shard. She struck something soft. Her captor yelped. He wrested the shard from her grasp, but in the process, his foot lost its purchase on the door.

It burst open. Grim shot into the room. Two blows and her captor went limp. A moment later Grim hauled the man off her.

Then Roxana was at her side, helping her sit up and untying the gag. "Praise God, we found you. Are you hurt, my lady?"

"I don't think so. I was fine until that oaf squashed me."

"This will help." Roxana held a water skin to her lips.

Livia drank greedily, surprised at how dry her throat had become. Then Roxana undid the knots and massaged life back into Livia's wrists and ankles while Grim used the ropes to bind her captor. When he was finished, he peered out the door. "Let's go before someone sees us."

Roxana draped a shawl around Livia's shoulders. "Wrap yourself in this, my lady." She took Livia by the arm and helped her to her feet. "Can you walk?"

"Yes."

Dap was waiting at the bottom of the stairway. "All clear?" Grim asked the boy.

"Yes, sir."

"Good." Grim ushered the women onto the street. "That way. No talking and go slowly. Dap, you take the rear and whistle if you see anyone following."

They zigged and zagged for three blocks. Nobody followed them so Livia judged they were safe. She called a halt.

"That's far enough, Grim. Avitus and Curio are walking into a trap and you must warn them."

"It's past midnight, my lady. Whatever trap Nepos planned is surely sprung by now."

"We don't know that for sure. Avitus needs to be warned that he's in danger and I'm all right. Now off you go."

Grim folded his arms. "I'm not going anywhere until you're home. The streets aren't safe for a woman at this time of night."

"We don't have time." Livia fought to keep her temper in control. "Where are we?"

"On the edge of the Caelian Hill."

"Then take me to my aunt's house."

Despite the late hour, Auntie's doorkeeper let them in immediately, concern plain on his face. "Are you in trouble, my lady? Has something happened to Avitus? What can I do?"

"I'm fine, but I'd like to talk with Aunt Livilla."

He hurried off without a word. Livia turned to Grim. "I'm safe now. Go! Find Avitus and tell him what happened."

"I don't know where to find him."

"He's at the shop of Nepos, the marble dealer. It's off the Via Tusculana, near the Shrine of Minerva."

Grim turned and jogged into the night.

CHAPTER 35

A few hours ago, Avitus had watched Nepos's doorway with eager anticipation. Now he viewed it with dread.

And fury. The thought of surrendering to Nepos's demands turned his stomach to acid, but he couldn't allow them to hurt Livia. If surrendering to Nepos was what it took to protect her, then so be it. His old enemy would gloat, believing Avitus had given up. But once again Nepos would be wrong, because Avitus had one final, desperate plan to rescue his wife.

It was late and the moon had set, so the sky was filled with thousands of stars. Avitus held out his hand, fingers spread wide, and sighted along it. When the stars moved one handspan, it would be time to go in and face Nepos.

Until then, Avitus would keep searching for his wife. He found Curio poking through the items in the vacant shop.

"You're back," Curio said. "Lots of interesting stuff here, but we'll talk about that later. Did you find Livia?"

"No. Any news at your end?"

"Not really. I've been watching Nepos and his men. The ones

you call Gimpy and Hairy appear too tough to break, but one of the others might be made to talk."

Avitus shook his head. No matter how desperate he was, he would not resort to torture. "You and I don't need to lower ourselves to the tactics of our enemy."

Curio let out a long, relieved breath. "Then what's our plan?"

Avitus told him about Grim and Roxana. "I've left runners. If Grim returns home with news, we'll hear it as quickly as possible."

"And if we don't hear from him?"

"If I surrender to Nepos, he'll have to send a messenger to Livia's captors. You and your men can follow the messenger to Livia and rescue her."

"That might just work." Curio clapped Avitus on the back. "Don't give up hope. We'll get her back, one way or another."

Yes, they would. Because they must.

"We still have an hour before I'll be forced to negotiate with Nepos. There's a chance Livia is being held somewhere near here."

"Then let's look. I'm sick of doing nothing but waiting."

Sorex took over guarding the prisoners while Curio and his men helped Avitus search for Livia or her slaves. They found nothing.

Nor did Timon appear with word from Grim.

When the stars said the hour was up, Curio and his attendants headed off to find their hiding places.

Avitus watched them go. *No point delaying any longer.* He breathed in a last view of the starry expanse. Then he girded himself to face the humiliation ahead and entered the shop.

He walked to the line of trussed prisoners and stopped in front of Nepos. He stared down at his enemy. The scum stared back, eyes burning with cruel anticipation. This was not going to be pleasant.

"Ungag him so we can talk."

Sorex obeyed, muttering something venomous in Germanic as he untied the gag. Nepos answered with a crude insult then pushed himself to his feet. "I told you you'd never find her."

"You win Nepos," Avitus said through gritted teeth. "What will it take to get Livia back?"

"You can start by untying me and my men. And tell your barbarian to treat me with more respect, or I'll raise your wife's ransom."

Avitus swallowed the bile rising in his throat. "Release him."

Scowling, Sorex sliced the cloth binding Nepos's wrists.

"Now my feet."

Sorex hesitated. Freeing this criminal went against everything slave and master stood for, but they must play this charade to the bitter end if they hoped to free Livia. "Do it."

Sorex knelt.

"Master! Wait."

Avitus spun around. Timon ran into the room, followed by Grim.

"We've found the mistress, sir. She's safe."

It was daybreak when Avitus arrived at Aunt Livilla's house. Despite the rigors of the night, Livia was awake and pacing her aunt's garden. She ran to him and wrapped her arms around his chest. "You're safe!"

He held her tight, the ferocity of her embrace confirming she was unhurt.

"When Nepos told me you'd been captured, I..." Avitus searched for words to describe how he'd felt. There were none. "I was ... I feared ... How did you escape?"

She told him. "Now tell me what happened to you. I was sick with worry when I realized you were heading into their trap."

He explained the cascade of events that had filled the night hours. "Meanwhile, forgive me for leaving you defenseless. I should have expected Nepos would follow Curio. I shouldn't have taken the extra guards. I—"

"Stop." Livia put a finger to his lips. "Don't brood over what should have happened. That's behind us now. Let's talk of all we have to be thankful for, instead."

"I allow you to be kidnapped and you want to talk about gratitude?"

"Yes." She gave him a squinty-eyed look.

He was too weary to argue. "As you wish, my dear. You go first."

"I'm thankful for God's protection," she said. "Secondly, I'm thankful for the actions of our capable slaves who helped us overcome Nepos and his evil plans. Finally, and most importantly, I'm blessed to have a husband who cares enough to give himself up to protect his wife." She took his face in her hands and kissed him soundly on the lips.

What a wondrous creature his wife was, to love him despite his failures.

She stepped back and crossed her arms. "Your turn. What are you thankful for?"

That she didn't despise him. That in spite of his faulty assumptions and poor planning, she was unhurt. Not that he could take any credit for that fact—

"Well? Are you going to answer?"

"I'm thankful you're safe."

"That's a good start. What else?"

Pollux. He wasn't capable of grappling with emotions after all he'd been through. He pressed his hands to his forehead and tried to think of an answer that would satisfy her.

She raised her eyebrows impatiently. This woman was the most exasperating, resilient, amazing, bewildering, enticing female he'd ever met.

"You're a gem among women. Who but you could be kidnapped by brigands and not only keep your head but spend your time worrying over the safety of others?"

That brought a smile. At least he could do that much right. "I don't deserve you."

"Nonsense. You're an honorable man with a good heart." Livia tapped his chest with a slender finger. "You deserve every blessing God chooses to give you."

"If the gods have blessed me, then I must make the proper thank offerings. To which gods do you refer?"

He watched a series of emotions flit across her face. Uncertainty, guilt, determination, relief.

She sighed, looked away then brought her gaze back to his face. "I've been meaning to tell you, but I never found the right moment."

He nodded, not daring to interrupt.

"The God I pray to is the One God worshiped by the Jews. Forgive me for not informing you before our marriage. It was dishonest and cowardly of me to keep it from you."

Her admission lifted another weight from his chest. "You've told me at last."

"You knew?"

"In part. Your brother didn't think it honorable to accept my betrothal without telling me you no longer worshiped the traditional gods. Why do you think I haven't forced you to participate in the rituals?"

"I . . . Thank you."

"You're welcome. And what offering of thanks will please this god of yours?"

"The Lord Jesus doesn't require sacrifices, but it would please him if I were allowed to worship with my fellow believers."

"You wish to join the Jews in their synagogue services?"

"No. I follow a sect of their faith called the Way. We believe that God has given us a new way to worship him that doesn't require adherence to the Jewish Laws. Instead of temples or synagogues, we meet in homes and shops. I used to attend morning prayer meetings at Pansa's bakery, but there's a closer option. A physician named Asyncritus, who has a shop near the base of the Quirinal."

"How large a gathering?"

"Small. Fewer than ten."

"You will continue to show respect to my gods?"

"Yes."

"Very well. You may join them once a week."

She gave him another kiss, this one gentle and quick. "Thank you. This secret has weighed on my heart. Curio and Placida have been scolding me for weeks about it. I should have listened a lot earlier."

He quirked an eyebrow at her. "Are there any other secrets you would like to unburden yourself of?"

She grinned at him. "There is one thing. I've asked the painter to include a black cat in one of the frescoes."

CHAPTER 36

Livia's redecorated dining room turned out even better than she'd expected. The paintings looked so realistic she could almost hear birdsong and smell the scent of the flowers. The embroidered couch cushions from Hermas blended perfectly. Best of all, Avitus was delighted with the results.

Her unemotional husband actually said, "I used to find this room unwelcoming but you've transformed it into a warm and relaxing room where I enjoy spending time."

Would wonders never cease?

He was so pleased, in fact, that he didn't balk when Livia suggested they should host a dinner party to celebrate. It took two days of (mostly) patient instruction and another lesson from Curio's cook to prepare Brisa for the ordeal.

By midafternoon on party day, Livia was exhausted but confident that the meal wouldn't be a disaster. She coached Roxana and Nissa on the final details then went to change into her best tunic before her guests showed up.

Damaris was the first to arrive. She oohed and aahed at the vivid colors. Curio said the room suited Livia perfectly. Aunt Livilla ran her discerning eye around the walls and proclaimed, "This was done by a true artist. I must have his name."

Babak and his wife preened at the compliments. "I am honored to bring delight to the advocate and his wife," Babak said. "Sending the painter was but a small thing compared to the debt I owe for the expert handling of my case. I find myself breaking into songs of victory whenever I remember the utter shock on my opponent's face when the verdict was given in my favor."

Livia and Curio exchanged smiles. They'd attended the trial together and witnessed Avitus's deft handling of the case. The cocky opponent had been rendered speechless, his face growing a dangerous shade of puce.

Publius and Hortensia were the last to arrive. Livia had been surprised when they'd accepted the invitation, considering the social standing of the other guests. Avitus claimed Publius accepted because he wanted to talk about Babak's case. The menfolk might think that was the reason, but Livia suspected otherwise. Hortensia had been scandalized to learn Livia had ignored her detailed instructions for redecorating the house. She would be eager for a chance to inspect the makeover and find reason to criticize Livia's flaunting of good taste (and her advice).

Publius stopped on the threshold to take in the room then whistled his approval. "For the past eleven years I've been trying to find my brother a suitable wife—one who could appreciate his true character and bring a woman's touch into his dreary home. If I had any doubts that Livia was the perfect wife, they're gone now. This room is brilliant, don't you agree, dear?"

"Yes," Hortensia said through unmoving jaws. "The cushions are an exact match to the greens in the paintings."

Livia stifled a smile. How it must pain her sister-in-law to offer even that small compliment.

Despite Hortensia's sour mood and Brisa's inadequate culinary skills, the dinner progressed smoothly. Babak proved an entertaining guest and soon had everyone smiling at his outrageous stories. Aunt Livilla took an instant liking to Damaris. The two of them were soon chatting like old friends. Avitus even joined the conversation from time to time.

When the last course had been taken away, conversation dwindled to a hush. Aunt Livilla cleared her throat. "Thank you for a lovely dinner. Now that we've finished, I'm bringing up the topic we've been studiously avoiding all evening. I want to hear how the whole thing happened from the beginning to the very end."

Everyone turned expectant eyes on Avitus. Livia was afraid he would grumble at the sudden attention, but he inclined his head to Aunt Livilla. "I will be happy to oblige."

The guests settled into comfortable positions, eager to hear the story. All of them had been impacted by the events in some way, but none of them had heard the entire saga.

"This mystery had many layers, and it's only with the clarity of hindsight that we can see how the various pieces fit together," Avitus said in his deep orator's voice. Then he turned to Publius and exchanged one of those nonverbal signals that so annoyed Livia. Could her husband communicate silently with every male?

Apparently he could, because Publius began to speak. "The story begins several weeks ago. A friend of mine complained that one of his cliens—a young man named Scaevola—had switched allegiances to Senator Gracchus. Gracchus is a particular enemy of mine, so I decided to look into the matter. I sent my most trustworthy servant, a freedman named Jonas, to find out what had caused Scaevola to switch allegiances. Unfortunately, Jonas was attacked by two thugs called Gimpy and Hairy for nosing into Scaevola's affairs. And that brings us to Damaris."

Who blushed as all eyes turned to look at her.

Avitus took up the tale. He explained how Damaris had witnessed Zeno being attacked and had told Jonas of the crime.

"Jonas must have suspected Gimpy and Hairy were the criminals she saw, and gone back to verify it. Unfortunately, the thugs were frantically searching for the ledger that Zeno had taken. When Jonas and Damaris appeared, they must have assumed Damaris knew about the ledger, so they attacked. Jonas sacrificed his life to protect Damaris."

"Have you caught the murderers, like you promised?" Damaris asked.

"We have," said Avitus. "Gimpy and Hairy confessed to killing Jonas and Zeno, as well as other crimes. The praetor of the murder court made quick work of the case, and the men face execution during the next gladiatorial games."

"I'm glad to hear justice was served," Aunt Livilla said. "But I don't understand how you discovered that Jonas's murder was tied to the water scheme."

"We would never have connected them if it hadn't been for Livia." Avitus raised his cup in salute and Livia felt her cheeks go warm. "My clever wife wondered why Zeno had been killed, and managed to track down his girlfriend."

Avitus related how Eleni had given them Zeno's tablet and the stolen ledger. "From that information, we realized the water theft was at the root of all these crimes. I assumed Scaevola was behind it all until I brought our discoveries to my brother."

Avitus raised an eyebrow, which signaled to Publius it was his turn to speak.

"When Avitus showed me the ledger, I immediately recognized that many of the customers listed there had recently become clientes of Gracchus. We set out to find proof that Gracchus was actually behind the fraud. Our biggest challenge was identifying the middleman who linked Gracchus to the men who installed the pipes."

Avitus took up the tale again. He described how they'd searched for marble dealers and discovered Nepos.

"But we still lacked proof, so we sent Curio to act as a customer, hoping to catch Nepos and his associates in the act of accepting payment for illegal water lines. Our trap didn't turn out the way we'd hoped, but the combined evidence we collected was sufficient to convince Senator Laenas. He brought the matter to the attention of the current commissioner, who has launched an investigation."

"What happened to Nepos?" Babak asked.

"Nepos has been heavily fined for his part in the water thefts. Plus he faces criminal charges for abducting Livia, as well as for other illegal activities that have come to light."

"And Gracchus?" Aunt Livilla said.

"We didn't find enough evidence to build a case against him," Publius said sourly.

"Gracchus gets away without a scratch?"

"Not exactly. The illegal water lines have been disconnected and the homeowners have been fined, which means Gracchus has a long list of disgruntled clientes to placate. We'll have to be content with that."

"Well, well, that was quite a story," Aunt Livilla said. "It took a lot of intelligence and courage on the part of many." She raised her cup. "I salute all of you for the parts you have played in this drama of criminals brought to justice."

Nemesis chose that moment to leap onto the dining couch beside Aunt Livilla. Grand lady that she was, Auntie barely hesitated before raising her cup a little higher. "And let us also thank Nemesis, goddess of retribution, who aided you in thwarting these brazen criminals."

As if she understood the words, the cat sat down and adopted a regal pose, tail draped artfully across her paws.

Hortensia's face was frozen in a mask of shock, but Publius chuckled and lifted his cup. "Well said, Livilla. We must honor all the gods who favored us that night."

Livia knew there was only one God who had protected and guided them throughout that terrible night. Perhaps one day Avitus would be prepared to acknowledge him as sole God over creation. For now, Livia raised her cup and sent a silent prayer of thanks to heaven.

GLOSSARY

Aedile: A Roman magistrate. The office of *aedile* was one of the less important magistracies a Roman gentleman could hold, open to senators who were at least thirty-six years of age.

Amphora: plural *amphoras* or *amphorae*. A large two-handled ceramic container with a narrow neck and a pointed bottom, used to store liquids such as wine, olive oil or *garum*.

Aqua Marcia: One of the eleven ancient aqueducts that supplied water to the city of Rome. It was over fifty-five miles long. Two other aqueducts piggybacked with the Aqua Marcia for part of its length, creating a triple-decker aqueduct.

As: plural *asses*. A low-value bronze coin roughly the size of a quarter, worth one-fourth of a *sestertius*.

Atrium: In a Roman house of this era, an open-roofed atrium typically served as the entrance hall and reception area for guests.

Castellum: plural *castella*. A tank that was part of the complex water system in an ancient Roman city. There were over two hundred *castella* in Rome's water network.

Cliens: plural *clientes*. Roman society functioned on a system of patronage—a mutually beneficial system where a more powerful man (*patronus*) collected a group of less-influential men (*clientes*). The *patronus* gave out small gifts and used their influence to aid their *cliens*. The *cliens* enhanced the prestige of their *patronus* and supported his causes. Many patrons were themselves a *cliens* of even more powerful men.

Consul: An important Roman magistrate. The most prestigious of the regular offices a senator could hold. Once a man had been a consul, he might serve as the *proconsul* of a province. Ex-consuls were also eligible for other special duties, such as becoming the water commissioner.

Denarius: plural *denarii*. A silver coin about the size of a dime. Roughly equivalent to a day's wages for a common laborer.

Dignitas: A Roman man's most important virtue. *Dignitas* was much more than dignity. It encompassed the honor and prestige a man enjoyed in society, and the personal influence he wielded. *Dignitas* was affected by such things as moral standing, fitness, appearance, reputation, rank, status, and standing among his peers. The higher one's *dignitas*, the more he was entitled to honor, respect and proper treatment (socially and legally). Insults to one's *dignitas* could lead to defamation lawsuits.

Fortuna: The Roman goddess of luck and fate (either good or bad).

Forum: A public square in a Roman city. The forum served as a marketplace and as a public gathering space for activities such as political speeches or legal hearings. Rome was so large it required multiple forums.

Forum of Augustus: When the main city forum became too crowded, Emperor Augustus built another forum adjoining it, where much of the legal activity was held.

Freedman: A freed slave. Freedmen were typically granted the same legal rights as freeborn citizens, but the taint of slavery meant they didn't have equal social standing. Some freedmen amassed great fortunes. Imperial slaves who became freedmen could wield significant power as well. Antonius Felix, who governed Judea during Paul's imprisonment, was an imperial freedman.

Garum: A substance made from fermented fish, highly regarded by Romans for its strong, salty flavor. Used in sauces or as a condiment. A relative of Asian fish sauces.

Gladius: A short, straight, double-bladed sword that was the standard weapon of the Roman legions.

Hours: The Roman day was broken into twelve hours, starting at daybreak. Thus the sixth hour would be the middle of the day and the ninth hour would be midafternoon.

Manumission: The term for officially freeing a slave. A *manumitted* slave was referred to as a *freedman.*

Must cakes: Must is freshly crushed grapes, including both juice and solids. When boiled down into a syrup, it was used as a sweetener for cakes, sauces, and drinks.

Palmyra: A wealthy city in ancient Syria, located along the silk road. Built around an oasis.

Patronus: A Roman man of influence. See *cliens.*

Peristyle: A private interior garden often surrounded by colonnades. The *peristyle* was the central living area of many wealthy Roman houses.

Praetor: A Roman magistrate who presided over one of the standing courts.

Sestertius: plural *sestertii.* A brass coin roughly the size of a half-dollar, worth one-fourth of a *denarius.* Although *denarii* were more common in circulation, monetary amounts were usually recorded in *sestertii.*

Strigil: A narrow, slightly curved metal tool used in bathing. Romans would rub their skin with olive oil and then use a *strigil* to scrape the skin clean.

Subura: A low-class section of Rome located in the valley between the Quirinal and Esquiline hills. The region was crowded with towering tenement buildings filled with poor laborers, and was known as a rough area. The poet Juvenal associated it with "the thousand dangers of a savage city."

Tenth Fretensis: The name of a Roman legion stationed in Syria during the first century. There were multiple legions with identical numbers (founded by different leaders in different eras), so to differentiate, each legion also had a name. *Fretensis* means "the legion of the sea straits," which commemorated an important victory. *Legio X Fretensis* was one of the four legions involved in the First Jewish War that resulted in the destruction of the Temple in AD 70.

Urban praetor: The magistrate who presided over civil cases involving Roman citizens. A different *praetor* administered the court for cases involving noncitizens.

Vigiles: The night watchmen and fire brigade for the city of Rome. Their main duty was to watch for and put out fires, but they also caught petty criminals and runaway slaves. The *vigile* cohorts were organized like military units and assigned to patrol different regions of the city. They were overseen by a Prefect.

Wax tablet: A booklet, usually of three wooden leaves hinged together. The leaves held an indented area covered in a layer of soft beeswax, into which messages could be inscribed with a stylus. The wax could be smoothed over and re-used many times. The Roman government used wax tablets by the thousands.

HISTORICAL NOTES

In the late first century, Sextus Julius Frontinus was appointed water commissioner of Rome. He undertook a comprehensive survey of the entire system to identify problems and presented Emperor Nerva with detailed report of his findings, called *De Aqueductibus Urbis Romae* (*On the Water Supply of Rome*).

On the Water Supply discusses everything from the history of the aqueducts to their discharge rates. It outlines standard pipe sizes, distribution routes, the various types of craftsmen required for the maintenance staff, and much else.

The report also includes a lengthy discussion of water theft, including details on various methods that unscrupulous men had devised to divert water for their personal profit. Frontinus reports finding extensive runs of secret pipes all over the city, which diverted so much water that only a fraction of the expected output was available for public use. He calls the men responsible "puncturers" because they punctured the walls of the distribution tanks to connect all their unauthorized pipes.

These passages from Frontinus's report are my inspiration for Gracchus's water theft scheme.

For more information on Rome's water system, I recommend Bill Thayer's very helpful annotated translation of *De Aqueductibus*, which can be found on his Lacus Curtius website.

Order Information

To order additional copies of this book, please visit
www.lisaebetz.com
Also available on Amazon.com and
BarnesandNoble.com

www.ingramcontent.com/pod-product-compliance
Lightning Source LLC
Chambersburg PA
CBHW022108310726
48972CB00007B/1945